4

The Spine Politic

A novel by Tom Levitt

The Spine Politic

ISBN 9798689805665

The Spine Politic

Politics, principles and progress mean different things to different people. It's 2005 and Ken Hemmings, a retired Midlands police Inspector, is coming to terms with the quiet life since moving to be near his son's family in rural Sussex. Asked by a new friend, a politician, to do a favour for the local primary school, the pensioner sleuth finds himself unwittingly on a collision course with a man who has dedicated his life to changing the world - by any means possible. Where did the fervour to destroy come from? Can a major political outrage be avoided?

'The body politic, as well as the human body, begins to die as soon as it is born, and carries in itself the causes of its destruction. But both may have a constitution that is more or less robust and suited to preserve them a longer or a shorter time. The constitution of man is the work of nature; that of the State the work of art. It is not in men's power to prolong their own lives; but it is for them to prolong as much as possible the life of the State, by giving it the best possible constitution. The best constituted State will have an end; but it will end later than any other, unless some unforeseen accident brings about its untimely destruction.'

Jean-Jacques Rousseau, The Social Contract

'The spine is our body's central support structure. It keeps us upright and connects the different parts of our skeleton to each other: our head, chest, pelvis, shoulders, arms and legs. Although the spine is made up of a chain of bones, it is flexible due to elastic ligaments and spinal discs.'

Any medical textbook

'The role of the spine is to keep your mouth and bum sufficiently far apart as to minimise the possibility of you talking out of your arse.'

Anonymous

The Author

Tom Levitt is a former Labour MP who also writes on responsible and sustainable business ('Welcome to GoodCo', 'The Company Citizen'). His last book was a biography of America's first female Cabinet minister: 'The Courage to Meddle: the Belief of Frances Perkins'. His first published work of fiction, 'The Spine Politic' draws on Tom's personal experience of half a century in politics in Britain and around the world.

The Spine Politic

Contents:

Chapter 1: Toledo, Spain, July 1978

'Welcome, my British friends, to Toledo! As you can see, our fort is most magnificent. In E-Spain we call it El Alcazar: the castle. Here, every express of civil war is being located: heroism, stoicism, gallantry, valour; conflict, vittoria and the losing. If we can see castle as symbol, it is of two threads of Spanish society in years of 1930s winding about each other throat, choking. Today it is 40 years more, you will follow course of most significant battle of 1936 as you walk through portals of this edifice, generator of deep emotions, revered there is no doubt same by Republican and Nationalist peoples.'

If the tourist guide's confident if slightly flawed English lacked authenticity it was compensated by his jaunty style and flowing moustache. The Alcazar towered over a sleepy, roasted town renowned for powerful, delicate sculptures in iron and steel. Much of the splendid medieval castle, now an exorbitant folly, had been rebuilt since its almost complete destruction in the Civil War; an attempt to recapture the majesty of its architect's dream.

'There are, how you say, notice for reading of English upon wall of castle, but your teacher, Mister Blend, he know this and he now tell you of history, I think. Thank you, very much, for visit to Toledo.'

With a brisk nod of his head the guide took his leave, directing the small group of students and their leader, Mr Bland the school teacher, towards the main entrance of the daunting fortress.

Mr Bland had a passion for Spain: 1978 marked his eighth occasion of bringing sixth form students here. His half dozen 17 and 18-year old companions were sixth formers either killing time between 'A' levels and results day or enjoying the first week of their holiday. They came from educational establishments across the whole of the Luton area and some of them shared his passion for Iberian history. The historian's pupil selection was almost always apt: there were seldom cries of 'Sir! Can we see a bullfight?'

Of the group of students Tony came from the least well off family, only able to afford the trip thanks to a small but timely inheritance and his family's blessing. A few weeks short of 17 he was also the youngest. Outside British shores for the first time, he shared the teacher's general interest in Spain: whilst Bland revelled in the medieval, the Moorish influence, the eloquence and splendour of Goya and Velazquez, Tony's heart was in the twentieth century.

Even at such a young age, simply by being in the country Tony was indulging a deep and congenital passion for politics. Every leftist, he knew, went through their own epiphanic experience of 'waking up' to political reality, which was not some sordid entertainment confined to television, council chambers or Parliament. His own 'Kennedy moment', that which opened his eyes to events in the big, bad world, was not the tanks that rolled into Wenceslas Square, the overthrow of Allende or even the horrors of Vietnam. For Tony it had been the death of Franco: November 19th, 1975, shortly after his own fourteenth birthday.

Tony's paternal grandfather, Wilfred, had 'the metaphorical teeshirt' in the form of a shrapnel wound from service with the International Brigade in these same, arid, fields of central Spain. Wilfred's seared memory of armed struggle, his burning passion for a cause and the thrill of taking on a heinous foe was bequeathed first to Tony's father, George, and thence to the boy himself: the family wore the inherited experience with pride, every day of their lives.

Franco was buried under only three bare years of history: Tony would not have graced Iberia with his presence, sullied his passport with its stamp, had the fascist dictator still been upon his self-appointed throne.

The boy had become aware of the British politics around him in the early nineteen seventies. His domestic eye-opener had been the candle-lit winter of 1973-74, celebrated by his father and grandfather and followed by a never-ending round of pushing leaflets through letter boxes at Dad's behest, as two general elections had come around in short order. The boy's political maturation galloped on: politics grew beyond being a hobby or a game. There would have to be another general election in 1979 and by then he would be defending his Labour government whilst urging it to be ever more radical, even though he would still be too young to vote himself. Juvenile certainty ('Labour will not lose in 1979!') was already giving way to the unpredictability of adulthood ('Labour might lose… and then what?').

The emergence of Bland on Tony's horizon presented an opportunity not just to see Spain but to visit, in Toledo, one of the most famous icons of the Civil War. This was an opportunity he was not going to miss.

With his dark, tousled hair, pale skin and lean gait the boy spoke not a word of Spanish but he knew that if he was to learn about the art of popular uprising, of revolution, he had to smell the truth as well as read about it, learn from defeat as well as from victory. No twentieth century experience had better claim to have been A People's War. He'd already explored Spain through immersion in Hemingway and Orwell over recent weeks, prompting his father's further re-telling of his own, now late, father's struggles.

The story of Toledo's Alcazar, thoroughly studied, inspired Tony so much that the thrills that suffused his spine that morning, when he first saw its profile break the horizon, then touched its walls and tasted its odours, were tangible. It was all part of the 'Toledo experience', as Bland was describing it. The teacher's nasal delivery penetrated the boy's consciousness: '1930 saw the collapse of the dictatorship of Primo de Rivera and the downfall of the monarchy. Azaña led a coalition of Socialists and Republicans who changed the Spanish constitution significantly. But in doing so they alienated the Catholic Church and the disillusioned army attempted an unsuccessful coup in 1932.'

He paused for effect. The whole group, to their credit, appeared rapt.

'Against the background of the rise of fascism in Germany and Italy, things weren't easy in Spain. Some poorer people, especially here in the centre of the country, were ripe for revolt - bringing the coalition government of February 1936 problems right from the start. When the Socialists decided to leave the alliance it became unstable and collapsed, whilst in the south ordinary people, urged on by anarchists and others, took control of thousands of acres from the landowners.

'In many towns there were street fights between left wing and right. The left was frustrated by economic injustice and the failure of the democratic process to deliver effective government. The right also wanted stability, but under a strong leader such as Primo de Rivera. He believed he was well placed for this role and the Church, always a powerful influence in Spain, agreed.'

It was hot. A small lizard ran across the yard in front of them. The group moved on.

'But no political faction had a real strategy,' Bland continued, as they walked. 'Feeling that everyone was against him the Republican Azaña became disillusioned, and no wonder: supporters of the monarchy, Primo de Rivera *and* the church were all plotting his downfall.

'In July 1936 a monarchist leader was murdered by soldiers loyal to Azaña and the floodgates opened. Within a week, the government had effectively fallen. A revolt of army officers split communities throughout Spain into separate camps; the Civil War had truly started.'

And it ended in defeat, thought Tony: defeat for democracy, for socialism, for dignity. He shivered as the late July morning approached thirty degrees.

Inspired by the need to fight fascism grandfather Wilfred had rallied to the socialist side through the International Brigade. Some of his comrades had given their lives for the cause and the boy regarded this week as a memorial to Wilfred.

In Tony's own universe there was a risk that Margaret Thatcher, already dubbed 'milk-snatcher', would come to power in Britain; things would be even less comfortable for working people than under 'good old Harold' or 'Sunny Jim'. Tony's generation needed to look to others' histories for their lessons.

That Thatcher – already stripped of both forename and gender – was evil, he had no doubt. Her confident rise was unnerving although Tony was barely politically mature enough to rationalise his reasons why. Tony knew he would put his cross by any Labour name once he was old enough to vote. Voting age had been reduced from 21 to 18 within his own lifetime and starting to vote would be a first step towards achieving the change he wanted in the world, the liberation of oppressed people everywhere.

He had already decided to explore the conventional party politics of his father whilst reserving the right to choose a different path in the future, should that be necessary. He was prepared to fight that good fight that grandfather Wilfred had fought before him.

Back in the real world Bland was knowledgeable if less than inspirational: 'In the early twentieth century Franco himself had done military training here in Toledo. His brother, Ramon, was a left wing antimonarchist - so the civil war existed even within the Franco family.'

Bland smiled wistfully at the irony as they moved to the next room of the Alcazar. He went on:

'Franco was a monarchist but above all he was loyal to his beloved Spain. In February 1936 the right wing Falangist and Nationalist forces asked him to lead a rebellion against the newly elected coalition, the Popular Front. But he turned them down. 'I'm a military man', he told them, 'not a politician'. He wrote to Prime Minister Azaña on June 25, 1936, alerting him to the danger of low morale in the army. Fatally, as we now know, Azaña took no notice of the warning.'

The tour took them up winding reconstructed staircases, through rooms and anterooms, across peach-coloured walkways and under atmospheric balconies. Everywhere the spoors of war were displayed – guns and cannon, uniforms, damaged stone.

The Alcazar had been base to 1,100 men of the Guardia Civil along with 200 residents of Toledo - mothers, the elderly, children and nuns - who sought security in its heavy, reassuring structure. In peaceful times those troops would have supported the government of the day without question, but 1936 was not peaceful.

In July the Republic collapsed and the insurrection began. Eight weeks later, even the massive bulk of this embattled medieval fortress felt fragile, vulnerable. Much had been literally blown away, along with half of the Guardia Civil and some of the citizens:

martyrs, dead, unburied. Many were pierced by bullets, their organs disrupted, their bodies crushed by masonry brought tumbling by cannon fire, others were brought to their knees from lack of food over many weeks.

The photographs on display, of the ruins of the fortress taken after the battle, made it difficult to see how anyone could have survived the onslaught.

Outside what was left of the Alcazar 16,000 Republicans massed, mostly men, boys, mostly Spanish but with many mercenaries amongst them. They maintained a siege throughout the summer and victory was eventually in sight. This so-called Popular Front was branded Communist, anti-Catholic, agents of the devil, yet their policy of attrition was gaining them the upper hand. Surely nothing could save the remaining Falangists inside the ruin?

Restored now from its former ignominy, the castle still held surprises. Tony blanched as he entered the room where the local commander had made his final call for assistance. An ancient bakelite telephone, left off the hook, filled the air with the crackle and creak of a reconstructed voice message: barely decipherable, its tone was clear.

In summary, it said: 'Help'.

The only hope for those imprisoned in the Toledo Alcazar was that their almost mythical saviour, Generalissimo Francisco Franco, would ride to their rescue. And so he did.

'One day,' said Bland, melodramatically, 'there was turmoil amongst the supporters of the Popular Front who'd besieged the Alcazar for so long. Were they really taken by surprise, or just exhausted? Did they simply not believe they could lose? We'll never know. But within a day the siege was over and the occupants had been liberated. The Popular Front had collapsed and the war changed direction. With Toledo so close to Madrid, Franco would use the town as a base to plan the successful completion of his campaign.'

They had nearly completed the tour. Bland himself appeared satisfied, his story almost done. The group stood in the midday heat, Tony's head swimming with a torrent of mixed emotions. The courtyard was surrounded by a shady, beckoning cloister.

'We come to the end of the story. Franco governed Spain without challenge for almost 40 years until he died of natural causes, in 1975. For 40 years he was the most hated man in Spain – but also the most loved.'

There was a dramatic pause.

Through the buzz of intensive listening Tony recalled his relief when he'd heard of the death of Europe's last Fascist dictator. His grandfather Wilfred, almost as though he'd been waiting for that day, had outlived the old bastard by just 24 hours.

The group was standing at the end of the tourist route.

There was something wrong with the story. This huge, square Alcazar had been shelled, bombed, attacked and almost destroyed in July, 1936: yet here it was today, 42 years later, almost as good as new.

It was as though Bland was reading his mind.

'On becoming President, Franco ordered that the Alcazar should be rebuilt, as a monument to those who'd died for their country.'

A monument to fascism, thought Tony. His flesh was creeping, his spine curling with disgust.

'Now I don't know whose side you'd have been on,' Bland said to the group, smiling in that teacher's way which means 'I'm about to put you on the spot'. 'Would you have chosen to be inside the Alcazar, fighting for survival, supporting strong and stable government, wishing to see the Holy Catholic church play a full role in Spanish society, defending your country's history? Or out there, in the fields, fighting for change, democracy, the right to vote, for separation between church and state?

'Both sides believed that they fought for justice. One thing's for sure: you'd certainly have been on one side or the other. In 1936, everybody was.'

Rather than rise to this intellectual challenge, the group's consensus was that more base needs, of toilets, food and drink, were the priority so Bland led the party towards the outside world where he declared a ten-minute respite. Inside Tony's head were whirls of confusion, his extremities tingling and emotions clattering, creating sparks and dents in his established beliefs. The burning sensation he could now feel was caused, he knew, by injustice. Was this to be his 'Kennedy' moment, a moment of nemesis, of revelation?

The Toledo day was heading to 35 degrees of dusty, arid heat. Tony was standing in a stone cauldron in which the rhythmic chorus of cicadas was getting louder. He staggered momentarily to reach the shade and relative cool of the colonnade where, around the walls of the open cloister, he found a row of commemorative plaques. Dry icons, he thought, self-aggrandising, meaningless junk.

Nevertheless, he gave them a second look. Even handed, they were not.

They were historical tributes to Franco's Falangists, to Franco himself, to the 'heroes' who had defeated the socialists and republicans at Toledo. This was why Franco had ordered the castle to be rebuilt: to honour the ignoble cause of fascism, creating a shrine where he himself and his deeds could be worshipped.

In the boy's opinion, that was poor taste. He felt sick.

The words of one particular plaque insisted on being read a second time. He knew little German, but it was easy to understand: 'From your friends in the National Socialist Party of Germany, 1937'. Then 'The Respect of the Hitler Youth Movement, February 1939'. And a personal tribute from Benito Mussolini.

As he walked through the cloisters the years, illustrated by the sequence of plaques, fell away.

Messages from dictators of South America, Portugal and the Caribbean in the 1960s were frightening.

These artefacts represented real people, real fascists celebrating other real fascists. How can this be so? Fascists believed in genocide, gas chambers, the denial of human dignity: how can anyone celebrate them?

Some movements were too modern for his school history books – and some were a bit too close to home. The shock was almost palpable as he read, in English, 'The British Movement celebrates its friends in the Fascist movement of Spain, 1974', 'The John Birch Society of Alabama, February 1975' and a memento from another visitor that year claiming to represent a Cuban government in exile.

No, fascism was not dead. It was alive today, in polite western societies, playing at being something else. It was in his home town, in the corridors of power and on the supermarket shelf. The conceited smile of bourgeois democracy would hide this reality from Tony no longer.

Some people were clearly willing to prostitute their intellects without even knowing what they were doing, debasing themselves and each other. He would not tolerate that happening to him; it was simply not right that fascists were free to inflict their bile upon others.

* * *

Over the next few days, over and above their wallow in history and culture, the group swam in Madrid's open air pools, admired bare, brown, stony countryside and took in the historic grandeur of Avila. None of it impressed Tony like the force of Toledo's ancient, reconstructed fort had done. It had stared him out and almost won, kicked him behind the knees and punched him in his kidneys until his very spine ached.

The trip would end with two nights in Santander before catching the ferry to Plymouth. On his final morning in Spain Tony set out to find sports news in an English newspaper. Before going a hundred yards he learned what it was to be 'taken aback'. Outside what appeared to be a police station a small crowd of perhaps 30 men was assembling, shouting, hostile. Every one wore a brown shirt. The Spanish chants meant nothing to the boy although it was clear that the group was angry.

From across the street Tony did not grasp the significance of what he could see. Those were not uniforms such as the military or boy scouts wore, they were more like those adopted by the mods of the 60s, or the 70s' own skinheads.

But the mob started to organise itself and the truth dawned: their chanting became regular, their stances more disciplined and now every man's right arm was bent at the elbow, right knuckles pressed to right shoulder in a parody of a salute. The police station, a totem of the new, post-Franco, democratic Spain, was the target of this demonstration of the politics of nostalgia. Were they demonstrating because they were free to do so, after a generation of repression? Were they flexing the muscles of democracy? Or was something more sinister going on?

He realised that these young men were fascists: walking, breathing, shouting fascists, Franco's Brown Shirts. They were demonstrating not in 1936 but here, today, in 1978. Tony had never before seen fascists in the flesh, with blood in their veins.

He was disturbed by his own ambiguous response: this was clearly an evil historical anachronism which should be in its death throes, so they could safely be ignored. Or could they? Dead, but they wouldn't lie down. There was nothing Tony could do. He was unnerved: he'd never smelt a fascist before yet here was a crowd of them.

Change was never an easy option and even the new Spain, a fledgling democratic monarchy, embodied contradictions which the Spanish would have to resolve. Opposition represented the birth pain of a new social order, it was nostalgia for the cosy certainty and stability of the past.

Discretion being the better part of valour he headed back to the sanctity of the hostel. 200 yards from his destination he glanced down a side street to espy a paper stand he'd missed on his outward journey. He grasped the pesetas in his pocket and headed towards it. Success! The solitary English newspaper amidst the Spanish papers was a three-day old, right wing Daily Mail, but at least it contained football stories.

Political sympathy for the late General within the Spanish media would not be stilled by something as insignificant as his death, but that was the media for you. Did he but know it, Spanish journals were reporting that Cantabrian nationalism was on the rise, that its respectable roots had been infiltrated by anarchists – and that Santander was on full alert.

Unable to read the language, however, Tony missed the news that the local Mayor was warning of an imminent heinous outrage.

Neither did the teenager realise, passing a dusty grey Seat, distracted by a story about a football transfer, that the abandoned car was illegally parked outside a Post Office, a symbol of the state.

But as it exploded behind him he became briefly aware of flame, smoke, an acrid stench of fireworks, of a choking, globby fluid in his mouth; of a steering wheel soaring through the air, a scintillation of shattered glass illuminating the morning sunlight, an intense roar followed by muted blurs and the sweet, warm taste of blood as he was thrown against a cold, hard wall, his spine thrust against a bruising drainpipe followed by the descent of pain.

At that point he lost consciousness.

His last, brief thought had been that the fucking Fascists had attacked him personally. They would pay for that affront.

From now on it would be Tony against the Fascists.

The consequences of those thoughts were still with him when he awoke in a bed, suffering from concussion, temporarily impaired hearing, a scratched cornea, a bruised back, the complete maceration of the top joint of one thumb and several superficial cuts to his face and arms.

He'd been lucky to survive the attack of the right wing scum relatively intact.

But survive he had.

Tony tried to turn over in his hospital bed but he was exhausted.

He knew what he had to do.

They would pay for inflicting these wounds to his body and his pride.

Chapter 2: Sussex, July 2005

Although village life was supposed to be every retired person's dream Ken Hemmings had not found Sussex easy over his first half year in residence. For someone more attuned to the pace of a bustling town it had risked being if not a living nightmare then certainly the first step on the long road to death.

There were good reasons for moving away from the East Midlands, of course, sensible, rational and logical reasons, but was the faint hint of sea spray over the horizon really adequate compensation for the lack of cough-inducing grime, for which Ken felt more than a pang of nostalgia?

His nice cottage was certainly more than sufficient for a single man, the neighbours were friendly-ish and the local pub served a pint sufficiently decent to justify an occasional visit. It had taken six months in the deep south for him to settle in, by any objective measure, but… it wasn't the same.

Perhaps nothing ever is, these days.

Back 'home' in Nottinghamshire the former police inspector had spent the years since his millennium retirement (at 55) working part time in a bookshop, listening to children read in the local primary school where Sheila had once taught, popping over to the cricket at Trent Bridge when the summer allowed and volunteering with Age Concern in whatever way was helpful. Now, at a time when most people were only just starting life in the third age, euphemistically dubbed 'the age of leisure', he had already had endured five years of it.

Five years earlier, in 2000, that early departure on a generous police pension had felt exciting. After Sheila had joined him retirement they spent long, enjoyable evenings drawing up great plans to see the world together. But six months after quitting work Sheila's cerebral haemorrhage, a stroke, had left her crippled both physically and mentally. The thirty more years they had planned, earned and anticipated for so long were not going to happen. Her death, six months later, after mountains of tears and hours spent staring into each others' eyes, had been something of a release for both, although Ken's relief was tinged with guilt.

The zest had gone from his life. Those great ambitions were no more and his life was now dedicated to solving not crimes but crosswords, walking the dog and reading too much detective fiction, much of it unconvincing.

At this point Ken's son had started talking seriously about Ken downsizing his home and moving closer to Clive's own family in Brighton. Feigning disinterest, Ken, forever a robust character with a good word to say for almost everyone, hated the idea of being a burden. At barely 60 he was still young, he insisted, but in great danger of feeling old.

Clive was a chip off the old block: he too was a police inspector, achieving the rank at only 36 years old and regarded as the backbone of the local constabulary. He persisted in his attempts at persuasion but it was Dixon (of Dog Green), Ken's faithful German Shepherd, who resolved the issue. After arguing that 'Dixon's 13, he doesn't want to move at his stage of life!' matters came to a head. People assumed that the Alsatian had once worked for the police himself but to the dog's eternal embarrassment he'd failed the fitness test as a puppy. After 80 dog-years Dixon's arthritis, deafness, weak heart and incontinence ultimately made canine euthanasia the only fair option. Ken's argument that 'the dog will never settle in Sussex' would never be tested. His waning reluctance to abide by the dictates of common sense was fatally undermined when Dixon, too, passed on.

The move south was thus inevitable and the relocation was completed in the January of 2005, six months prior to this sunny July day.

Ken knew that he had to make an emotional investment in Sussex, not confine life to family alone, but that he could take his time in doing so. He had to accept a lifestyle which didn't absolutely require him to move more than a hundred yards from his home, a home in which PD James was his most constant companion and the greatest moments of anticipatory thrill were found in checking those last inscrutable clues from yesterday's Times crossword. There was a danger that his could become a wasted life. As when up in Nottinghamshire, Ken discovered opportunities to volunteer, with the even more elderly, but it wasn't the same; they weren't 'his' people. He became a member of Sussex County Cricket Club and spent many a happy hour in Hove watching the game he loved, making up for all the times when he wished he could have seen more of it at Trent Bridge over the last half century.

At Clive's suggestion Ken even tried learning golf, so that the men could share a common pastime. The game had previously been anathema to him and after a couple of sessions designed for 'the older beginner' he concluded – part reluctantly, mostly in relief – that his conviction that it was just not for him had been fully justified. Nevertheless, the Clubhouse was a convenient alternative to the village pub, being both pleasant and nearby. Becoming a social member (cheaper than joining as a player) allowed him to court a variety of occasional drinking companions, on the occasions he might choose to avail himself of their company. On the whole, however, Ken preferred to keep himself to himself of an evening.

Since Dixon's passing Ken had done little in the way of waistline-controlling exercise. He was not a tall man and he possessed a physique for which portliness was always a risk. That was another reason for considering golf although someone had once, persuasively, described it as spoiling a good walk. He needed a hobby which was more than jigsaws and crosswords.

Ken's cottage was small but perfectly formed. Against his initial better judgment he'd come to enjoy the rural idyll and its opportunities to see more of his only son and his lovely young family. Chris, Clive's wife, lectured part time at the University. Ken habitually called her Christine, for reasons he could never quite explain, and although she taught law it wasn't 'proper' law, in Ken's eyes, not criminal law. Ken had always thought that company law was an oxymoron: too many companies he'd come across had sought, in one way or another, to get around it.

Then there was Troy, 8 and Sable, 6 and he could forgive their mother anything - except for her taste in forenames. Though Ken enjoyed his delightful and lively grandchildren in every single respect, what on earth had possessed her to dream up those monikers?

The cottage had a stone roof, climbing roses over the door and a garden of just the right size. Although he lived barely a stone's throw from the village primary school Ken couldn't quite bring himself to offer to listen to the children read; the memories of Sheila were still too strong. He was happy, he was fine, but he'd rather not be constantly reminded of his wife's pedagogical calling, nor the partner he missed so much.

The time Ken spent reading detective novels was a real indulgence even if it rendered him vulnerable to his son's teasing. On one occasion Clive suggested that Ken write about his own experiences as a Nottinghamshire cop, perhaps as the basis of a work of fiction, though Ken could summon little enthusiasm for the idea. A few weeks later, however, the son discovered that his father had indeed committed several hundred words to paper, sprawling long-hand on a lined A4 pad, so he suggested buying a computer and getting broadband installed.

Ken Hemmings was of a generation that hadn't appreciated the power of computing during his career, despite the IT explosion within public services which had started on his watch. The new laptop, Ken's first, was a godsend. Little in the way of creative writing actually flowed from Ken's fingers but he became an expert at Solitaire - and was delighted to find that many friends and former acquaintances were 'into' email. Inevitably Ken became a fully paid up member of the on-line community. Through the internet he could 'research' everything under the sun, not least crossword clues. Thank heavens he would always be vulnerable to his son's powers of persuasion!

From time to time the two men discussed policing, sometimes over a pint, frequently at Sunday lunch (when the children allowed it) and increasingly by email. Ken had truly loved his job, his career, and he subscribed to the philosophy that the police were a 'service' rather than a 'force'. To his delight his son was cut from the same cloth.

Over his career Ken had saved vulnerable children from dastardly fates, been a champion for justice and put more than his share of villains behind bars. He had climbed the greasy pole sufficiently to justify some self-confidence without ever getting too distant from the front line. He had reason to be proud of his life; a man with thinning hair, a well-groomed small moustache, a contented heart; a man with no regrets about anything he had ever done.

* * *

On the last Sunday in July it rained. Ken's drive to Hove to watch a day's cricket had ended in disappointment as, after a handful of overs and the loss of a couple of home wickets, the downpour had descended in earnest. The promise of more play later in the day, should the clouds lift, was insufficient incentive to remain huddled in the cold wind. This was not supposed to be what July – heavens, nearly August – was about.

At least, he mused, as he drove home through damp countryside, the disgusting weather would make it possible to sidle along to the Golf Club later without having to justify why he'd not been 'up for a round' that afternoon.

He sat at the bar with a pint and the Sunday crossword and, despite his cricketing disappointment, was generally content with the world. The clues were challenging, the solutions rewarding and the atmosphere warm and benign. A regular, a committee member named Graham Seward, came in from the cold accompanied by his golfing partner. The former police officer assessed the couple with a single glance but, aware of the dangers of engaging with 'boring Graham', he returned to his challenge.

However, he'd been spotted.

'Hello there, Ken. Stuck on the crossword? You intellectuals, I don't know! Been out today? Thought not. You did well to stay indoors, I'll say.' Seward removed a damp jacket and hung up his cap.

'Hello, Graham. There are limits to enjoyment, you know. I've never yet caught flu from a crossword.'

'Indeed! Bit of a risk, I agree. I think a little precautionary tipple would go down very well right now.' He called to the barman: 'Shaun? When you're ready, son. Will you have one, Ken?'

Ken's glass was only just too full for good manners to allow him to accept. 'No, I don't think so, I'm alright. But thanks. Another time, Graham, certainly. I must go and have some supper shortly.'

'Righty-ho, then. No problem-o. Ken, let me, let me introduce you. This is Peter.'

'Hello, Ken!' said the golfing companion, a man with brown, expensively cut hair flecked with grey.

'Hello, Peter. I'm Ken Hemmings.' Ken reached over to shake the proffered hand. The newcomer was stocky, confident, smart. He was wearing a large signet ring on his left pinky and clearly not short of a bob or two. Peter's face suggested he'd had acne badly as a child, the scarring making it difficult to tell whether he was closer to 35 or 45 years old. 'Have I seen you in here before, Peter?'

'Occasionally, perhaps. This isn't my usual links, but I'm addicted, I'm afraid. I'm often here as a guest.'

'I see.'

Peter's voice suggested years of smoking but there was no smell, no excessive wrinkling of the skin and no staining of the fingers. If the man still smoked, it was rarely. Peter handed Ken a business card which Ken took and scrutinised; its design was plain, name, address, email and phone but no business title, though it felt important. Ken smiled kindly, then assumed a puzzled look. 'Peter Elder: do I know that name?'

'Watch out, Peter! Ken used to be a police officer. Not so much Old Ken as Old Bill, eh? Can you tell?' Graham teased and Ken played the game.

'Graham, please! He's always giving the game away. How am I ever going to chat up girls when you keep telling them that?'

Peter smiled. 'You may have come across me. I'm Councillor Peter Elder. I'm often in the local paper.'

'Yes, of course!' Ken wrinkled his brow as he addressed his memory: 'You're a Labour councillor, is that right?'

'Indeed. You don't get many like me in Sussex Golf Clubs!' Elder was right: whilst Ken had never been overtly into party politics, not least for obvious professional reasons, he hadn't been slow in appreciating the stark difference in the political wallpaper between Nottinghamshire and rural Sussex.

'The Mystery of the Golf-Playing Socialist!' declared Graham. 'Sounds like something - what's her name? - Agatha Christie might dream up! You know, I don't really care what bloody revolution Peter's plotting when I'm thrashing him over 18 holes! As long as I keep winning I'll be keeping the nationalisation of private industry at bay, I think. He plays off a mean handicap, better than any of his friends in the Labour Cabinet, I'll bet. Hold the fort, boys, I'm off for a pee.'

Ken knew that politicians deserved to be taken seriously. He respected their calling and had always made a point of voting, though he'd often made his choice of candidate on the day of the poll. Over the years he had voted for all three major parties at one time or another.

'But you don't represent this area, do you? Not the village itself..?'

'Oh, no!' Elder laughed. 'Standing for Labour is still a hanging offence in this village. But I do live nearby – and I'm sure I've seen you around. They deign to let me chair the board of governors at the primary school here. The ward I represent is much closer to Brighton.'

'I see. So why haven't they hung you yet, then?'

'Because I don't fit the archetypal image of a socialist, I suppose. Look, are you sure you don't want a drink? Graham's gone off without ordering.'

Ken demurred, this time more reluctantly. 'I'm fine, but thanks.'

Elder was right. Even back when the Ragged Trousered Philanthropists had inhabited Hastings, Sussex as a whole would not have been a socialist community.

Ken was intrigued. 'So where do you...'

'Aha, the policeman again! I live at The Grange.'

Elder had named one of the larger grand detached properties in the area. Ken had once wondered whether the pile had been converted to flats, though he'd later established that The Grange was a single residence.

'I'm actually a property developer, in real life. Yes, a double black sheep: a socialist living in an aristocratic heap; a practitioner in the capitalist system; a Labour councillor for over a decade. It's all great fun.'

Ken raised an eyebrow and a quizzical smile.

'I'm sorry, Ken, I don't know where Graham has got to. I'm his guest, so I can't order at the bar...'

Ken took the hint. 'Of course. What will you have, Peter?'

'I'm sure Graham's got a slate. Gin and tonic, please.'

Ken indicated the order to Shaun, who nodded. Elder took a small cigar from a box but made no move to light it.

'So, how do you square the circle, Peter? I would have thought that being a property developer was beyond the pale in Labour circles.'

'Oh it's even worse than that! I've got inherited wealth, too, I'm afraid. My wife's family owns The Grange. My political colleagues respect the fact that I do have some principles and my conscience is clear. I build homes that people need, decent homes for ordinary folk to live in. I build them of good quality at a fair price - a fair proportion are what they call 'social housing'. Housing Associations like working with me. And my company sponsors a charitable trust which, after the local authorities, probably does more for homeless young people than any other group in this county.'

'Hmm…' Ken approved of what he was hearing. His purr was calculated to be neither enthusiastic nor dismissive.

'I'm sorry, Ken. I get challenged on this quite a lot, as you can imagine. You've just had the summary answer. I was first elected before I was quite so stinking rich – I'm not *that* stinking rich, by the way – and I've always been upfront about what I do. And I've been re-elected a couple of times, so I've nothing to apologise for!'

'I can see that,' said Ken, genuinely impressed. 'Gosh, I'm surprised you've the time to be a councillor, let alone an active one!'

'That's a good point, actually. Many people – especially on lower incomes, in jobs where they've less control over their own time than I do – might have the motivation or ability to be councillors but they can't afford it, either in time or money.'

'I hadn't thought of it like that.'

'It's better than it used to be. Councillors get reasonable allowances now, but if it wasn't for people like me in years gone by then Labour, especially, might have struggled to get the candidates for council seats, even winnable ones. Lots of people think being a councillor is a lot of work, bother and effort for little reward, but I think it's fascinating.'

Graham had rejoined them: 'Trying to convert you, is he? Recruit you to the people's socialist militia? So, about this drink, then. Are you sure, Ken? Peter?'

'It's sorted, thanks, Graham,' said Peter. 'No, I haven't come here to talk politics…'

'Oh, don't mind me!' said Graham, in mock disbelief.

The barman placed two gin and tonics on the bar. Graham smiled and, as predicted, indicated that they should go on his 'tab'. 'Are you sure, Ken?'

'Positive, thanks. So – who won the golf?'

Graham took a philosophical view. 'It's not so much the winning, Ken…'

'So, congratulations to you, Peter!'

'Thank you.'

'Well done! That's what you meant by 'a thrashing', is it, Graham?'

The men laughed and continued in idle banter for several minutes. At one point Ken summoned the courage to raise a matter of common interest with Peter Elder: 'So you're chair of governors at the school… My late wife was a teacher. Primary, like yours, but in Nottinghamshire. I moved down here after she died. She loved the job, it was her life.'

'We've some very good and dedicated teachers in the village school; we're very lucky. Of course, having more money around in education under this government helps a lot too.'

Graham laughed: 'My God, Peter, you don't miss a trick! Political animal or what?'

'Well, it's true.'

'Oh, I know,' said Ken. 'Sheila used to say it, too. We saw it in the police service, as well. More officers, Community Support Officers, technology. I was involved in the school too, after a fashion.'

'Oh, yes? How?'

'After I retired, I used to go in to hear the children read. Very enjoyable.'

'Right! We'll have to recruit you here, then! We could do with someone of your experience listening to the children.'

Ken engaged in mock protest: 'Well, maybe, but I'm even older now, too old. I've got a vested interest in doing what I can for Age Concern, something like that...'

His audience chuckled.

'I'm sorry to hear that. Seriously, if you change your mind, let me know, we could use you. May I mention your interest to the Head? If I can find him...'

'What d'you mean, 'find him'?' The hint of mystery awoke the retired policeman in Ken.

'Oh, it's nothing. Teachers are entitled to their holidays, like everyone else. I just didn't expect him to disappear into thin air on the first day of the summer break without a word. No, I thought he was planning two or three weeks away a little later in August. There were things I needed to talk to him about last week but I couldn't find him.'

'Are you seriously worried about him?'

'Do you know, I'd forgotten you were a policeman! Former policeman.'

Ken smiled. 'Inspector, actually.'

Peter nodded, continued.

'Right... No, I'm not worried about the Head, not really. Norman Flagg's a grown man, he can look after himself, got a good brain on his shoulders. I'll tell you what, Ken, if he's not back by the start of September I'll let you know,' Peter joked. 'Then I might really have a job for you: with all your experience, you might be sitting in the Head's chair!'

More laughter.

Shortly afterwards, Ken made his excuses and left. As he walked down a rhododendron-lined drive, past thatch and stone, bramble and rose-hip, he thought that the village wasn't such a bad place to live. The sun was visible at last, after hiding all day. He didn't spend a lot of his retirement thinking of the past, but the conversation with the councillor had sparked rosy memories of when Sheila was alive and working. He'd enjoyed being involved with the school, working beside his wife and together with the children, the mouldable human clay of the future.

Maybe there was something he could do with the local school, after all. Was this the idea for which he'd been waiting? He put it to one side but promised himself he'd return to it, one day. For now, the priority was the pork chop in the fridge with his name on it, some cold mashed potato that could be fried up, a few fresh green beans his neighbour had given him and, as he'd been really good, a Marks & Spencer's crème caramel for afters.

* * *

Ken Hemmings' summer continued according to plan. Watching cricket around the county, listening to an Ashes series on the radio, dabbling in the garden, even taking a coach trip to London to see *Phantom of the Opera* and the National Gallery. The season even allowed him time to acquaint himself with the walking trails of the Sussex Downs. Clive, Chris and the children were away for two August weeks in Portugal during which he missed their contact more than he'd expected. Was this because he was closer to them, that the children had developed recognisable and missable personalities, or was he was just getting old, sentimental and lonely? The current Inspector Hemmings had pressed him to join them on the Algarve but it would have been too hot for Ken. There was also this to consider: was dad being asked to join the works outing from filial duty or did the invitation come from a genuine wish to share quality time with him? He didn't want to risk asking that question.

The day following the family's return from Portugal Clive was still on leave so he invited Ken over for the day. The grandfather went, gladly. His enjoyment at sharing the family's meal and perusing their somewhat repetitive holiday photographs was genuine. He couldn't quite get used to seeing such pictures on a computer screen instead of on tangible glossy paper, but such was modern life. Fancy, seeing the fruits of their photographic labours just the day after they'd returned home – digital cameras were truly wonderful.

Ken saw the Bank Holiday approach and then rapidly recede behind him. He started to look forward to the cooler, more varied, quintessentially more English month of September.

And so August drained away. On the evening of Friday, 2nd September Ken received an unexpected phone call.

'Is that Ken? It's Peter Elder. Do you recall we met at the Golf Club a few weeks back?'

'Of course – Councillor. What a pleasant surprise! What can I do for you?'

Ken had quite taken to the man on their only meeting and had intended to stay in touch.

'How's your summer been? Did you get away?'

'Not far, Peter, no, I'm not tied down, not restricted to school holidays. You?'

'We've a cottage near Perpignon, had three weeks there. Look, you know what I said about being a Head Teacher light?'

'Yes…?' Ken replied, hesitantly. He had a vision, instantly dismissed, of standing in front of a school assembly, *in loco dominis*.

'Well, that's still the situation. I got back from France a couple of days ago to find that the silly sod still hasn't checked in. You're actually the only person I've mentioned this business to and, although I don't know you very well, I wondered…'

'With me being an ex-policeman?' Ken teased.

'An ex-Inspector… look, could we have a word? May I pop over to see you this evening?'

It was seven o'clock. Eastenders had reached a critical point but Ken could programme the video recorder. The only intellectual stimulation he'd had that day was a particularly frustrating crossword.

'Aye, of course'.

Within half an hour the conference had started. Peter Elder took readily to Ken's sitting room. He sat in a well-padded chair with the air of an accustomed visitor and accepted the proffered whisky.

'It's a puzzle, Ken, I don't mind admitting. I've spoken to the deputy. She's been in school the last couple of days, she's no idea where Norman might be. Term starts on Tuesday and it could get embarrassing if we start without a Head, to say the least.'

'Does he have family locally?'

'No, I don't think so.'

'Where did he come from?'

'His last job was in London, in the East End, quite a difficult school. He was deputy head for a couple of years, helped turn it round. Successfully, I might add. That dynamism was partly what attracted us when we appointed him.'

'And before that?'

'Originally… home counties. He came here three years ago, to the day.'

'Does he like his holidays? I mean… where did he go last year?'

'Yes, he gets away. Goes to some fairly exotic places, I understand. Not too difficult when you're single, especially on a Head's salary. Bit of a workaholic though, doesn't disappear when the bell goes at home time. During the shorter holidays he'll come in every day to prepare and manage his school.'

'You picked a good Head.'

'Indeed, he's been a godsend, fitted in from day one. The East End doesn't have a lot in common with leafy Sussex but… well, as chair of governors I chaired the panel which appointed him and we knew straight away he was the one for us. Excellent references. No regrets about appointing him, none at all.'

'And you know nothing more about his family?'

Elder hesitated. 'There is no one local. I don't know if his parents are still alive.'

'So, there's been no one else to miss him over the past four weeks?'

'Not that I know of, no.'

'No girlfriend?'

'Not as far as I know.'

'During the past three years?'

'I wouldn't know. Actually… I don't really know him socially.' Peter's hesitation had waned. 'Probably should,' he went on, almost to himself.

'Does he have particular friends on the staff?'

'Not really… he's very professional. There are only twelve teaching staff here, mostly women, and I think he gets on well with all of them. There's a very good atmosphere in the staff room. A group have a girls' night out every now and then, but I shouldn't think he's part of that!'

'I take it you've checked his home. Where does he live?'

'About ten miles away. I've written his details here for you' - he took a folded paper from his pocket and proffered it - 'He used to say that teachers shouldn't live too close to their school, shouldn't meet parents and kids in the street too much. Professional at work, but careful to defend his private life, I'd say. Quite right, too. Useful if you want to go out and get drunk! Not that I have any evidence that he does.'

'Have you been to the house?'

'Yes…'

'This week? This summer?'

'No.'

'If you don't mind me saying so, it might be reasonable…'

'To call in? Of course. No, I haven't. But I know someone who has.'

'Really?'

'Mrs Goose. She lives in the village, she cleans for Laura and me. When Norman arrived he asked if I knew someone who'd clean for him and she was happy to take him on. It's a bit of a drive for her, ten miles, but her daughter lives over that way. I think she goes once a fortnight. She's got a key; she was there yesterday.'

'You've spoken to her?'

'Nothing in the house has been touched. Norman apparently hasn't been there over the holidays.'

'And you've telephoned him, does he have a mobile?'

'No reply. Voicemail turned off.'

'Are you planning to speak to anyone else about this, Peter?'

'You mean the police? The real police? Sorry! No. No, I haven't.'

'You don't want to make a fuss?'

'It's not that, I'm no stranger to fuss! It's just that... well, I almost feel it's none of my business.'

'You say 'almost'?'

Peter was frustrated. 'Except I've got a school to look after and I need to talk to the Head before term starts on Tuesday. It's about being responsible, I feel, and I know he feels that, too. I want to know that he'll be there on Tuesday, when the kids come back, and at the staff meeting on Monday, come to that. And frankly I feel let down by someone I've come to trust. As of now he's not technically in breach of his contract, I've no reason to believe he's in danger, and it's just that – well, who else will report their concern, if not me?'

'I see. So you're seeking my professional advice without having to put those concerns officially on the record.'

Peter looked briefly sheepish. 'I think that's about it. Thanks for listening. I must say, your interrogation technique's effective!'

'It was once, perhaps. I'm a bit out of practice. But I can understand why you're worried. It's unusual that there doesn't appear to be anyone else who's noticed his absence all summer. You said the Deputy was in school today: I can't imagine she's too happy about all this. Who's she, by the way?'

'Jane Moore.'

'Miss? Mrs?'

'She's prefers 'Ms'.'

'Did Mr Flagg call her 'Ms'?'

'It wouldn't have been an issue for him. School documents list her – and a couple of the others – as Ms.'

There was a pause as Ken thought things through.

'The difficulty's this, Peter. Either we have a genuine disappearance here, which should be reported to the police properly, or we don't. If it's the latter, then we're very limited as to what anyone in officialdom can do to help you or your school. The first thing we need to do is find out whether or not someone else has actually reported the absence.'

'How do we do that?'

'I have my methods…'

'Your son? He's a police officer too, isn't he? Graham told me.'

'Let's keep this off the record, Peter, at least until we know something more.'

'I understand.'

'I'd certainly like to help. You're concerned, as a conscientious Chair of Governors, of course. As you can imagine, I do like a bit of a mystery every now and again! It'd be best if we could have everything cleared up within hours, though that would take half the fun out of it.'

'What do you think about… I mean, if we had some more clues? Evidence. As I told you, we share the same cleaner.' He reached into his trouser pocket. 'This is Mrs Goose's key, for Norman's house. There's no burglar alarm. Couldn't we just… see what we can find?'

Ken pursed his lips and tutted. 'I'm not sure that's entirely kosher.' There was a twinkle in his eye. 'But it could be fun. Let's see what I can find out before we do any James Bond stuff.'

'Time's of the essence. You know, I don't think I've ever used that expression before!'

Ken smiled. He was not the only one enjoying the conversation.

'So, are you free tomorrow morning, Ken? Could you go over then?'

Ken resisted the temptation to leap up and shout 'Yes!' at the top of his voice. He'd come to respect Peter Elder over their brief acquaintance and he sensed that if the councillor had judged that there was a problem, there probably was… and potentially an intriguing one. For his answer, he made do with: 'I think it could be arranged. If absolutely necessary, of course.'

He took the folded paper that was still in Elder's hand. 'His phone number's there, too, for good measure. The houses in the village all have names but his is easy to find, it's next to the church. It's small, with the front door opening onto the street. The key's for the back door.' He smiled. 'More discreet.'

'You appear to have decided what needs to be done. But... are we going together?'

'Well, no. I've got to give a presentation tomorrow morning. Local government stuff.'

'We could go later?'

'I'd really rather you...'

'We'll see.' The retired policeman was not wanting to say 'no'. The whole exercise could drop a toe on the wrong side of the law, but on the other hand there was no reason to take up police time, no evidence that the absence was sinister or that any crime had been committed. Norman Flagg was a mature adult responsible for his own actions, within the law.

If someone needed to take an unofficial look around the Head teacher's house it was probably better that it were Ken, and Ken alone.

'We'll see.'

'Thanks.'

Peter had not intended to stay long at his neighbour's house. But the company was good, the whisky smoky and the conversation fascinating. Over many minutes the topic ranged widely. Ken found out more about his 'partner in crime': Peter had been born and bred in Luton, son of Arthur Elder, a car worker and lifetime official of the Transport and General Workers Union who had once fought a (predictably unsuccessful) Parliamentary campaign in a rural seat for the Labour Party. Peter was 45 and his father was no longer alive, but his character and views were in his father's mould. However similar those views had been, however, their life experience had differed vastly. Peter went to a comprehensive school and then became the first Elder to go to university - where he had met Laura, the love of his life, whom he subsequently married.

'Were you involved in politics back then?'

'At University?' He thought about how best to answer the question. 'I was quite active in Luton, whilst still at school, late '70s. At University I had to choose between a rather right wing Labour Club, you might call it the David Owen tendency, middle class types, a pre-pubescent SDP, or the vanguard Trotskyists who would become the Militant Tendency. Neither was for me, I wanted neither sitting room socialism nor anti-democratic opportunism. I stuck with the Labour 'brand' because there was nowhere else to go, but basically I opted out of active politics for several years. I was a member in name only.'

'Was yours a typical University experience for someone on the left?'

'Probably not. But I'm sure it was the right way to go.'

Ken had put some peanuts in a bowl. He reached forward for them but they were just out of his reach.

'Here, let me!' Peter picked up the bowl with both hands and proffered it to his host. The hands were immaculately groomed, thought Ken, the nails were even polished. This is a man who doesn't rely on manual work for a living.

'Thank you. So, what changed your mind later on? Did something happen?'

'Yes. The miners' strike, in the early '80s, funnily enough! I knew Scargill wasn't leading them well, my head was very clear about that, very clear indeed. But my heart said that these communities deserved better from the employers and the government, that Scargill had been set up like an Aunt Sally by a conspiracy of the right and that if my socialism meant anything at all I had to campaign alongside the miners. I still had that little dormant Party card in my pocket and the time had come to take a stand.'

Ken let the younger man talk.

'It meant showing some sort of commitment when it mattered. Writing a cheque every now and again wasn't enough. This sounds silly now: I arranged fundraising dinner parties - Sussex is a bit short of actual coal pits. I raised thousands of pounds for the miners' campaign. I moved in wealthy circles and within those circles, both here and in London, enough of us had come up – not exactly from the gutter – but our fathers had been factory workers. It wasn't difficult to find people who supported the miners' cause - though they generally didn't like Scargill, the man.'

'Interesting, thank you.'

After a brief pause Peter said 'Ken, I'm sorry for mentioning the miners' strike. It can't have been an easy time for you, with you being in the police at the time, and Nottinghamshire being... on the front line. But you did ask.'

'That's OK.'

'Were you involved in the strike?'

'Yes, of course. I was a uniformed sergeant, in Nottinghamshire, back then. Things were a bit different there compared to the rest of the country.'

'You mean the UDM business? Miners squabbling with each other?'

'I almost felt that it was a family affair, something we police officers shouldn't have had to be involved in. Working class communities do appreciate law and order, as I'm sure you know. They've more to gain from safer streets, more to lose from disorder than other communities do. It was a tragedy to see members of the same family pitted against their brothers, literally, in the way that they were.'

Ken shifted to the edge of his seat.

'And, Peter, I also think it was a tragedy to see those communities die over the years that followed; Mr Scargill's predictions about the future of the industry came true.'

Peter looked up, slightly taken aback by the former policeman's sympathetic position. Rationalising, he smiled, and both men contemplated their glasses pensively.

By the end of the evening a couple more social whiskies had been dispensed and the two neighbours, no longer strangers, regarded each other as friends.

* * *

It took Ken under twenty minutes to drive to Norman Flagg's home the following morning. He drove past the modest end-of-terrace cottage, once around the block and more slowly past the house again. He parked against the wall of the church yard, fifty yards away, and walked back to the house.

The street was deserted, the gate easy to open. The key slipped into the back door lock as though oiled: before he knew it Ken was in a modest, sparsely furnished sitting room.

There was no mail on the floor. No doubt it would be in a tidy, Mrs Goose-constructed, pile somewhere convenient.

Beneath the window looking out onto the street was an ovate gate-leg table, one leaf folded down against the wall, with two modest piles of school-related paperwork upon it. On fitted bookshelves, in recesses either side of a featureless fireplace, Ken found fewer books than he might have expected in a teacher's home. Their content, however, was not inconsistent with what might interest a primary school head. They included educational theory, grey and dour, a couple of historical coffee-table style books, travel guides and learned tomes on the Second World War and the Spanish Civil War. There were biographies of Attlee, Kinnock, Thatcher, Saddam, Gaddafi, Franco, Jimmy Reid and the Upper Clyde Shipbuilders. Almost without exception the books were political, though this was not an offence.

There were atlases, much thumbed, and maps, ditto. Ramblers' magazines. There were paperback novels by Grisham, Wilbur Smith, Ruth Rendell, Le Carré. 'Cooking for the Single Person' was there, less thumbed, and several books of poetry of which Shelley was clearly a favourite.

In the alcove under the stairs was a computer on a dedicated desk. Later, Ken told himself, he could study that later.

A small filing cabinet was next on his search. Ken took a pair of thin latex gloves, Boots' best, from his pocket and pulled the top drawer open. The contents were domestic rather than professional; the bills showed Flagg to be a light user of utilities, a prompt payer of bills.

Behind them was more official correspondence, not very interesting. He found a diary for 2002, which he would also leave for another day, having ascertained that its contents were modest and dry. There was a letter from a dentist, three months old, informing Mr N A Flagg that his appointment was being postponed.

In a folder was Flagg's NHS card, a letter confirming the qualified teacher status of Norman Anthony Flagg and several out of date membership cards of the National Union of Teachers. The oldest letter, from 1983, was a faded circular concerning the arrangements for a degree ceremony at the University of East England.

This was not helping. A cursory look around the kitchen and two small bedrooms revealed nothing of where Flagg was now. All of this was ordinary, there was nothing special here. The mail, when found, and the computer were likely to be richer sources of information.

A quick rifle through the rest of the filing cabinet revealed more information about the school but nothing more about Norman Flagg, a man who lived in a certain sort of limelight.

Gently, Ken pressed the 'on' switch of the computer with gloved finger and waited for the mature beast to cough and groan into action. He looked again along the shelves. As the PC warmed up he found, in a kitchen drawer, Mrs Goose's neat pile of mail and other communication: 'I paid the window cleaner for you,' said a note signed 'MG'. 'Please buy more toilet cleaner' said another, unsigned, in the same handwriting. Considering his status, age and income Mr Flagg received little mail. None of the three personalised envelopes amongst the circulars promised much at all.

The fridge was empty, save for a jar of mayonnaise with a screw top, an open jar of mustard and two apparently empty plastic boxes with tight-fitting lids. Mr Flagg had not left his home in a hurry.

Back to the computer: the blue screen was requesting a password. Damn! Ken's limited knowledge of information technology (such a pompous phrase, he thought) was such that he could not risk attempting to circumvent this obstruction. If he'd have believed that Flagg had been murdered, perhaps he would have tried. In an official enquiry a constable would no doubt be allocated this routine task. It would never be up to a retired officer to decide on such an action.

Back to the three letters. Steaming the envelopes open was not an option. One was manila and handwritten. One was white with a window and a PO Box return address which ought to belong to a bank or building society. The third had a computer-generated personalised address label on the outside and half-hearted adhesive under the flap, which needed very little encouragement to fall conveniently open. Within was a letter inviting Flagg to a grand dinner celebrating the 50th anniversary of the founding of the University of East England's Combined Cadet Force, taking place later that month. Nothing of great interest here.

He placed the invitation back in its envelope and reconstructed Mrs Goose's pile of papers in the drawer.

Before leaving the building empty-handed, the former police officer took a more thorough look at the folder of personal documents in the filing cabinet. In a plastic wallet at the back of the drawer were two photocopies of the teacher's birth certificate: Norman Anthony Flagg, son of George Norman Flagg, lathe operator, and Beryl Flagg, nurse; born 11th September, 1961, in Luton, Bedfordshire.

'Small world,' thought Ken. Did Peter Elder know that he shared a birthplace with the missing Head? And that they were almost twins?

Driving home, confident that neither arrival nor departure had been witnessed, no spoor left behind, Ken thought about all the information he had not found. Apart from the birth certificate, there was no evidence of family, not a hint of wife or former wife, no letter from any other personal acquaintance, nothing from the Child Support Agency, no greetings cards and no postcards from friends. Either this vacuum was genuine or they'd all been cleared away before the errant teacher's departure. If so, why? Over the whole of August no friend had bothered to send Flagg a holiday greeting. But the biggest mystery was that amongst all this data there was nothing to suggest a mystery at all.

* * *

Ken made a diversion to the supermarket for his Saturday 'big' shop and spent the rest of the day in routine mode. Promptly at six his doorbell rang and, by prior arrangement, Peter Elder arrived to collect both the key and the report of the newly employed private eye.

'So how did your conference go, Peter?' Ken asked as he handed the key over.

'Very well, thanks. I'm inspired! I'll spend tomorrow writing fifteen hundred words about strategic partnerships in the delivery of local government services and try to get it published. How was your day?'

'I'll tell you in a moment. I think we deserve a whisky, don't you?'

'It is after six, Ken.'

Five minutes later Hemmings and Elder sat once more in their comfortable chairs, whiskies in hand, but the nibbles, this time, were within easy reach. Ken was consulting his list of recollections from his morning's foray, printed from his own computer.

The former policeman described the fruitless nature of his work. Then:

'Were you born in 1960, Peter? Or 1959?'

Peter looked puzzled. 'Why?' Ken replied only with an inscrutable wink.

'1960, actually, June. And you?'

Ken laughed. 'Don't worry about me. You lived in Luton?'

'Yes... why?'

'Now, I don't know how many schools there were in Luton in the 1970s, but did you know Norman Flagg then?'

Peter stopped chewing his peanut. 'Why do you ask?'

'He's a year younger than you and he was also born in Luton. I don't know if he grew up there or maybe moved away, but your school years overlapped. If he did go to school there you might've come across him.'

Ken had not previously seen the politician stumped for words. The moment passed and Peter regained his composure.

'Yes, I did know him. Well done! At any rate, I knew of him. But it's not important. I didn't know him well, we may have met once or twice, it's... really just coincidence.'

'You genuinely have no idea of where he is now?'

'Ken, you have my word: I'm not sending you on a wild goose chase.'

Ken Hemmings wanted to believe his new friend, yet the two socialists had lived in the same town at the same time and it did not feel as though these 'reds' were necessarily herrings. On the other hand, years of police work had taught him that some coincidences were indeed just that: yes, coincidences did sometimes genuinely happen. But not very often.

'Remind me, Peter, where were you at University?'

'Oh...' Peter took a deep breath. 'Ken, believe me, this isn't... I mean – you obviously know the answer to that! Otherwise you wouldn't ask... it's an old politician's trick.'

It hadn't been difficult to find the councillor's curriculum vitae on the internet.

'You were at the University of East of England.'

'Indeed.'

Ken put on his 'more in sorrow than in anger' face for the first time since he'd left the Division.

'Peter, what am I supposed to believe?'

'Oh, this tangled web is worse than you think. Yes, we were at the same school, I was a year above Norman. We were in the Labour Party Young Socialists together and yes, we ended up at the same university. But we were on different courses and in different years, you'll be relieved to know. And we mixed with different people - very different people.'

'So, how well do you know him now? And what about the intervening years, did you keep in touch?'

Peter put his glass down.

'Let me tell you exactly. It doesn't change anything at all of what I said last night, or my worries about him, or my concern for the school. It doesn't actually change a thing.'

The councillor, the man who described himself as so centre-left as to be 'middle of the road', told his story earnestly. Ken, anticipating a significant period of intellectual stimulation and entertainment, relaxed.

'We hardly met when we were at school but our dads did work together at Vauxhall, and Tony and I – sorry, Tony is Norman's middle name.'

'I know.'

'The name he went by at school.'

That made sense. Norman was an unusual moniker for someone of the Head's generation.

'So we were at the same University, in different years. We were two years apart, actually, because he missed a year - took a gap year or something like that. We were both in the Young Socialists in Luton. In a town environment politics isn't the same as at University. The town group wasn't as radical as student groups tended to be, we were small and pretty mainstream, I suppose. Anyway, the branch saw itself as existing to support the Party, support the then government - essentially as part of the Party's infrastructure. When Wilson was PM, then Callaghan, everything was all right with the world. We just got on with things and - in a way, there wasn't a lot of politics in our activities - do you know what I mean? We weren't the blatant dating agency that the Young Conservatives were, and we did discuss political matters, passed resolutions and so on, but the fire in our bellies was pretty much… under control.'

'Go on.'

'Norman and I weren't close. It wasn't a large group, but large enough that we didn't get forced together. I didn't really get to know him. Look, I'll show you how close we weren't: I went to university in October 1978. He came along in, must have been 1980, so I was starting my final year. He'd been there more than a term before I bumped into him - February '81? I guess I might have heard on the Luton grapevine that he was coming up to Eastie but neither of us had bothered to look the other up.

'As it turned out, East of England, stuck out in East Anglia, hadn't been his first choice of University. He got in to read - was it Russian or was it politics? – on clearing.'

'What did you read? And what's 'clearing'?'

'I did Business Studies - of course!' He smiled with a touch of self deprecation. 'It paid off... 'Clearing' is where your grades don't quite get you onto your first choice of course or university, so they allocate you to somewhere else. To a course that doesn't demand such high grades.'

'I see.'

'So, early '81 at Eastie we renewed our acquaintance slightly – for a few weeks, at least.'

'What happened then? Did you fall out?'

'Let me go back to what I told you yesterday. Back then, an active member of the Party who went to University had to make a choice. Should you veer towards the complacent, intellectual, academic, relatively right wing University Labour Club? Or should you be more radical, less patient, look for simpler solutions to the problems of society, the economy and the world? And they don't get more simple, infantile and dangerous than Militant, I can tell you.'

'Yes, I remember Militant. So... you chose the soft route and Norman chose Militant?'

'He was calling himself Anthony then. Tony at school, Anthony then, Norman now. That's absolutely it, yes, he threw himself into it with huge amounts of energy. He didn't exactly speak at student union meetings, he ranted. He pointed his finger, you know, jabbed his finger in the air as he spoke' - Elder demonstrated the action - 'It's a sort of 'in' joke on the left, revolutionaries always stab the air when they pontificate.'

'You grew apart?'

'I should say so! We renewed our acquaintance in the February, by March he had shown his true political colours, a Trotskyist, he was more Trot than Labour if the truth were known, and he argued with all and sundry. By April I'd got my head down cramming for finals and wasn't active politically any more. I don't think I spoke to him once in that summer term, my last.'

'So what did he get up to? Politically?'

'He stopped coming to Labour Party meetings, not that he was ever a regular attender. Militant was technically a caucus of Labour Party members but in reality it was a separate organisation. 'A party within a party', Kinnock called it, a few years later. No, the Trots met separately. Some of them did come to moribund Labour Party gatherings, enough to force motions through that were not just hostile to the Tories but hostile to the university, hostile to – well, hostile generally, really. My reaction was to become pissed off by the railroading, by and large, leave them to it and get on with my finals. It was not the left's proudest period as a political movement.

'In public meetings, as I say, Union meetings, he'd rant. He'd grown his hair a bit since school but he always dressed smartly. He was especially critical of Russia, the Soviet Union - a typical Trotskyist position. In his second year I understand he became quite a dominant, influential, almost charismatic figure, acquired a personal following. I don't think he ever actually ran for office but whenever he proposed a motion he could rely on support from younger, more naive and impressionable elements. My lot regarded him as pretty dangerous, but in retrospect that intense goldfish bowl of student politics didn't matter a hill of beans off campus.'

Ken smiled, recognising the quote from his favourite film, *Casablanca*. But he wouldn't divert Peter from his story.

'So, less than two terms after meeting him again I left University - and I didn't look back. I remember wondering if he'd dropped out, he'd seemed so little interested in studying. But no, he saw it through. They had a 'modern', modular curriculum, if you recognise that? I guess he wasn't obliged to be on campus day in, day out.'

'Did he get his degree?'

'Yes, of course, it's on his CV. 2:1. No one ever disputed that he was bright, he just... didn't apply himself in a conventional manner.'

'And after University?'

'I don't think I ever gave him another thought until three years ago. I've no idea what he did.'

'I didn't see a CV in his house. Of course, I didn't look everywhere.'

'Oh, there was one in my files: here it is, I printed it off for you.'

He took a single sheet of paper from his pocket and handed it to Ken. It was printed on both sides but the lines were well spaced; it was a nicely produced, highly readable if not over-informative document.

It listed Flagg's academic qualifications including a Postgraduate Certificate of Education, completed four years after graduation, from a University with a more ancient history than the East of England could boast. There was then another gap, of three years, before he started work at a rural primary school in East Anglia. Five years were spent there, followed by two in Cambridge. The third employment was four years in the East End of London, the last three as a deputy head, from where he moved to Sussex three years ago.

'Isn't this CV a bit 'thin'?'

'There are some years missing at the start of his career, I don't know what was in them. But it pushes all the right buttons: 'succinct' is the word. His covering letter was strong enough to justify shortlisting for Head. Another governor had connections with east London schools and we heard some good things about Norman through that channel, informally. We took up references before interviewing him and they were impressive, I tell you. And he's done a good job for us, just what we wanted. He was the right man for the job and we haven't been disappointed.'

'When did you realise that you'd known him previously?'

'Not immediately. That Norman / Anthony stuff. I didn't put two and two together straight away, but I sussed it might be him shortly before the interview.'

'Did you tell anyone?'

'Actually, yes, I discussed it with the Clerk to the Governors and my Vice Chair. I offered to step down from the interview panel but they convinced me I didn't need to. We all agreed that on paper he was strong enough to merit an interview. I hadn't known Norman well before, as I said, it'd been a long time ago and there was no good reason for me to withdraw.'

'When did you first mention it to Norman?'

'After the interview, but before we decided to appoint. The Governors had previously agreed not to announce our decision on the day of the interviews but provisionally on the next. Norman was the last one to be seen. As he was leaving he said, I don't know... 'It's been twenty years,' something like that. It was hardly two brothers throwing themselves into each others' arms, the old prodigal son stuff, but it was polite, pleasant. Professional. I guess he knew that the interview had gone well and it was better to come clean then than later. Canny.'

'Since then? Have you discussed your common past with him since then?'

'No... Well, no. We don't exactly have fond memories of our times together. But I think it's known on the staff that we knew each other long ago. If we'd made a mistake and appointed the wrong man you can be pretty sure that this would all have been thrown back at me, but no one's ever mentioned it in a hostile way.'

Ken changed tack.

'Is he still politically active?'

'No. 'Given all that up,' he told me. I've no reason to believe he hasn't. In the three years we've been working together I've seen no evidence that he still 'indulges', as you might say. He's not even voiced a political opinion in my hearing - on anything outside education, at least. He was – is – passionate about schooling, but he doesn't stab the air any more, I'm pleased to say!'

'Going back to Luton; you told me about his father. Were there any brothers or sisters?'

'Ooh, now you're asking! I really can't remember.'

The conversation continued in a similar vein for several minutes, establishing that Flagg drove a relatively new Renault. Peter was preparing to leave when Ken said 'Did you know that Norman was a member of the CCF at University?'

'The CCF?'

'The Combined Cadet Force. A volunteer military unit.'

'You're joking!' Peter was bemused. 'I'm pretty sure he wasn't a pacifist, but he wouldn't have had much time for the army. At University he condemned Soviet invasions, American invasions, Vietnam, Chile. What would be the attraction of the army to him?'

Peter paused to think: Ken respected the moment.

'Thinking about it, they were awful people in the CCF. Public school types, Tories to a man. They'd have really got up Tony's nose. No, I can't believe he was in CCF.'

'When you were at school in Luton, did any of the schools have links to the CCF?'

'No, of course not. They only attach to public schools, surely? Ours was a comprehensive, they wouldn't have had that sort of thing.'

'You'd be surprised. When I was a young police officer I used to go to some state schools to check the security of their gun cupboards. The army provided them, installed them, but we had to make sure they were secure, in accordance with their licence.'

'Well... that's a new one on me.'

'There was a letter at his house, inviting him to a dinner at the University shortly, the fiftieth anniversary of the CCF. They'd only invite members to that sort of thing, wouldn't they?'

'I guess so. Why don't you ask them?'

'To do that would mean...'

'Going to the house again. Here's the key back.' Peter looked wistfully at the older man.

Here was a conscientious and responsible citizen, thought Ken, genuinely frustrated that without his Head Teacher he can't discharge his responsibilities to the children and their families. The former policeman had decided to return to the house even before the councillor looked into his eyes and proffered the key.

'Please?' asked Peter.

After Elder had left, Ken put the whisky glasses on the draining board and the remaining nuts into his mouth. He pressed 'rewind' on the video recorder and switched on the television; it was time to catch up with last night's fictions from Walford. Before sitting down he reached for the telephone.

'Clive?'

'Hello, Dad.'

'Glad I've caught you. Have you got a minute?'

'Literally! You know what it's like, on the job 24 hours a day. What can I do for you?'

Ken knew his son was on duty but it was still relatively early in the evening, thus probably quiet. Nevertheless, he still had to screw up his courage to make the call to Inspector Hemmings of Brighton police station.

'Can I ask a favour? I'll keep it brief.'

'Go on, I can't promise.'

'A chap who works in my village, local primary school Head, seems to have gone missing. There's no reason to suspect foul play, by him or on him, but the Chair of Governors is a... pal of mine and, well, he's going frantic. His school re-opens after the holidays on Tuesday, and he hasn't seen the Head since July.'

'And?' Clive asked, guessing what was coming.

'Any chance you could do a quick persons check for me? If we knew that the chap was dead or had already been reported missing, or in hospital, then a lot of heartache could be avoided down here.'

'Dad...' started Clive's protest.

'If I could just know if he's dead or been arrested, I've really no reason to believe he was up to anything. Whilst it's quiet, before the Saturday night rush starts...'

'Dad, you know I can't...'

'Clive, I know you can if you want to. You have the authority to interrogate PNC and it won't take you a minute...'

The son took a deep breath. Access to the Police National Computer was sacrosanct.

'Why don't you formally report him missing?'

'It's not up to me. If you tell me he's not been arrested or died then my friend might then take this into his own hands and formally report Norman Flagg missing.'

'Flagg?'

Ken spelt it out. 'Foxtrot, Lima, Alpha, Golf, Golf. Drives a red Renault, fairly new, model and registration unknown. Norman Anthony, born 1961, Luton.'

'Dad, I'm not going to argue. That would waste more time than doing the bloody search.'

'My thought entirely, Clive. Thank you.'

'But I disapprove, you know that. You've given all this up, Dad, you can't go round playing at coppers, you've no authority.'

'I know.'

'And I'm not going to do it again, OK? Dead or arrested, that's all.'

'I'd be very grateful. Peter will be very relieved.'

'Peter who?'

'Elder. Chairman of the Governors at the school.'

'Oh yes, you said. That's Councillor Peter Elder?'

'You know him?'

'I know who he is. I know he lives in your village, he's an important man.'

'So you'll do it?'

There was a significant pause. 'Are you coming for lunch tomorrow, Dad?'

'If I'm still invited.'

'We'll talk then.'

'It's a deal. Thank you, Clive.'

'Don't mention it. Oh, I mean that, Dad: don't mention it to anyone.'

* * *

Over Sunday lunch the grandfather revelled in his grandchildren's paintings, music and stories. The roast was as good as ever and Chris's stories of her mother's declining health were graphic but mercifully brief. Ken had rarely seen eye to eye with the woman whose legal relationship to him – the daughter-in-law's mother – had, perhaps significantly, never merited a title of its own.

After the meal Troy went to play with friends, Sable had a painting to finish in the playroom and Chris needed to prepare for her Monday classes. Ken and his son were alone, the dishwasher was whirring, each man held a glass of red wine and there was more in the bottle.

'You haven't asked me, Dad.'

'I didn't want to rush you!'

'But you knew I'd do it.'

'Thank you.'

'Norman Anthony Flagg, since 20th July: no admission to hospital, not reported dead or arrested, passport not scanned anywhere, though that doesn't tell you much. His car's a red Renault Megane, 2001 vintage, and it hasn't worried any speed or Congestion Charge camera.'

'Was there anything else on the PNC?'

'That's not what you asked.'

'Thank you, anyway.'

'Please don't ask me again.'

'I won't. Thanks, son.'

An hour later Ken was driving home, itching to report to his new friend.

Chapter 3: Afghanistan, November 1979

'Mr Darcey - you asked to see me?'

The young American rose from his seat in the corridor. 'Hi, there! Yes, sure. You're Mister, er…'

'I'm with airport security.'

The man in a suit opened a featureless white door in a plain white wall and ushered in his guest. 'Do come in. Please take a seat.' His manner was the epitome of English courtesy.

Darcey sat on a simple chair beside a basic table, deep in the bowels of London's Heathrow airport. The room was austere, with no natural light; a large window in one wall revealed blackness. Darcey wondered if it was one-way glass with a darkened cavity on the other side. Believing that listeners were sitting there made him feel important.

'How can I help you, Mr Darcey?' It was early November, 1979.

The middle aged man in a suit also wore a sober tie and a crisp white shirt. He placed a virgin pad of lined, A4 writing paper and a fountain pen neatly on the table and sat down behind them. Darcey felt conspicuous. The wavy blond locks that significantly overlapped his collar compensated for a forehead that was extending backwards with ridiculous prematurity. His two-day stubble lacked the definition enjoyed by men with darker complexions, his cotton shirt had been bought for a few cents in a Delhi market just a few days earlier; it wouldn't suit the autumnal weather outside this cocoon. He'd purchased his woollen jacket in a Himalayan village a month ago. On the floor alongside him was his battered, nylon, aluminium-framed rucksack sporting a red maple leaf emblem on a white background. Whilst Darcey would never deny being an American (his west coast accent told its own story) it was sometimes convenient, when travelling, to be taken for a native of a country with a more benign foreign policy than his own.

Whilst the rucksack had served him well over weeks of sub-continental travel, most of his possessions were still in the basement of his millionaire parents' home in Marin County, California. Thanks to their spontaneous generosity Darcey, 26, who possessed a third class degree in Comparative Religions and no career, had been 'seeing the world' for some years, prior to enacting some vague plans to 'settle down'.

His life was built on euphemisms, he sometimes thought.

At the end of this particular excursion the American's seasonal migration had seen him arrive in London from Frankfurt earlier that morning, but he had not requested this interview in advance. He had some hours to kill before his connection to LA would depart. He was a citizen of the United States and sometimes a citizen just had to do his duty.

'I have a story which I guess might interest you. I've just come from India.'

'Yes, you were on the flight from Frankfurt.'

Darcey paused momentarily, expecting a question but being presented with a statement of fact.

'That's right, Ariana Afghan Airways. Hey, you know they've only got one 747? No shit, only one! And the pilots, they're American! The national airline of a pro-Soviet country has American pilots, how about that? Some sort of deal with Pan Am. Not what you'd expect.'

The self-invited guest was showing his nerves, moving from quiet reticence to rambling in a matter of seconds.

The interrogator raised his eyebrows and smiled briefly. 'It's not what some people would expect, I'm sure. But you are Matthew Darcey's son and you would notice things like that.'

Darcey was taken aback for a moment; then he smiled. 'Hey, that's right! Do you know my dad?'

For the first time in his life he felt proud of his family's renown. Perhaps others, from less significant backgrounds, seeking to perform their American duty, might not have been granted an interview quite so readily. Hell, after all those years of trying to disown his parents there had to be some compensation for being the son of a retired head honcho spook.

'You departed from New Delhi, had one night stop-over in Kabul, flew out this morning, refuelled in Tehran, disembarked in Frankfurt and caught the shuttle to London. You're booked on a Los Angeles flight in five hours time.'

'Hey, that's right!' The young man's confidence was growing. He found this knowledge of his circumstances strangely reassuring. He smiled.

His interlocutor said nothing, now or later, about current events in Tehran. Darcey, who'd been high in the air over Europe as it was happening, had not yet heard of the US Embassy hostage crisis, which would see 52 Americans besieged in their own Iranian embassy for more than a year.

'Before we start, Mr Darcey, do you mind telling me why you chose that particular flight?'

'Sure... I'd been four months in India, it was time to move on. I'd heard that this flight had the stopover in Kabul and I thought hey, why not add Afghanistan to my list? Just spend a night there, you know, see what's cool. Hey, is it true they're thinking of stopping that stopover, because of the situation out there?'

Jet lag was not assisting Darcey's efforts to maintain equilibrium, but obtaining this meeting with the spy man was literally awesome.

'I believe it's on the cards. There is, as you say, insufficient stability in that country for the airlines to guarantee reliability of the service. I'll put it no stronger than that.'

'So I was lucky?'

'In a sense.'

'There was a guy on the plane.'

'And you want to tell me about him.'

'Yeah. There was something, you know, not quite right. And then I lost him.'

'Please tell me. In your own time.'

'OK, here goes. We got talking in the lounge at Delhi, the flight was delayed coupla hours. He was British, he called himself Gnat, or Ant, some insect or another: weird! I guess I just didn't hear his name properly when he introduced himself. I was embarrassed to ask him to repeat it. Not a good start, huh?'

The man's thin lips smiled, without conviction.

'I never saw the inside of his passport, but I did see it was British. Black, with a big, like, emblem on it, round holes for the name and number. Like you Brits have. I didn't catch his surname. So, it turns out we're on the same flight, all the way to London. Anyway, we just passed the time, talked about where we'd been in India. I did most of the talking, I guess. I'd been out in the Thar desert, Rajahstan? You know it? The Himalayas, Kulu, you been there? It's kinda nice. Maybe not your scene, huh? I had more to talk about than him, I guess. So... when we got on the plane, well, there were lots of empty seats, so I sat next to him, to continue our conversation.

'Turns out he's much younger than me, guess he's just finishing high school. He's been in India travelling for a coupla weeks and now he's getting back for the new semester. Looks a bit, like, 'tidy', for someone who's been travelling but what the heck, some people can carry it, I guess.'

'Go on.'

'He had a carryall with him, cabin luggage. Just a hunch, but I think that's all he had; nothing in the hold.'

The interrogator made a gesture which said: 'It doesn't matter. Carry on.'

'We talked a bit about Afghanistan, you know? He knew a bit about it: he told me about President Babrak Kamal, pro-Soviet guy, is that right?'

'Yes…'

'And like, this guy really governed just three cities, like the heart of the Afghan economy, culture, what have you. President of the nation but very little authority in the countryside. And that was fine, things were stable, not a problem, for years. The cities were communist but the countryside was Muslim. But that wasn't good enough for some people in Afghanistan and the new President who came after Kamal, he wanted it all his way, everywhere. Is his name Amin? Same name like the African guy?'

'Yes, it's Amin. Hafizullah Amin, not Idi.'

'OK, so that's the guy. Now he was pro-Soviet too, but he clamped down on the dissidents who were really like, Muslims. He closed mosques and that and like this was a Muslim country? I mean, that was their religion? They weren't happy. The Soviets weren't happy either. They wanted peace and quiet, like they'd never had any trouble from Muslims inside the Soviet Union and they didn't want them getting ideas now, in Tashkent and places like that, right? So Afghanistan's got a Soviet border? And this guy told me that a guerrilla army, the Muslim forces, were out to take revenge. Did you know that? They're planning something?'

'We're listening, Mr Darcey.'

"We?"

Darcey saw no one else in the room. His father had told him very little about matters professional, life inside the State. On the rare occasions he did mention his work, Darcey Senior had always referred to 'we' or 'us', never 'I'.

'Anyhow, I knew there were problems out there in Afghanistan but it seems like maybe I'd not done my homework too good. I'm telling you, this conversation was a bit frightening. That's when he told me there might not be another flight back with a stopover in Kabul after this one and I really wanted to get off that plane! But thirty thousand feet above the Punjab that's really not a good idea.'

Darcey smiled; the passive interrogator shrugged.

'So we land at Kabul, what an amazing airport! Like, is it under-developed or what? We were due on that famous 747 out of there the next day. But can you imagine? Taking off in a jumbo on a runway that's basically mud and ends with a wall of solid mountain? Awesome.'

The listener's patience was infinite. He raised an eyebrow to show he had registered the boy's excitement.

'I'm ahead of myself... So we get off the plane and across the airport building there's this slogan in huge writing: 'Welcome to the Land of the New Style Revolution', like, it's in English? And they don't just check our passports, they keep them. We get them back next day when we leave, I guess it's their way of making sure everyone who comes in leaves again.

'So they put us on a bus and take us to the hotel. And I'm still with this guy, Ant or Nat, and he's calm as you like but I'm shitting myself. Hey, did I say this guy had a bit of his thumb missing? Like, no thumbnail? That's a 'distinguishing feature', isn't it? Isn't that what the passport calls it?'

'Yes, it is. No, you didn't say.'

For the first time, the interrogator made a note: fountain pen, black ink, clean sheet.

'We passed a modern housing estate? Big, square, white apartment blocks. My friend says 'That's where the Russians live'. And guys with guns are on the bus. It's creepy.

'So we get to the hotel, more armed guards. There's a well dressed guy, western style, he's the manager, standing on the step saying hello to everyone, literally. He shakes each one of us by the hand and says hello, in English. We only have our hand luggage, everything else is still at the airport. He says, 'Hello, please stand over there.' And he asks me to stand one side of the foyer and this Nat guy on the other. And everyone is standing on one side or the other.

'It's 6pm by now, local time, and the manager gives a speech. He says 'Welcome to our hotel, but I gotta tell you that we have a curfew, so you guys shouldn't go out on the streets after nine o'clock'. Now, I wasn't planning much sight-seeing in the dark, but, shit, I don't like being told that I can't. It got worse: 'This certainly applies to you guys,' he says to the other group, the group with my friend in it, 'but to you' - that's me and my guys - 'you shouldn't leave the hotel at all.' Then I get it. My hair, right? My skin? Like, I do not look like an Afghan. Afghan hound maybe, you wouldn't be the first to say that, my aunt says that, my mother's sister, you know, what with the hair? But Afghan person, no. Nor do any of the others in my group look like Muslims. We're the blonds, we're the fair skinned group. It seems to me – and later Nat agreed – that my group looked like we could be Russians. In poor light. The Mujaheddin, they shoot first, ask questions later if they think you're Russian.'

The silent interrogator continued to write longhand.

'So the manager says, 'Dinner will be served in half an hour, please collect your keys.' Turns out I'm sharing a twin room with you know who. So I said, 'You know a bit about this place, don't you? What with the cool approach to all these guns and knowing where the Russians all live.' And he says 'Yes, I do.' End of story. This guy's young, remember. And he does look like an Afghan. Maybe. But at his age he can't be a spook. I mean, can he?'

The interrogator stared Darcey in the eye but ignored the rhetorical question.

'And he's in the 'home' group. I mean the 'slightly safer to go out' group. How cool's that? He's a skinny guy, straight dark hair, not pale like me.

'So, we're talking. He's so confident, he must have been there before. This hotel, I don't know, but Kabul, yes. Twenty years old, tops, maybe less, and I think he's been to Afghanistan before.

'Anyway, it's dinner time and we go down. Great food, goat stew. You had it? You should try that some time. The bread wasn't too hot, all doughy, like sticky, bland. Czech beer, in bottles. You go all that way to mysterious Asia and they give you Czechoslovakian lite beer. If I was European that would piss me, you know? But under the circumstances, hell, I guess it was OK. Not exactly Good Ol' Bud, but good stuff.

'Hey, did you know that they have Budweiser in Europe too? It's not like American beer, though. How about that?'

'Go on.'

'OK. Now there's a German guy with us, big guy, and, of course, he's blond. The waiter's brought a big pan of this stuff and the guy wants some salt. The waiter doesn't speak English, looks confused. This guy is miming shaking the salt but like he's not connecting? So Nat leans across to the waiter and says a word. Literally, can't have been more than two or three words. The guy goes off and brings out some salt! So this young guy speaks the lingo! What do they call it out there?'

'Pushtu, probably.'

'Pushtu. How about that? Eighteen, twenty, years old, whatever, he speaks the lingo! I'm sitting opposite and I say to myself I'll ask him about that later.

'So the food's over, he says 'I gotta go' and he goes. I just assume he's gone to the bathroom, but – like, I never see him again! I don't think much about it, I'm having a good time. I don't think any of my companions left the hotel at all. Except one. You know who.'

Darcey paused to reflect. The man listened stoically.

'Anyway, this beer's going down fine, but like we have to be up early next day so I bid these guys good night and go upstairs. He's not in our room and his carry-all ain't there, either. Closet, empty. I stand on the balcony, it's 9.30, maybe ten, and I look out, maybe I can see him in the street. No. There are searchlights on top of buildings and one beam's moving towards our hotel, what's that they say about discretion? I step back inside and I'm onto the bed and I'm straight out, like a light.

'Next morning, his bed's not been slept in. After breakfast we're herded back on the bus. I ask the manager what happened to my room mate and he says 'Sir, your bus is waiting' and turns his back. How about that?

'So, the guy's not on the bus and at the airport I get my passport back and mine's the last one, so his passport's not there. You've guessed, he's not on the plane either. He'd told me he was changing at Frankfurt for London, same as me.

'So the plane, the jumbo, is not busy. There's maybe 50 of us altogether. When we're up in the air I ask the steward, have we lost someone? He just smiles and tells me we've got everyone we were expecting.

'I guess that's the end of my story. Here I am. I know things are, like, delicate with the Soviets right now, talk of them invading Afghanistan… and I thought you ought to know this story, you know…?'

The Englishman was still writing.

'Once a Darcey, I suppose…' the younger man reflected. He leaned back in his chair and smiled. 'I'm sure my dad would, like, want me to talk to you.'

'I'm sure he would. Thank you. You've done the right thing.'

The interrogator wrote a few more words, then put his fountain pen down. Then: 'That's been very helpful, Mr Darcey.'

'I didn't get a chance to take a photo of him. Sorry. I didn't even get this guy's proper name,' said Darcey.

The interrogator smiled.

'Don't worry, sir. I think we know his name.'

Chapter 4: Sussex, September 2005

A more thorough examination chez Flagg was called for. The Head Teacher had more holes in his past than a string vest, but did they amount to a reason for disappearing?

As surreptitiously as before, Ken entered the small home. He looked around the main room again, this time not missing an inch. Within minutes his decision to return had been vindicated as several observations which he could have made previously, but had not, presented themselves.

Oversight 1: next to the computer was a device which Ken recognised as a docking station. So Flagg had a laptop too, which must still be in his possession. Hardly a killer fact. Perhaps he'd left the laptop at work? Ken was already planning to visit the school on the Wednesday, if it were still a Head-free zone, to talk to Flagg's Deputy, Jane Moore.

Another, smaller, docking station was labelled 'Nokia'. Flagg's mobile phone would be capable of synchronising contacts and diary with the computer, so finding either that or the laptop would be significant.

Oversight 2: the copy of Jimmy Reid's autobiography, 'Reflections of a Clyde-Built Man', was signed on the title page: 'To Anthony. Keep up the struggle. Jimmy Reid.' Flagg had still been in short trousers at the time of the Upper Clyde Shipbuilders strike but Reid, as leader of the insurrection, had undoubtedly been an icon for pubescent socialists of Anthony and Peter's generation. The signed book would be much sought-after in certain circles.

Oversight 3: to the left of the largest shelf of coffee table literature, the pile of magazines was not entirely contemporary. Underneath June's Education Review, a May New Statesman and a June Economist, was an amateur, photocopied publication dated June, 1982. This 'People's Struggle' coincided with Flagg's final year at University, reasoned Ken. There are very few reasons why people hold on to cheap magazines: it must contain an article written either by or about them, or someone close to them. It deserved a closer look.

The banner across the cover was bold and strident; its logo was two clenched fists crossed at the wrist, rampant. Beside a photograph so stark and grainy that the poor contrast made the black faces unrecognisable was an article in which a member of a South African revolutionary group was urging the ANC to bring down apartheid by rekindling its 'direct action' roots. The editorial proclaimed that Thatcher must be removed by a working class insurgency followed by the establishment of a People's Parliament to repeal 'Tory anti-working class laws'.

The publisher's address was in SE1, central London, south of the river. Ken recognised neither the magazine nor the street; printed over twenty years ago, the location was probably no longer valid.

Flagg's reason for keeping the magazine, well thumbed but not part of a set, was unclear. His name wasn't listed on the contents page so perhaps one of the revolutionary authors bore his pseudonym.

On closer inspection, the inside of the back cover might just contain a clue. The lower half of each column contained personal ads ('Non-smoking male admirer of Leon Trotsky seeks similar, female, for touring European sites of working class history this summer') and notices of meetings: 'Why true Revolutionaries should support the Argentinian People'; 'Call a General Strike Now!' and 'Revisionist TUC are selling out British Workers'. Above this was a diary column, of half a dozen very short stories. Some were libellous commentaries on public figures, mostly of the conventional left, purporting to demonstrate that Labour Party leaders were unfit for office for reasons of alcoholism, sexual infidelity (possibly involving animals), incompetence or congenital class treachery. One paragraph sought to establish support for an obscure revolutionary dance group from Bulgaria hoping to tour British universities. The rest were thumbnail accounts of meetings, including one at East of England University, also a venue on the Bulgarians' proposed itinerary. In larger, italic script at the foot of the column was the author's pseudonym: 'Red Flag'.

OK, so it was missing a 'g' and mention of that particular campus might just be another coincidence, but the article dated from a period when student radicalism was rife and Ken was no fan of coincidences. If 'Red Flag(g)' was not the most obvious name for an anonymous left wing columnist to adopt for a diary piece then Ken didn't know what was.

In any case, he reasoned, a columnist doesn't just write a single column; he writes several, periodically. So why keep this particular heirloom in the family archive for over 20 years?

Several of the articles were unsigned and the Editor unnamed, though an explanatory paragraph at the foot of the editorial page revealed that he was, in fact, a workers' collective.

Ken scanned the first of the unsigned pieces.

'In the twenty years since Jack Kennedy was elected President of the USA the depth of his lies, the fragility of his image and the purposelessness of his followers have all been exposed...

'Lee Harvey Oswald did us all a favour when he made the middle class pretenders of the western world open their eyes by executing the plastic messiah...

'JFK was a do-gooder, a superficial benefactor, his record was an excuse for leadership. His words were balm to liberal western conscience both in America and in Britain. Yes, he was right to say that the problems of the starving world had to be solved by his generation but did he ever intend to tackle that problem seriously? No. The American military industrial complex would never allow it and he knew that, even if he had the courage or intention or desire to pursue acts of popular liberation, which he clearly did not...

'Kennedy was Yankee aristocracy, the epitome of American nobility. He was psychologically, politically and intellectually incapable of leading ordinary people into an era of workers' power and people's democracy. The very fact that he held himself up as a leader, elected by a system in which many black people, poor and disadvantaged people, do not even register to vote undermined his claims to authority...

'Harold Wilson saw himself as Kennedy's equal. Today, some younger members of Foot's shadow cabinet see themselves as the President's natural heirs. One day they will be vying for the Labour leadership, each trying to out-Kennedy the others. It will be a pathetic, sickening sight as British class traitors squabble in the nursery over the right to mislead and deceive the working class...'

It takes all sorts, thought Ken.

He looked further along the bookshelf, peering inside covers for further handwritten inscriptions. There were a few, though none had the resonance of the Reid dedication. A green, fabric-covered book with no title on the spine was a short history of the Spanish civil war. Inside its cover, pencil marks suggested that it had inhabited more than one second-hand bookshop. The name of the owner was also pencilled in, printed rather than signed: A Flagg.

Oversight 4: behind the book was a crumpled piece of paper advertising a meeting in Bethnal Green, in London's east end, on 'Workers' Gauntlet: the Movement for the 21st Century', where the speaker was Arthur Birch. That name rang a bell. The meeting was arranged for Friday, 15th February in a community hall. The paper looked younger than the 'People's Struggle' newsletter: Ken's personal organiser told him that the last time

15th February had been a Friday was 2002. Prior to that it was in 1991, before Flagg was teaching in the East End, thus this was probably from 2002.

Arthur Birch.

Ken remembered a more distant era: the 1984 miners' strike. As a member of Nottinghamshire Constabulary, Sergeant Ken Hemmings had attended a clandestine briefing at which an unmemorable man from Special Branch in London had met a few select local plods. Arthur Birch's name had been near the top of an unofficial list of men (they were all men) deemed dangerous in the current context. Although Birch was due to visit the county to conduct a public meeting at the height of the conflict, local attention was focused not on visitors but on the local antagonism between the National Union of Mineworkers and the Union of Democratic Miners. This division at the coalface had caused visceral local strife, setting village against village, miner against miner and father against son. The theme of the Birch crusade was that the then seven-month old strike was the ideal basis for overthrowing the Thatcher government and bourgeois democracy in general. Having such a gathering take place in the Nottinghamshire coalfield could only be unhelpful.

Sergeant Hemmings never got to meet the redoubtable Mr Birch. He did, however, meet the caretaker of a certain community hall, the Chairman of its management committee, a friendly locksmith, a senior regional official of the National Union of Mineworkers (in a very private capacity indeed) and several discreet UDM activists. Suddenly the hall became unavailable, causing Birch's meeting to be cancelled at 48 hours notice, whilst Birch himself was firmly advised not to make his planned journey. The revolutionary hero had complied without demur and taken his campaign elsewhere.

Two thoughts crossed Ken's mind. The first was that three of the oversights so far addressed related to a single shelf in the teacher's living room. How many more were still to come? The second was that had he still been a serving officer he would now have been straight onto the telephone to find out if his subject was still politically active: despite the fact that Flagg had told Peter Elder that he was not.

The rest of the bookshelves were less fertile but the theme of revolutionary politics, the very fringe of democracy, as Ken saw it, was common to much of the content. He'd never heard of Workers' Gauntlet, which remained the only hint of Flagg's continuing political involvement of a remotely contemporary nature, though Ken was aware that such groups came and went on the extremes of politics, both left and right, with alarming frequency. Today, as long as Trotskyists, anarchists and other minority organisations kept their activities within the law (abstaining from violence, intimidation or sabotage) they were of little interest to the police. Generations of ineffectiveness had neutralised any general threat they might pose to 'law and order'. These days such groups competed amongst themselves more on the volume of their shouting or how often they got a dozen people to a 'public' meeting rather than on how much social change they actually achieved. As long as they left little behind but echoes of chanting and splintered placards it was allowed to let them fall below all but the most assiduous police radar. That had not been the case back in Ken's time on the Force, when Special Branch had wanted to know the whereabouts and activities of key people on a weekly basis, just for the hell of it, and a register of potential troublemakers was actively maintained.

Understandably, police attention in 2005 was more focused on the men with bombs and quasi-religious motives than on conventional left wing political conspiracists. Mohammed, rather than Trotsky, was the flavour of the month in such quarters. Here in the 21st century the values of the 6th were more of a threat than those of early 20th century Bolshevism. At least those committed to the hegemony of the working class – whoever they might be – resisted spilling innocent blood better than the plane hijackers who committed the outrage of 11th September, 2001, forever to be known as 9/11. That day, only four years ago, had marked the start of a new and more dangerous era. The bombs that had exploded in London earlier in that summer of 2005, known predictably by the euphemism '7/7', ensured that people like Ken's own son had to live and breathe the anti-terrorist cause in a way that their predecessors, such as Ken himself, had rarely experienced.

Inspired by a newfound determination he picked up the handwritten envelope that he had deigned to open previously for fear of leaving evidence of his presence. He slit it carefully along the top with his penknife to reveal… a request that Flagg return an overdue library book. So much for that.

Oversight 5 was extraordinary. Ken kicked himself that he had not thought of checking the telephone answering service on his last visit. He could see no answering machine and had forgotten about the 1571 answering service, which hadn't existed during his professional years. Even though he now used it at home, it hadn't occurred to him to try it on his earlier visit

With latex glove he picked up the landline telephone handset and heard a distinctive dial tone, indicating that messages awaited. He dialled 1571 and listened, notebook at the ready.

'You have ten new messages,' a female voice told him.

'Message 1,' the machine went on. There was a silence followed by a long beep, followed by the machine-spoken date of the call, in late July. 'Message 2' was similar, as was 3. So were numbers 4, 5 and then 6. But 7 was more revealing.

'Norman? It's Jane. I thought I might have heard from you. Give me a call at school, please. It's Friday. Thanks.'

That message was three days old.

A familiar voice had left message 8: 'Norman, can you call me back when you get this, please. We need to talk. It's Peter. Peter Elder.'

The absence of those messages would have been more significant than their presence.

Messages 9 and 10 were back to the usual brief silences. So this time he dialled 1471 and received another automated message: 'You were called, yesterday, at 18:03. The caller did not leave their number.' The dial tone resumed, back to normal.

This was extraordinary. If he assumed that all of the silent messages were from the same unknown source, which was not an unreasonable assumption for at least some of them, then maybe as few as three people had called Norman Flagg over several weeks. Either everyone knew he was away or no one was close enough to him to care. Flagg clearly would not have returned to his house over the period to collect his messages, then delete those that were meaningful to leave only the silent ones.

Oversights 6, 7 and 8 were revealed by the filing cabinet. As before, it was almost empty of anything of interest, including any reference to Flagg's mobile phone account. That could be checked by other means, should this whole thing go 'official'.

On the floor of one drawer, clearly misfiled, was a sheet of paper. It was a printed page from the internet – confirming Mr Flagg's ticketless booking of a budget airline flight to Barcelona, dated 28th July! And the flight was one way only, explaining in a flash both where the missing teacher had gone and his intention not to return. This was surely it, thought Ken, the breakthrough! Problem solved. It was now only a matter of time before…

Hmm. The flight was indeed for 28th July but 28th July 2003, two years previously. Oversight 6 exposed no clue at all. Flagg was as unlikely to be in Barcelona as anywhere else.

Seven, similarly neglected in the bottom of the drawer, was a receipt for a car service from a local garage, confirming the registration number of Flagg's car. If he'd known this earlier he could have saved Clive some trouble, but this find was no longer of much help.

Eight was a shoebox of trinkets in a cupboard in the bedroom. Every home has one; an orderless collection of souvenirs of sentimental value which mean nothing to the independent observer in the absence of context. There was a small piece of coal and a couple of small rocks, origin unknown. Some well worn campaign badges proclaimed student and political campaigns of the past. A tattered old address book was almost certainly too old to be helpful. Many of the addresses in it were from Luton and Dunstable, none from the vicinity of 'Eastie'. Some of the handwriting was adolescent, convincing Ken that this was a memento of teenage years of little relevance to his current detection. After noting that some of the Luton names were Asian, no surprise for that multicultural town, he abandoned it.

Folded neatly in the bottom of the box was a press cutting from the Socialist Worker newspaper. Under a headline 'The Eastie Uprising' was a grainy photograph of students marching, banner aloft. The text spoke of a demonstration in the local town to support a student rent strike, the justification for which was not immediately obvious. But that was newspapers for you, Ken reasoned, and this was typical student politics of the 1970s and 80s. On the picture, six or seven students were prominent. All had shoulder length hair and each was adorned with some combination of dark-rimmed glasses, leather jacket, sleeveless sweater and/or moustache. None were identified on the caption.

So his quarry may have possessed dark glasses, a leather jacket or a moustache 25 years previously. This was hardly cutting edge detective work.

Ken now realised that he didn't know what Norman Anthony Flagg looked like; there were no pictures of him in the house. Exactly what sort of detective did that make the old man to be?

Tuesday 6 September
Lamonde Associates was a successful insurance underwriter which didn't try to hide its affluence. Their office was on the twelfth floor of a recently constructed monstrosity near London's Liverpool Street Station: to the casual visitor the suite of rooms looked and felt like it belonged in a plush, grand hotel.

Ken Hemmings was unfamiliar with this way of life, although he'd tried to anticipate it on that morning's coach journey. Despite his legitimate reason for being in London - going to the theatre - he wore his smartest suit and a pair of shoes he'd bought the previous day. He held his macintosh over his arm and his trilby, as ever, in his hand as he looked down on the ant-like folk of the industrious City from a plate glass window. It was enough to bring on vertigo, so he didn't stand too close.

This day in the metropolis had been planned for some time so, in one sense, Ken had fallen lucky. The coach, organised by a local pensioners' group, had left Arundel at a civilised hour of the morning and was due to return from Victoria coach station after the show, arriving back in Sussex after midnight. In the in-between-time of the afternoon it was anticipated that the company would indulge in a spending spree before meeting at the theatre in the Strand. Ken had been looking forward to seeing 'Chicago'; he liked gutsy musicals. Now the day was here and the opportunity to combine business and pleasure was too good to miss.

'Mr Hemmings?' A pleasant voice distracted him from the ever changing view.

'Yes?'

'Gordon Sloane will see you now.'

The girl was all long legs and dark-rimmed glasses. Thirty years old at most, she wore a well cut blue dress which made attractive features of her slim waist and naked calves. She wore a wedding ring and a large diamond. No mere receptionist, she was probably a 'PA', whatever one of those was.

He followed her across the twelfth floor foyer obediently, unconsciously admiring her smooth locomotion underneath that soft blue fabric and momentarily reflecting upon his own age and mortality.

They approached a blank wooden wall, highly polished to an almost mirror-like state. As they all but walked into it Ken saw there was a door, which yielded to the young woman's touch. She turned, smiled him a smile that would have melted a younger man and introduced him to Gordon Sloane.

'Good morning, Mr Hemmings.'

'Mr Sloane. Thank you for seeing me at such short notice.'

'Not at all. Let me get you a coffee.'

'Please.'

Sloane was a growler: whether he was recovering from a cold, had a heavy smoking habit or was just suffering from a hangover it was difficult to tell.

'Take a seat. Cappuccino? Latte? Over here, let's take the easy chairs. Tremendous view, don't you think? The teeming metropolis.'

'Indeed, it's splendid.'

'Caf or decaf?'

'Oh... Just an ordinary white, please, as it comes.'

'Americano it is.'

The host pressed a button on his desk and when the device bleeped he asked Alison, no doubt a minion of lower rank than the gatekeeper, to bring coffee. Sloane was young, mid-thirties. He was stockily built, a rugby player capped by a quiff which stood to attention unaided, so blond it was almost unnatural. His chin was so smooth it might have been professionally shaven especially for their meeting. His hoarse voice seemed his only imperfection. 'O brave new world, that has such people in it!' thought Ken.

Sloane was Lamonde's 'client director', whatever one of those was. He had agreed to see Ken just the day after the latter's telephone call; the coincidence of his diary window with Ken's pre-planned trip to the capital had been serendipitous.

Sloane was an important man, no doubt, though it transpired that the haste to meet had not been entirely on Ken's account. The minor fabrications the investigator had prepared to ease his way into the appointment may not even have been needed. Today it felt as though he was going to be in luck.

'You're lucky to catch me, Mr Hemmings! I'm off to Washington tomorrow to fix a deal, taking two weeks R&R after that. I'm only in the office today to clear up a few odds and sods, so, yes, you've been very lucky to catch me.'

'Thank you for seeing me. I'm sorry it was such very short notice. And it won't take long, I assure you.'

'You've been lucky for another reason, but before I tell you let me just get one thing straight in my head.'

Ken raised his eyebrows as if to say: 'Go ahead.'

'You're a private investigator, is that right?'

Ken smiled at Sloane and let him think what he wanted to think. He congratulated himself on replying so silently, competently: illusion did not come naturally.

'You're looking for this Mr Flagg because…?'

'Can I just say 'domestic reasons'? You'll appreciate that in my line of work discretion is…'

'Of course.' Sloane's face erupted in a knowing wink. This was man talk. 'Yes, I understand, totally. 'Domestic', eh? So his wife's hired you to see if he's having an affair, is that it?' Ken smiled another inscrutable smile. 'I'll try to be as helpful as I can, of course, though I'm not sure how. Don't actually know the chap personally. But fire away - I can literally only spare ten minutes.'

'I'm sure we don't need longer than that,' Ken admitted, wondering whether that would leave him time to finish the coffee that had not yet arrived. Almost on cue, there was a knock on the door. It opened and the aforementioned Alison – a younger but similar, equally beautiful version of his greeter, but in an orange matching skirt and top – brought in the coffee. From the size of the cups Ken surmised that ten minutes would probably allow him time to drink four of them. The trend to microscopic coffee shots was another modern phenomenon which Ken did not regard as progress.

'And you got my name from…?' asked the businessman.

'You wrote a letter to Mr Flagg, a few weeks ago? You invited him to a dinner, a CCF reunion. It's an anniversary, I think? I mentioned on the phone that I'd seen the letter.'

'Of course,' said Gordon Sloane. 'Look, as I said, I'm going away tomorrow. But one of the ends I want to tie up today, before I leave this office, is indeed this bloody CCF dinner. Fiftieth anno, half a bloody century. Bit of a bore. Hotel wants to know final numbers PDQ so I've actually got the file here with me, which is your good news. The bad news is that I don't personally recall meeting your Mr Fagg.'

'Flagg. Oh, he was involved long before you were. It's Foxtrot –'

'Flagg, yes. And I don't think he's replied to me, has he? Let me have a look…'

Sloane picked up a pink folder and thumbed through its contents. He took out a printed spreadsheet. 'Yes, here he is: Mr A Flagg, Sussex, that the one?'

'Yes… he called himself Anthony when he was younger. It's Norman now. Norman's actually the first name on his birth certificate.'

'Hmm… Yes, he certainly had an invite to the 'do' but no, he's not replied. I'd hoped we'd have a pretty damn final list by last week. The dinner's in October but it's amazing how quickly these things creep up on one.'

Sloane was almost certainly a public school boy which was where, as Peter had pointed out, the CCF movement had its traditional roots.

'Fifty years old? But the University isn't that old, is it?'

'No, well spotted! That's right. It's one of those odd things where the CCF – the Combined Cadet Force – actually pre-dates the Uni. East of England started life as an FE college, but not your common or garden one. No, Eastie was a sort of finishing school for those public school types who didn't make it to Uni. The inbred, the congenitally ignorant! Well, that's the reputation, isn't it? Not true, of course, and I should know! About 1970 it was upgraded to a University. One of the first, before the rush in the 1980s.

'Actually, CCF is also a bit of a misnomer for what happened at Eastie. There are 240 CCF units across the country, almost all of them attached to schools, including about 60 in state schools, did you know that?'

Ken smiled. 'Funnily enough, I did.'

'Not what most people think. Anyway, back in the '60s, as a college Eastie took kids from age 16 so it qualified for having a CCF. In actual fact, since it's been a University and only open to 18-year olds and upwards, it's not technically a CCF.'

'No?'

'No. It's a UOTC – a University Officer Training Corps. Technically it's a branch of the Territorials. For those of us who were in the CCF at school it's a grown-up version, a bit more management skills-inclined. In practice it's the same sort of stuff, same attraction.'

'You still call it CCF in your letter.'

Sloane's face split in a huge grin. 'Sentimental softies! Back in the '70s it became a UOTC and no one really noticed. They called it CCF before that, they called it CCF afterwards.'

Sloane shrugged, and went on:

'I wasn't round back then, I graduated in '90, Business Studies. God, that was basic. You learn more in two weeks on the job in this place than two years at Eastie, I can tell you. Make or break stuff. Working here is testosterone, you might say, whereas Eastie's… Horlicks.'

He beamed with pleasure at his metaphor.

'So what can you tell me…'

'About Mr F? Sorry, of course. Well, let's see… my records show that he was a member for three years.'

'And that would be?'

'Let me see.' He perused the file. 'It was '80 to '83.'

The date matched what Elder had said, that Flagg had graduated in 1983.

'Would it have been unusual to have a member of the CCF – UOTC – who was… left wing?'

The blond man did a double take then laughed aloud. 'What? Left wing? Ha! You're joking, aren't you? We had the odd one who was pinko in sexual preference terms, but not pink in politics, oh no! No, I wouldn't have thought so.'

That was sufficient reply. Ken moved on.

'What would Mr Flagg have done? I mean, what do people do, as members of a UOTC?'

'Done? Well, he would have had army discipline, camp craft, fitness, rifle training, first aid, combat courses. Strategic thinking. Most of our members would have been in the CCF at school. I know Eastie's a redbrick, but, like I said, it was still a sort of home from home for those public school types who didn't make it to Oxbridge and wouldn't be seen dead at Warwick or Lancaster. Perish the thought. But every year there are one or two not from that background. Real beginners. Did you know that there are about 40,000 youngsters in the CCF these days?'

'Really?'

'Camps, kayaking, rifle range, all that sort of thing.'

'On campus?'

'What?'

'The rifle range?'

'Yes, actually. Funny, really. Every few years some hairy type' - here he waved his fingers to illustrate quotation marks - 'would 'discover' where the rifle range was and do an exposé in the student rag. Six months later they'd forget about it and leave us alone. Three years after that the student population would've changed and it would happen all over again! Wasn't secret: but we didn't exactly go around shouting about where we popped a few rounds off, either.'

'Do your records show whether Mr Flagg was an active member? Of the UOTC at University or of this alumni group that you run, after leaving the University?'

'Alumni, no, well, certainly not now. I'd know if he'd been active since about 1988. As far as when he was at Uni, it's difficult to tell from my records - before my time. But people who didn't take part – take the tests, powers that be were pretty rigid about that – didn't last the course. Your friend Flagg obviously did.'

'I see.'

'But what's this got to do with his infidelity?'

For a moment Ken was genuinely puzzled by the question. Then he remembered.

'Who said anything about infidelity?'

Sloane smiled again, a big, broad, beaming, conspiratorial grin. 'Aha, Mr Hemmings! Very clever. The discretion of the private eye, I see! Very good. Very good!'

Ken resumed on safer territory. 'Mr Flagg had a comprehensive school background.'

'Did he, now? Well, that's unusual. Did he play rugger?'

'I don't know.'

Ken realised that he'd finished his coffee. Had it been two sips or three?

'I've been in my current position five years now, Mr Hemmings. That's a long time in my profession. Insurance is a cut-throat business, live by the sword, die by it. Know what I mean? I used to work with comprehensive school types, when I was lower down the food chain. They were useless, absolutely useless, degree or no degree. It comes down to the schooling - do they have the character for an important job like this? That's the question. By and large, the answer is 'do they, buggery'. Or, in real money, 'no'.

'Do you know, I've never knowingly seen a state school boy promoted to anything in Lamonde, since I've been here?'

Ken didn't know how to respond. He may not have been a political animal, but he could recognise prejudice when he saw it. A man of Sloane's relatively tender age was not capable of making judgements about the lives and careers of others, he thought, taking his own career progress as a guide. Sloane might be in his thirties, but he was still a boy in many ways.

'Look, we've had our ten minutes and I'm really going to have to get on. I've told you a bit about Eastie CCF and a tiny bit, I suppose, about your man, Alan Flagg.'

'Anthony. Anthony Flagg.'

'Whatever. I hope it's been helpful, I realise it's not much, so I also hope you don't feel you've been brought up to London on a wild goose chase.'

'Not at all, Mr Sloane. You've been very helpful. Thank you.'

* * *

Ken still had several hours to kill before 'Chicago'. He was looking forward to the colour, the pizzazz, the excitement of the lustful Fosse masterpiece and its pulsating noise: it was his treat to himself, his indulgence.

He took a diversion on foot over Southwark Bridge, then headed south, following his 'A to Z' guide. Within five minutes he'd answered another outstanding question: there was no sign of The People's Struggle editorial office at the address in the newsletter. In its place, shielded by plywood fences, was a very large hole in the ground, crawling with diggers and men in hard yellow hats.

Wednesday 7 September

Ken put down his tea towel when he heard the car horn. He waved through the kitchen window at Peter Elder, who sat in his Volvo in the street, then took his jacket from its hook. It was 9.20 on Wednesday morning. Shutting the front door behind him he strode eight paces to his garden gate and got in the car.

'Good morning, Ken!'

'Peter! What a swish car! We're travelling in luxury…'

'Just think of it as a workhorse. D'you find anything out yesterday?'

'You're quick off the mark!'

'I don't want to talk about it at the school. We'll be there in three minutes.'

'Well, no killer clues, if that's what you mean. Quite a lot about his political past. He went on holiday to Spain two years ago. So there's been no news?'

'No. I've spoken to Jane Moore…'

'The Deputy.'

'Indeed. They had a pre-term staff meeting on Monday, which I sat in on. They spent five minutes collectively worrying where Norman had got to, but then they just continued as though nothing had happened. That's the sign of a good Head: he has a system, even on day one of the school year, that can look after itself when he's not there.

And a good deputy, too. I'm not saying they didn't notice his absence, obviously they did, but I didn't worry them with my concerns.'

'Did you share them with Jane?'

'Well… no, not really. She knows you're interested and that you're a retired policeman. My priority – and hers – has to be to keep the school running. But I'm worried about him, as you know.'

'Where did you say he was?'

'I had to be honest, so everything I said was true, even if not complete. I admitted I didn't know where Norman was and that he hadn't been in touch. I didn't speculate… and I didn't tell anyone, other than Jane, about you.'

'So why am I here with you? Officially.'

Peter looked at his watch. 'School will have started and Jane will be finishing assembly. I've booked to see her at 9.30 but she might not be expecting you today.'

They approached the school grounds. Peter leaned out of the car window and punched a security code to open the gate. He took the last remaining vacancy in the staff car park and the two men walked the twenty metres to the school door and a second security code.

The receptionist was matronly; she was busy feeding register forms into a computer via a bar code reader. Peter smiled at her as he signed the visitors' book and picked up a visitor's badge. Ken waited his turn.

'Jane's expecting you, Mr Elder. Please go on through.'

'Thanks, Irene.'

'Gosh,' said Ken, 'it was never like this when I was at school, all this security. And that was only a few years ago!'

'It's a sign of the times. All schools are like this now: pederasts, angry absent fathers, terrorists: in theory, we're ready for all of them. Security's one of the things Norman brought from the East End, I suppose, one of the first things he introduced.'

The two men entered the Head's office and Elder gestured towards the two easy chairs.

'Just before I sit down, Peter – may I look at these pictures?'

'Of course.'

Photographs hung along the walls. On closer inspection, pictures of adults were very few and far between; most were of children, achieving things. When a new play facility had been installed children had performed the opening ceremony. When the school had received an Arts award children had led the celebration, and when the star of the local pantomime visited it was children who had welcomed her. This was child-centred education with a vengeance, yet no youngster was identified by name on the photos. Security ruled in this school.

If there was a photograph of Norman Flagg amongst the collection it did not stand out.

'Peter, what does Norman look like?'

'Oh... dark haired, receding, my age – as you know – taller than me and slimmer, damn him, don't know how he does it. Narrow face with a five o'clock shadow... there'll be a photo in the book.'

Elder indicated a photograph album on a shelf behind them, but a cursory glance failed to locate a suitable picture here, either.

'I know! When he started here, three years ago, there was a photo in the local paper. I'll get Irene to look out the old album, I don't know where it's kept. If the worse comes to the worst I'll have a copy at home somewhere.'

'The newspaper will have a copy.'

'Indeed. Aha! Jane!'

The Deputy Head had entered the room. She too was tall, slim, dark haired – but there the similarity with her line manager ended. Her dark eyes were apparently not enhanced by make-up but her lips were plastic red. Ken noted that she exuded confidence, wore no wedding ring and dressed in a manner that was both sober and snappy. Her blouse had narrow black and white vertical stripes and a flamboyant collar with a modest décolleté; she had well fitted, comfortable black trousers and workmanlike, sensible shoes.

'Peter, it's good to see you!'

'Jane!'

Each touched the left upper arm of the other and allowed the other to come cheek to cheek in a momentary kiss-substitute gesture.

'Jane – Ken Hemmings. I mentioned Ken might be with me.'

'Of course,' she smiled at the visitor.

'Miss Moore.' Ken returned the smile.

'So – how's it going?' asked Peter.

It was second nature for Jane Moore to take the seat at the Head's desk.

'We're coping, Peter. School's been up and running now for a full day plus half an hour.'

Peter 'came over all formal', as Ken later described it. 'You know that both I and the governing body have the utmost confidence in you.'

'Thank you. I'm sure we'll manage. Have you any news about Norman?'

'I was going to ask you the same question.'

'No. No news.'

'If there's anything I can do, Jane...'

'I'm sure we'll manage.'

'I'll call in each day to check if...'

'That won't be necessary, Peter, really. But thank you. I'll phone if I need you, but you really don't need to worry. I've a full complement of teaching staff, everything's under control.'

'If you need to take on a supply teacher...'

'I've engaged one already, thanks. I've taken myself completely off timetable, at least for this week, and – I'm not being awkward, Peter – but decisions about supply teachers and the day to day management of the budget have got to be my responsibility. Where strategic decisions need to be taken you'll be the first to be consulted. Sorry, I mean 'involved'. Forgive me.'

Ken felt as though he was witnessing a private family tiff. It clearly showed on Peter's face.

'I'm sorry, Mr Hemmings,' said the Acting Head. 'This isn't what you came about.'

Ken smiled, almost apologetically. He wondered exactly how much Jane Moore knew about his mission.

Peter looked almost embarrassed, but it passed within moments. The politician's sangfroid was soon reasserted.

'Jane, Ken's a friend of mine from the village. Over the last few days he's been trying to find some clues about where Norman might be. Ken's a... private investigator. Don't worry, this isn't going to cost the school anything.'

'Actually, I'm a retired police officer. My services are voluntary.'

'And have you found anything?'

Peter took control: 'Nothing categorical. We've ruled one or two things out. We don't think he's... dead... but the absence of meaningful clues is... interesting.'

The Deputy Head was unmoved; having a detective in her office seemed the most natural thing in the world.

Peter addressed Jane. 'You don't have *any* idea where Norman might be?'

She thought for a moment. 'His absence has taxed my imagination from time to time but I'd no reason to worry about it seriously until you mentioned your concerns last week, Peter. You were trying to play it down, you said you expected him back over the weekend, if you remember. I'm trying to follow your example. It was only the day before yesterday, the day before term started, that it really hit me that we had a problem

- and that I was going to have to deal with it. I really haven't had much time to wonder where Norman might be. Sorry.'

'Nothing at all?'

'If anything occurs to me you'll be the first to know, Peter.'

There was a brief impasse.

'You'll let me know if there is anything I can do, Jane.'

'Peter, of course I will. I thank you for your concern, really. I'm sorry if I sound officious. But I just don't need to have my eye taken off the ball right now, I'm sure you see. I've got a school to run.'

'Of course.'

'I'm an experienced Deputy and I'd like to be a Head one day. Right now there's so much to do; I know I can do it.'

Peter started to protest mildly, but Jane continued: 'You know this school, Peter. We have a great staff, manageable class sizes – at last – new resources and a budget that's just about in balance. Thanks to Norman we have good systems which work and I want to keep it that way. But you should see my inbox this morning, not to mention the backlog of parcels and letters.'

She went on: 'You know, the council, the government, the civil servants at the Department, they all think they know how to run schools better than the professionals.' She ought to sound angry, thought Ken; instead she was matter-of-fact. 'We're being suffocated by paperwork. A lot of the fun's gone for staff, teachers and Heads with all this dry bureaucracy, delivering other people's agendas. But what we do is good for our kids and we know how to do it well. If I didn't get a thrill, a tingle down my spine, every time I see a kid smile because of something we've done, or see the realisation on their faces when some new skill clicks, new knowledge sinks in – if it wasn't for all that I wouldn't be here, Peter.'

Peter edged forward, wanting to speak, but again she continued:

'When you told me the other day that it was all down to me now, I wanted to run a mile. But I didn't. I'm here, enjoying the challenge. I've got that tingle here and now, it's my second day in charge of a school of kids. My leadership, experience, skills are on the line. Keeping it happy, keeping everyone on board.'

She dropped her voice, almost to an exultant whisper: 'And I love it!'

Peter, chastened, again edged forward on his chair; then paused in response to a brief upraised forefinger.

'I'm grateful to you, Peter. You're a good Chair. You're supportive, you understand the issues, you've got the right balance of legitimate concern combined with the need to be a bit – well – hands-off.'

Peter smiled ruefully. This was admonition of the highest quality, a stylish stiletto rather than the blunderbuss of political put-downs with which the councillor would be more familiar.

He took a breath: 'I think we need to leave you to let you get on with it. Sorry about this, Ken... I thought we might talk a bit more about Norman, but perhaps... another time.'

Jane addressed the visitor: 'It's not that I'm not willing to talk, Mr Hemmings, even though I really can't think what I might say that might help.'

'You'd be surprised, Miss Moore.' Ken noticed one of the teacher's eyebrows rise and fall. 'In my years as a police officer I learned most from those who thought they could tell me nothing.'

'Hmm, perhaps later in the week?'

'Of course. Tomorrow – how about after school?' Ken suggested.

Jane Moore turned effortlessly to her computer screen and clicked the mouse twice on her calendar page.

'Four thirty?'

'No problem.'

Peter looked inexplicably at his watch. 'I'm not sure I can make that...'

'Between Jane and myself I'm sure we can manage, Peter. Thank you for arranging this introduction. If I may, though, perhaps just ask one question for now; one which I am sure Peter has already asked. Did Norman give any hint of where he was going this summer? How long he would be away?'

'We excel at numeracy in this school, Mr Hemmings. That was two questions.'

Ken smiled enigmatically.

'No, nothing. Two summers ago he went to Barcelona, I remember; he had a passion for Gaudi, he always wanted to climb the towers of the Sagrada Familia. Last year... let me see. He was away for three weeks during the children's summer break, but I can't recall where.

'This summer, the deal was that he would be away for two weeks and then I was going to do the same, so that one of us was around, if needed, all of the time. On call, as it were. I only got back on Thursday and I called him on Friday' – 'I know', thought Ken – 'but he didn't call me back.'

Ken asked a question to which he knew the answer, a technique which can sometimes elicit an unexpected response.

'Was that on his mobile or landline?'

'Landline. I tried his mobile a couple of times but it wasn't taking messages. We pray for peace from our own phones then get exasperated when others switch theirs off!'

'Indeed,' murmured Ken. He brought the conversation to a conclusion. 'Until tomorrow, then... Jane.'

The school had a quiet air of order and organisation as they walked through the foyer. The men signed themselves out. It brought back memories of Ken's days as a reading mentor and husband of a primary school teacher: good days.

In the car, Peter said 'Do you remember I said that Jane Moore is a Ms, not a Miss?'

'Pardon?'

'Did you notice she riled when you called her 'Miss'?'

'Is that what it was...'

'She prefers Ms.'

'I'll try to remember that. In my experience it's normally the other way round. A lot of women are offended by the modern term.'

'So what do you call a woman when you don't know her marital status, Ken?'

'But we do know Jane Moore's status, don't we?'

'Some married women don't wear a ring... but yes, she's single. But that's not the point. Why should a woman be known by an epithet which denotes her marital status, both when a man isn't and when she prefers not to be? Did you know that in Spain all women over about 20 are called Senora these days?'

'Do you mind, Peter? I really don't want to get into an argument! I'll call her 'Ms', if it helps.'

'Fine. So, what now?'

'Let me think.'

Clearly more thinking was required than the brief journey allowed. Neither man said anything more until they reached Ken's home. Getting out of the car Ken said to the driver: 'If you had a 'passion' for Gaudi, Peter, wouldn't you have at least one book about the master on your shelves at home? Or, indeed, one book about art or architecture at all?'

Thursday 8 September

Sheila used to call it 'pottering'. Ken let a whole morning go by without achieving very much, though in retrospect he did a lot: weeded the window boxes, placed an internet order with the supermarket, did more washing up than it seemed possible for a conscientious singleton to accumulate, washed and dried a light load of underwear, socks and shirts. During the laundry time he honed his recently acquired Sudoku skills.

He squeezed in some of the thinking he'd promised to do about Peter Elder's problem of the missing Head Teacher. It seemed to Ken that he had four options of which two were reasonable, two not.

The first was to hand the whole thing over to his son with a request that Flagg be formally classed as 'missing'. This was an inadequate solution. Flagg hadn't been reported missing by his family. He wasn't 'vulnerable', not mentally deficient, a child, a disabled person, a frail pensioner or a young female. He appeared to have no dependants. The police procedure would make superficial enquiries and computer checks in the first 36 hours and then the case would be filed. There wouldn't even be a photo of the elusive Flagg with 'Have you seen this man?' beneath it in relevant police stations, launderettes or post offices.

At least the question of the photograph had been resolved. Early that morning, whilst Ken had been reading in bed, vaguely following the progress of the Today programme on the radio, he'd heard his letterbox clatter. The manila envelope bore the words

'Out all day. Got to rush. Peter. PS Talk tonight.'

Inside was a photocopy of a story from the local newspaper about the welcome given to the new head teacher at the village school by parents, governors and children. Three years ago, almost to the day. At the heart of the grainy photograph was Councillor Peter Elder, Chair of Governors, shaking hands with the new Head, Norman Flagg.

Ken's technique for remembering faces was tried and tested: Norman Flagg was a clean shaven Jeremy Irons, with the same slim face and top-heavy mop of hair the actor had adopted in the film *The French Lieutenant's Woman*. The photo showed no trace of Flagg's legendary five o'clock shadow, but it was taken on his first day in post and he would have wanted to look at his best that morning.

The second option was to admit to Peter what was probably the truth, that they had insufficient resources to carry on the search and there was little they could expect, in reality, to achieve. Norman had probably decided to disappear, for some perfectly rational reason. This would mean simply leaving Jane to get on with her job of being Head Teacher Designate until, at least, such time as Norman could be dismissed from his contract (assuming he didn't turn up later).

Then, leaving the realms of reality, were options three and four.

Three, Peter would finance a major search starting by sending Ken to Barcelona, chasing two-year old leads. Such a search was probably doomed to failure, but so what?

Between Barcelona, delightful at this time of year, or the east end of London Ken knew which he would prefer to investigate.

Number four involved coming clean with his son and recruiting the Inspector to a surreptitious search campaign, using the Police National Computer in what would effectively be an undercover operation at taxpayers' expense, under Ken's direction. Ethically, this had to be a complete and utter non-starter.

With Peter away for the day, the decision could wait. Time flew in the hours leading up to 4.30, when Ken found himself in the Head's office once more.

By 4.35 nothing had changed and the computer's screen saver had become hypnotic. At 4.37 Jane Moore entered.

'Ken, I'm really sorry, I've a couple of parents to see, we've had bit of a crisis with a new boy this afternoon, I'll be ten more minutes, is that OK? Or would you rather come back tomorrow?'

That was not an option. If either option 1 or option 2 were chosen tonight then this interview would never take place and that would be a pity. The case was interesting, after all.

'No, I'll wait, if that's all right with you. Do you need your office?'

'No, no. I don't want them to feel intimidated, I prefer to see them in a classroom. Small chairs, not Head's territory. Inclusive. Reduces stress.'

'Fine. I'll wait here then.'

'Ten minutes. Cup of tea?'

'No, you're busy.'

'Just ask Irene if you want one.'

For the first time in their brief acquaintance Jane displayed a sweet and enchanting smile. She was feeling the pressure even though clearly coping with – perhaps enjoying – her first week as Acting Head.

So Ken had ten minutes in her office, on his own. Ten minutes would be long enough to... there was an elderly, large brown photograph album on the desk, similar to the one he had glanced at previously, so it would be no crime to look at it in more detail. He sat in the Head's chair to get purchase on the large pages and leafed through it.

The photograph in question was not hard to find. Of better definition than the copy he'd already seen, the original print of the newspaper image told him nothing he didn't already know. The rest of the album confirmed Norman Flagg's reticence to have his photo taken at all, as he appeared nowhere else.

As he closed the book, Ken's hand touched the computer mouse and the screen lit up. Several programmes were running including Internet Explorer, open at Teacher Net.

Ken glanced through the vertical glass panel in the door to the office and saw no one. Just out of interest, of course, he used the mouse to hit Explorer's 'History' button. The computer had been used several times in recent days but before that it had clearly lain untouched for several weeks. Unless the History settings were set in an austere manner, some of the web sites listed would be those last accessed by Flagg.

At last! His hunch had paid off: here was some new information. Four sites at the bottom of the list had no obvious connection with the primary school curriculum. They were for Hathersage Homes which, counterintuitively, turned out to be an estate agent in Brighton; Fintons (ditto); Searchlight, the organisation which monitors the activities of far right organisations in Britain and Ken's old acquaintance, workersgauntlet.org.uk.

He had no time to investigate further. He made sure the web browser was back on the page it had started from and hoped to hell that the screensaver would be triggered before evidence of his exploration could be detected. As an insurance policy, he noted that the screen itself was not visible from the door so he should be able to stall before anyone who entered the room could see it.

He returned to perusing the unhelpful school album. Sure enough, exactly as the door opened the computer screen reverted to black, with geometric designs rotating and bouncing all over it.

'Right! You've not had tea? Let's have it now, shall we?'

Jane Moore was brighter and more breezy than previously; this woman was seriously enjoying herself. She disappeared but returned within a moment.

'On its way! No news?'

'About Norman? No, none.'

'So... fire away, Ken.'

The two occupied the comfortable chairs. Jane Moore sat formally, her body well back in the seat, knees crossed, stockingless feet in sensible court shoes. Ken Hemmings wore a pale grey suit and striped tie, his face and shoulders pushed forward in an attempt to inject security and intimacy into the conversation. The study of body language and its use was something that had come to Ken only relatively late in his career.

'How well would you say you knew Norman Flagg?'

'As well as any deputy knows her Head. I've been his deputy for two years.'

'Were you teaching here before that?'

'Yes, four years. Altogether I've been teaching for 12.'

'You were Norman's choice as Deputy?'

'Erm…' She smiled. 'I wouldn't want you to think that. I was the only internal candidate for the job and yes, he encouraged me for to go for it, but it was a completely open and fair selection. He never let me believe it was in the bag; he wanted the best for the school. Three others were interviewed and we were all put through the mill for a day. I got the job on merit. Ask Peter Elder.'

'Oh, I'm sure you did. I've never been a teacher but I was married to a primary school teacher so I know a little about it. Without being patronising, I'm sure you deserve your position and that you'll go far.'

'Thank you.'

'May I ask you the same question again? This time I would like a qualitative answer. How well would you say you knew Norman Flagg?'

She considered her response. 'He's a very good Head, very professional. He confided in me a lot, but it was always clear that he was the Head and I was number two.'

'He confided in you?'

'Professionally, yes. I know as much about what is happening in this school – and with individual children – as anyone does or could. He's paid to take the responsibility of making the decisions; I'm paid to help him make the right ones and help deliver on them. Together we run this school and run it well. It's like I said yesterday, his systems are good enough for us to run the place even without him. For a while, at least.'

'Is he a reliable person?'

'Totally.'

'So how do you feel about him disappearing?'

'If I had the time to think about it I'd be pretty upset, I suppose. Disappointed. Worried. I don't know what's happened to him, I really don't, but if he needs to take time out then he needs to take time out. I trust his judgement, at least until there's good reason not to. I… would've liked to have known about this absence and planned for it. More than that, I'd like to think he would trust me with the reason for it.'

'Of course.' The woman was being very open with him.

There was a knock at the door and Irene, the school secretary, entered. She placed two mugs of tea and a bowl of sugar on the table between the two.

'I'm off now, Jane.'

'No problem, Irene. Thanks for today.'

'I'll be in by eight tomorrow? Just in case you need anything.'

'I'm sure you don't need to come so early, but thanks.'

They exchanged smiles and Irene left.

'Are all your staff as co-operative and helpful as that, Jane?'

After a moment's thought she replied 'Pretty much. Norman and I treat them professionally. We don't ask them to do what's not reasonable - within the framework of what our lords and masters regard as 'reasonable', that is.' Ken recalled the teacher's view of the various education authorities from the previous conversation. 'It does pay dividends.'

'Is that ethos something Norman's built up or did he inherit it? You were a foot soldier back then.'

'Oh, the previous Head wasn't bad. He took early retirement and I think he was coasting for a couple of years at the end. This is a profession of constant change, Mr Hemmings. It's traditionally very demanding but when the rules change about this, that and the other, virtually every term, anyone in a position of responsibility who tries to take it easy is risking failure. You have to embrace a culture of change whilst giving the impression of stability. This school was ready for Norman. He challenged our plateau of confidence, gave us new aspirations.'

'Impressive. What d'you make of Peter Elder?'

'Peter? Goodness, are you investigating him, now?'

Ken smiled. 'Not at all.'

'He's fine.'

'Do you know if people – I mean the staff – are generally aware that Peter and Norman knew each other in their childhood?'

'I think so, now you mention it. People aren't responsible for accidents of geography and history. I don't think anyone thinks anything of it. I don't know that they knew each other very well.'

Ken motioned her to continue: she did.

'They make a good team, Peter and Norman. Norman's professional, passionate, capable. Peter's supportive, sensible, very caring about the school. He does what a Chair of Governors ought to, stands up for our interests in the corridors of power – or so he would have us believe.'

'Would 'passionate and professional' describe Peter, too?'

'Hmm.' She pulled a pensive face. 'I'm not sure I didn't use the words deliberately. But it's true. Peter's capable and competent but 'passionate' isn't... he's more clinical. I know he's a politician, so maybe you'd expect some passion from him, but with Peter it's – I don't know – a systematic, meritocratic approach. He's keen to do whatever Blair and the Secretary of State of the day might want him to do, he wants to be the first in the area with the Brownie point, while Norman... well, Norman takes a more child-centred approach.'

'Do they argue?'

'No. As I said, Norman is one hundred per cent professional. And Peter respects a well honed argument so what we end up with is an interpretation, strategy and time scale designed by Norman presented in a way in which Peter can happily imagine was all his doing. Norman's a successful manager who never looks for the limelight and Peter, well, Peter's a politician...'

Ken smiled again at the slight hint of cynicism and moved on.

'So, you'd been here a year; and Norman Flagg inspired you to want to be his Deputy?'

Jane smiled. 'I suppose that's right. I wouldn't have wanted the job under the old regime. That's not to say I wouldn't have applied for it – I may have done, for the experience – but my heart wouldn't have been in it. I always wanted to move on to being a Deputy, then probably a Head somewhere. Yes, having Norman here made that decision quite easy.'

Ken surveyed the room whilst they spoke. He'd been in several Heads' studies over the years and this was no different from any other.

'Norman has a laptop, I assume? Aren't they standard issue?'

'That's right. If it's not at his home he'd keep it in a locked drawer here in the desk.'

'Is it there?'

'No. I've got a key. I looked all through the office on Monday, I wanted to make sure I knew where everything was. There's no laptop here, but that's no surprise.'

'Does the authority or the school provide a home computer as well, for Heads?'

'I don't think so. I find the laptop to be sufficient for my own needs, but I'm not a computer nerd.'

'Was – is – Norman?'

Jane spluttered, the closest she had been to giggling. 'No! He hated the things! He could see they were useful, of course, but if you asked him where to find a USB cable he'd think you were talking about a pop group. That tells you something about his engagement with popular culture too.'

'So what sort of a 'nerd' was he, then, if you don't mind me asking?'

The teacher hesitated. 'Nerd's not the right word. As I said, he was an icon of professional commitment, truly dedicated. And he could talk to children about what was on telly last night or who's in the charts, but... I don't know... you got the impression that this was part of his professional duty too. I don't think he'd choose to watch Top of the Pops, but then I don't, either.'

'I'm sorry to ask this next question. I'm sure that Peter will have explained why he asked me to ask a few things, but: what do you know about his personal life? His family, personal relationships?'

'Of course, I expected... I'm going to disappoint you: I know nothing about his family, just that he comes from the Home Counties, north of London. He's never spoken to me about a life partner - of any sort.'

Ken resisted asking if this was unusual, as no simple answer would add to his understanding.

'Has he been absent like this before?'

'Not unplanned, no. I've never known him go sick, go to a funeral, even have a dentist's appointment. Teachers learn to do that sort of thing in the children's holidays.'

Ken noted the phrase 'children's holidays'. This was a teacher who would not describe her annual 13 'non-contact' weeks as 'holiday'. Sheila had been the same.

She went on: 'Of course he had meetings to attend, courses to go to, training events – so do I – but either he or I were on the premises every minute the school was open, ready to provide leadership wherever necessary. That was our commitment to our school.'

'Is he active politically? In his union, perhaps?'

'He's in the Head Teachers' union. I'm entitled to be, as a Deputy, but I've always been in the National Union of Teachers and I want to stay there. I wouldn't say he was active, I've not known him take time off for union work. He's attended NAHT meetings after school, I know that. He was conscientious in reading up union advice, just as he was conscientious about everything else. I'm sorry – I've lapsed into using the past tense and that's not appropriate.'

'Party politics?'

'I don't understand where you're going. How's that relevant?'

'I suppose I'm grasping at straws.'

'As I said, he was – is – very professional, in all he does. His political views don't affect his job.'

'Is he a political animal?'

'I didn't say that.'

'Are you a political animal?'

Jane was bristling, but she took a deep breath and controlled herself. She drew back her shoulders to say 'You can't be a teacher and care about children, and be aware of the role of government in education, and value the professionalism of your fellow teachers, yet not be concerned about the sort of society in which those children are growing up. You understand what I'm saying?'

Her tone was reasonable and sincere. She was no longer angry.

'So how would you describe your politics?'

'I vote Labour, if that's what you mean.'

'Is it what *you* mean?'

She smiled. She was now enjoying the exchange. 'I'm not a member of the Labour Party, I don't agree with a lot of what they're doing, especially in education. But they are infinitely better than the Tories so I guess they will always get my vote.'

'Even here in Sussex?'

She laughed. 'I know what you're saying. This little rural idyll is a bit of an indulgence for me, I admit. But I don't live here, I vote in Hove where the politics are a bit more interesting.'

'Have you always lived in Hove? As an adult?'

'About six years. Why?'

'Happy there?'

Jane had an air of puzzlement but she played along.

'I've got a nice flat, not planning to move. I have a cat, and she's not planning to move, either.'

A key question had been answered.

'So what about Norman? How would you describe his politics?'

'I think he votes Labour too, but with the same sort of caveats.'

Ken decided to fly a kite.

'From what my wife used to tell me – she used to be a teacher, did I say? – teacher politics has a number of fringe left wing groups – I'm not having a go at trade unions, but you know what I mean. There's the Socialist Teachers' Alliance, is that what they're called?' Jane nodded. 'And others. Have you ever heard of an organisation called Gauntlet, or Workers' Gauntlet?'

'No.' No hesitation; a slightly furrowed brow.

'But you talk politics together, you and Norman.'

'No… not really.' She did not take the bait. 'We talk education.'

'Meaning?'

'I'm not interested in sectarianism, factionalism. I don't get involved in 'teacher politics', as you call it. Teachers shouldn't be the focus at the end of the day: children should. There's nothing more important than education in the whole field of politics, Mr Hemmings. You've some knowledge of that, so you'll know what I mean. Every child should be able to fulfil his or her potential, be open to the world of knowledge and skills, not just because it's good for society but because it's good for every child. But society benefits because an educated and skilled workforce is an effective one. Every child who doesn't have opportunities created for them is not only losing out on the chance of self-fulfilment and the enjoyment of culture but is also a lost resource to the economy. Investing in education is win-win.'

'So you approve of Tony Blair's investment in recent years?'

'That's not what I said. Providing the money – which he's done, God knows it's better than under the Tories, as I said. But money isn't the be all and end all. It's *how* the money's provided is what matters, what it's spent on. Sometimes there's so much string attached to the cash that it strangles you, it becomes a poisoned chalice. Overbearing reporting, the administrative burden, is so high you sometimes wonder if the extra cash is worthwhile. And as for testing, of children and of schools, just don't go there! Don't get me started on that. You don't make pigs fatter by constantly weighing them.'

'The children come first.'

'Of course! That's the whole argument about teaching being 'vocational'. We're like nurses. Just because we care about our jobs and we put our pupils first they know they can take liberties with us and get away with murder. The bottom line is that conscientious teachers would never do anything to damage the interests of the children.'

'Like going on strike?'

Jane thought about her answer. 'Sometimes their long term interest is best served by a painful short term response to an unacceptable situation. It doesn't mean we're not putting the children first. I've never known teachers strike without being very heavily provoked.'

'Was Norman of one mind with you on these issues?'

'I think so.'

The certainty of the evangelist, thought Ken. On the one hand she couldn't bring herself to believe that someone she respected, with whom she worked closely, someone who clearly respected her and shared her educational principles, could differ from her on their wider political analysis. On the other, it appeared that if Flagg did have any views which differed from the 'party line' then he kept them to himself, well hidden from the angelic if not quite evangelical New Labourite, Peter Elder, and the school staff in general.

Jane may just have got that one right.

* * *

That evening Ken started up his computer and thanked heaven he'd let Clive persuade him to invest in broadband. He went straight to Google, knowing that he would be on line for most of the evening.

'Norman Flagg' was the first entry he made and bingo! Ignoring several men of that name in America, close scrutiny of the initial trawl revealed the very Norman Flagg Ken was searching for, exclusively in his role as the head of the local primary school. But the stories were brief, telling the searcher nothing he didn't already know. The now familiar 'welcome' photo was the only image of him online.

Then there was a poorly spelt article about the banners held aloft by William the Conqueror's forces at the Battle of Hastings and Ken kicked himself for thinking that this might be easy.

'Anthony Flagg' – the Headmaster's youthful soubriquet – was even less forthcoming.

He took a deep breath and asked the oracle about Workers' Gauntlet. There were surprisingly few references to an organisation with leading capitals and a well-placed apostrophe which (presumably) sought to win over mainstream opinion and perhaps rule a significant part of the world. In his relatively limited experience of Google he knew that the 1,344 references constituted a relatively small number.

The organisation's home page stood out.

> 'Workers' Gauntlet is a concept which is self explanatory. If, like us, you reject capitalism but accept order; reject oligarchy but embrace liberation; and believe that bourgeois democracy cannot deliver the legitimate aspiration of emancipation to working people, then please join our discussion group.'

Discussion group? Ken wondered if he'd stumbled across an Adult Education collective funded by a well-meaning 'Old Labour' council somewhere, rather than the dawn of a movement intended to be as potent as Soviet Communism.

There was an index which led the reader to a number of different 'rooms' where the discussions followed themes. They included 'Why Workers' Gauntlet is better than anarchy'; 'A timetable for achieving Workers' Gauntlet's aims' and 'The traitors of the conventional left'.

The latter contained the anonymous views of 17 adherents. It was predictably libellous of both the living and the dead: as in the publication, Jack Kennedy again took the brunt of fierce attacks which, even to Ken's limited political savvy, were both self-indulgent and ill informed. Neil Kinnock, 'who had the opportunity to turn Labour into a truly revolutionary party but failed spectacularly to do so,' was slated and Tony Blair was so beyond the pale as to receive only a single mention in the whole discussion; it was not complimentary.

Only one name received anything like praise in the whole proceedings: Arthur Birch.

'When considering the state of exploitation in which more than 95% of the world's population exist, Workers' Gauntlet has the obvious solution. Workers' Gauntlet offers hope where there is none by inspiring workers to have confidence in themselves both as individuals and collectively. Getting this balance right, between individual interest and collective need, is essential.

'Whilst of course every worker is of equal value to every other, and in an ideal world Workers' Gauntlet would bestow absolute parity of esteem, the transition to a true workers' democracy will, in the short to medium term, require committed and focused leadership of the very highest order. Leadership of the calibre which those who know him believe Arthur Birch is capable of giving.

'The selection of our temporary leader is a practical necessity even though our philosophy maintains that the cult of personality does not serve the best interests of workers in the longer term.'

That was called having your cake and eating it, thought Ken.

Flagg had been a conscientious member of his trade union. What did Workers' Gauntlet have to say about trade unions?

'Trade union membership is a necessity for all who wish to work for our cause, but we should have no illusions. Trade unions are the pupae of the working class movement: an essential phase of adolescence but immature, unable to thrive in an adult world. If they perform any useful purpose in practice it is to give us access to rudimentary communications webs upon which we can build the sophisticated infrastructure that will be essential to mobilise workers in acts of revolution.'

At least he'd found a writer with a degree of imagination, if not identity.

In a brief contribution from 'An activist in Bristol', Ken found something to chill the spine of a former police officer:

'We know that Workers' Gauntlet's programme is essential if we are to operate an economy based on fair shares for all and collective decision-making on every issue in which the common interest is paramount. But we cannot trust the corrupt and outmoded concept of western democracy to deliver power to the workers and we have to consider how therefore we might achieve it by other means.'

The web site was boring, with no pictures and few graphics. Apparently the cult of personality had not developed sufficiently to let the world know what Arthur Birch looked like. From all those years ago, the one photo Ken had seen of the man demonstrated, from a ragged memory, that the charisma-free leader was not particularly photogenic.

But of Flagg, Norman, Anthony or Tony, there was no mention under the banner of Workers' Gauntlet.

Friday 9 September

Friday being market day in the nearby town, it was Ken's habit to wander around the stalls, ostensibly shopping for the weekend. He usually ended the day with a collection of comestibles which bore some slight resemblance to the list which he habitually compiled over breakfast and then generally left on his kitchen table. Ken saw Fridays as his weekly opportunity to connect with what passed for real life in rural Sussex.

In the open market, amidst plastic-roofed stalls, he couldn't resist working out who the pickpockets were and spotting where opportunities for theft presented themselves. He saw a woman whose purse projected from a shopping bag, a stall-holder so deep in conversation with his neighbour that a plastic box of loose change was accessible to any passer-by. A 'hoodie', a boy of perhaps fourteen who ought to have been at school, exchanged a meaningful signal with an acquaintance before loitering near a stall which sold batteries, razors and other favourite targets of low level, organised crime - a set-up reminiscent of Fagin's time. This extension of the supply chain would lead to illicit trading in goods which may already have been 'hot' themselves, as they lay displayed and open to the elements on the market stalls.

Ken leaned against a bollard and took a rolled up newspaper from his pocket. He was well versed at appearing engrossed whilst secretly focusing his attention elsewhere. He braced his legs, pulled his trilby down over his eyes and opened the paper whilst scrutinising the pantomime before him.

Just as it seemed the hoodie was to pounce, Ken's mobile phone sounded. Damn! His first impulse was to let it ring. Its conventional tone made it very distinctive but leaving it to ring unanswered was more conspicuous than answering it. He received so few calls that he ought to respond, he reasoned. The hoodie had disappeared, leaving no sign of crime or disquiet behind him.

'Hello?' Flustered, Ken struggled to press the appropriate button. By some miracle instinct served him well.

'Hello, yes?' he said again.

'Dad?'

'Clive! What do you want? I'm sorry, I didn't mean... I wasn't expecting a call from you. Aren't you at work?'

'Are you at the market? It's Friday, and I thought…'

'Yes, I am. Is that all right? Am I supposed to be somewhere else?'

'Not at all,' the Inspector laughed. 'Actually, I'm just around the corner, with some time to spare, and I've got something to show you. How about lunch?'

Ken held the phone in his right hand and studied his left wrist. Ten to twelve.

'Isn't it a bit early?'

'Well, if you're not keen…'

'Oh, no! I mean yes, let's do that. Where would you like to go?'

They agreed to meet ten minutes later in a pub renowned for its reasonably-priced menu, only 200 yards from where Ken was standing. He was there in six.

Selecting a table by a bay window, one he had shared with Clive on a previous occasion, Ken waited for his son. His thoughts returned to Norman Flagg and the disappointing progress he was making in finding his friend's missing head teacher. Maybe Clive had news? Perhaps Flagg's name had turned up on a list of road accident victims, speed merchants or travellers detained without charge in North African jails.

Speculation halted as his son arrived and a church clock struck the final stroke of noon. Clive, in civvies, put an attaché case on the table, touched his already seated father affectionately on the shoulder and offered to buy drinks. Ken resisted the temptation to rifle the contents of the case as his son went to the bar and instead sat calmly awaiting his refreshment.

Two sparkling mineral waters upon the table, two baskets of chicken and chips on their way.

'Mineral water? You're on duty. Are you under cover?' Ken asked, with a fake conspiratorial air.

'Not exactly.'

'I'm dying to know what's in the bag!'

'Aha! Cheers.'

They each took a sip of water.

'Wait no longer. Look at this…'

Clive took a slim box, about the size of a pack of 50 pages of copier paper, from the case. In it was a diaphanous silk scarf, blood red, in which golden threads wove a delicate pattern enhanced by a sprinkling of tiny, delicate, pearl-like beads.

'Isn't that gorgeous, Dad?'

Ken was bemused. 'Is red your colour?'

'It's not for me! It's our wedding anniversary tomorrow, Chris was looking at this in a shop window when we were in town a couple of weeks ago. It wasn't cheap, but I'm sure she'll like it.'

'I'd forgotten it was September...'

'Don't worry. It's eleven years, it's not a special one. Not paper or tin, or anything like that. We'll go out for dinner tomorrow night, somewhere swish.'

Ken remembered that Sheila had been put out at the time. 'I've got six weeks off school, then two weeks after term starts he's having his wedding! Now that's not good timing, Ken, is it?' She had never hinted at this frustration in the presence of her only child; Ken alone had been privy to these innermost thoughts.

One concept Sheila would not have accepted was that a particular anniversary was 'nothing special.' Every year meant something to Sheila, as it did to Ken... he supposed. Even if a party had only two guests it was still a celebration of the time spent in partnership. For Ken and Sheila every year was 'special' and Sheila, in particular, had not wanted to miss the opportunity to celebrate a single one.

Which was what, he supposed, Clive was really saying: eleven did not warrant a big family 'do', but it was important enough for a significant present and a candle-lit dinner for two.

'It's very nice, Clive. I'm sure she'll like it.'

Ken didn't let his sense of anticlimax show as they sipped and then ate. He'd quite worked himself up into believing that his son might have some key evidence revealing the whereabouts of the errant teacher.

Small talk dominated the conversation whilst neither raised the subject that was occupying Ken's thoughts and he declined the offer of dessert. When the meal was over:

'So... has that teacher of yours turned up, Dad? The one you asked me to look for?'

'No, he hasn't.'

'Bit irresponsible, isn't it? He's paid to be there, to teach and manage the place, isn't he?'

'Well, yes.'

'Have you any reason to think that he's deliberately hoofed it?'

'No...'

'Or otherwise? Still no clue, no message?'

'No.'

'Some people, eh! If one of my sergeants gave us grief like that, not turning up for shifts, he wouldn't have a job to come back to, I can tell you.'

'I don't imagine he would. Still, they seem to be coping.'

'But that's not the point, Dad, is it?'

'No… it's not. You're right.'

'So, how far have you got?'

'Pardon?'

'What have you found out? About the Head?'

'I thought you weren't interested.'

Clive hesitated, seeking a diplomatic course: 'I'm interested in whatever interests my dad.'

'Oh, that's nice. You're in danger of sounding patronising, son.'

Clive smiled. 'So d'you want to tell me?'

Ken assumed a professional air.

'Norman Anthony Flagg. Born 11 September 1961, Luton. Active in the Labour Party as a youth. Got a degree in Politics from East of England University where he was active on the far left. Unusually, he appears to have undertaken some military training whilst at University. He eventually resurfaces as a primary school teacher in Bethnal Green, perhaps still with an interest in the far left but… I've found no *direct* evidence of any recent political activity of any kind.'

Clive nodded, listening.

'He came to Sussex three years ago where he's been a very successful Head Teacher. He values his staff, takes them with him. He's not only bred loyalty amongst them but self-sufficiency and independence, too.'

'So where d'you think he's gone? And why?'

'Heaven knows. He's admired professionally but has no known close friends. No evidence of contact with family -'

'How do you know?'

Ken had said too much. 'I have my methods!' The two men smiled.

'He went to Spain two years ago…'

'It's not much, is it? How's your friend, Councillor Elder, taking it?'

'Peter would be frantic if Jane Moore – she's the deputy, acting head – didn't keep him in his box. His other responsibilities are keeping his mind off this - just about. As long as there's no problem at the school I guess he'll be all right.'

Clive started to prepare to go.

'When I thought I might see you today I checked that data again. You know, hospital admissions, congestion charge cameras and so on for Mr Flagg. Still nothing.'

'You did all that just now? What, on the phone?'

'What do you mean?'

'You didn't know you were going to see me until ten minutes before we met.'

'No... but I knew you'd be at the market this morning. Once I decided to pop out and buy the scarf for Chris, first thing this morning, I thought it'd be nice to see you, so I... did the checks.'

'Well... thank you.' Of course this was the right explanation. He trusted his son, an upright and professional policeman, implicitly.

Five minutes later Clive concluded: 'See you again on Sunday, then. Lunch at ours, as usual?'

'That would be nice. And thanks for lunch.'

'No problem, Dad. No problem.'

* * *

Ken spent the afternoon productively: two hours doing The Times crossword and a challenging Sudoku followed by a brief, unsatisfying, foray into daytime television: the embodiment of the perennial conflict between hope and experience.

Come four o'clock his mind returned to Norman Flagg. It was possible that the web pages of the estate agent carried the key to the Head's whereabouts, but how to access that information?

He would try the Lamonde approach that had recently worked so well. He would call into the two estate agents' offices, in due course – assuming Flagg had not turned up – and introduce himself as Ken Hemmings, Private Investigator. He would be up front: let them think that Flagg was an errant husband, all he wanted to know was if they'd had an enquiry. The chances were that the answer would be 'no'. That was the beauty of the internet: Flagg's initial approach to Hathersage Homes and to Finton's would have been electronic, anonymous and probably brief. He would only show up on their client list if they had something he might want and had approached them in person. This was going to be fun. He was looking forward to it, as much as he was also looking forward to joining Peter Elder in the Golf Club later for his regular report back. Elder had been away for a couple of days on political business. It would be good to find out how he thought the first week at the school had gone.

Ken jumped as a thud rang through the house; then relaxed. It was only the weekly paper falling from the letter box onto his mat. It could stay there for a few moments.

Was it possible to buy or rent a property under an assumed name? He dismissed the thought. Perhaps as a company... This was the meandering mind of a former policeman allocating base motives on the flimsiest of pretext. There was no justification for this – at least, not yet.

What he'd read about Workers' Gauntlet on the web had disturbed him. Its naivety might be quaint, its sneering disdain offensive, its ambitions simply arrogant, but its hatred was profoundly repulsive. But what did it all mean? Were these the ramblings of a hard core of ineffectual students, bearded vengeful pensioners or psychotics, from the safety of their padded rooms? And where was the evidence that Norman Flagg had done more than look at the site once, let alone contributed to its inane ramblings?

Ken thought of the names of some academics of his former acquaintance, people who might know someone who knew someone who knew something about the politics of the hard left. It was a long shot, which could wait a few days - if it was still needed.

It was 5pm: time for a cup of tea.

Ken walked to the kitchen via the hallway and instinctively picked up the newspaper from the mat. The back page lead was a speculation about Albion's chances of three points the following day; Ken thought it obscene to give soccer priority when the last ball of another glorious cricket season was not yet bowled.

He did some washing up as the tea brewed, poured it and sat down. At last he turned the newspaper front side up - but had to read the headline twice before it registered.

'Where is he?' a huge headline screamed from the page.

The subheading read 'School Head leaves kids in lurch'.

There was no photograph but before he'd read the name of the school Ken knew that this was his story – and that it was not welcome.

> 'Mystery deepened today as a Sussex primary school completed its first week of the new academic year – without a Head Teacher in charge.
>
> '44-year old Head teacher Norman Flagg went AWOL over the summer holidays without letting his deputy, the governors or the local authority know when he would be back.
>
> 'Debbie Pearce, mother of ten-year old Wayne and pretty Samantha (7), who attend the school, said: 'It's disgraceful. What does this man think he's paid for?'

The story included four more paragraphs in similarly negative vein. Jane Moore was cited as refusing to comment; Peter Elder was not mentioned. The story was not designed to serve the interests of the school - it would undermine confidence in Jane, attract attention for the wrong reasons and potentially destabilise what was, despite the Head's absence, a good working environment for all concerned.

Ken itched to talk to Peter about the story but reasoned that, like him, Peter might have only just seen it. The politically experienced Chair of Governors was in a much better position to deal with it than was the retired copper whose impatient curiosity must wait until the Golf Club rendezvous.

* * *

They chose a discreet corner of the lounge. The bar was popular on Fridays but they had arrived early enough to avoid the golfers' rush.

'I agree, it's not good,' said Peter. There was enough of a Friday night feel to his voice already – strained after a long week – without this extra burden.

'I spoke to Jane as soon as I saw the story, about quarter past four. I won't say she was distraught, she's too professional for that, but it was clear she could have done without it. Obviously, we've not had time to get any feedback from the parents yet.'

'Having them stew over a whole weekend is not a good idea.'

'Exactly. I just wish she'd contacted me when she first had an inkling. I gather the reporter spoke to her just as she was leaving school, about six last night.'

'Spoke to her? I thought she wouldn't speak to them.'

'She didn't tell them anything. But I ought to be told when a reporter's harassing my Head for a story, shouldn't I? She has my mobile number.'

'I don't suppose you were the first thing on her mind.'

'No... I guess you're right.'

'Anyway, Peter, what would you have done? Called the reporter and confirmed their story? It seems to me Jane was probably right not to talk. Would you've done things differently?'

'No, you're right. It's just that... You know, I enjoy the challenge of politics. This is a 'damned if you speak and damned if you don't' situation, what would the right thing to say have been? I just think I should have known what was going on.'

'Who's Debbie Pearce?'

'She's well known to us, unfortunately. D'you know what? We've had three of her kids through the school. Charlie, the oldest, left us in July. With every one we've come close to prosecuting her for non-attendance. Norman never wanted to go down that route, he bent over backwards to help that family. He was very good at trying to understand people like Debbie: socially deprived, many problems. He last spoke to me about her only in about June. I think if Nathan – I don't know why the paper called him Wayne – had missed more than a week in September, even Norman's legendary tolerance might've snapped. He's done so much for them but there are limits, even for him.'

'So Mrs Pearce was hardly going to take a sympathetic view of Norman's unfortunate absence?'

'Indeed, that's her outlook on life: hard and hardened. Actually, this time it really is 'Miss'. Three children, three different fathers, so I believe. Her mother's a cleaner at the school and Gran absolutely tears her hair out about the kids, the poor things. No, if Debbie Pearce thought she'd a reason to slag off the school she'd go for it, big time. The good thing is that we've never given her a hostage to fortune – until now.'

'So this isn't the course of events you anticipated.'

'No, but the politician in me should've thought of it. I've had a busy week, conferences, meetings, council stuff – oh, and a business to run.'

'You're a glutton for punishment! Still, it means you've allowed Jane to do it her way, stamp her authority on things. Is she doing OK, otherwise?'

'Can't fault her. But I'm calling an extraordinary meeting of the governors for next week. We do need to be doing something. At the very least we have to formally write to Norman and demand an explanation of his absence. We ought to suspend him, pending investigation of allegations of breach of contract.'

'This is bizarre! How can you write to someone who's not there or suspend him from a job he's not doing?'

'I'm checking to see whether we have powers to stop his pay. At the moment I'm paying for two Heads out of a tight budget and it's just wasting money. We're having to buy someone in to cover, too. If Jane's going to be doing the job for any period she has to be paid the right rate. As for him not being there – yes, I had noticed that, Ken! – the letter has to be sent in order to cover the governors legally for any future action we might have to take. It's less about communicating with him. Unless, of course, you've got any useful information for me?'

This question was inevitable. It was, after all, what the meeting had been convened to discuss. Ken had spent some time earlier in the day worrying about how he was going to respond to it.

To discuss the possibility that revolutionary or fanatical politics explained Flagg's absence was going to sound far-fetched. Peter already knew of Norman's involvement in that field over twenty years ago, of course, but neither man had any evidence that the subject was of anything more than passing interest to the Head today. Peter would likely find the notion that Norman had disappeared off to some terrorist training camp absurd.

'Not much, I'm afraid. I've spoken to Jane at some length, found out a bit more about the man – thanks for the photo, by the way – and I can confirm that there's still no evidence that he's been knocked down by a bus, failed to pay the Congestion Charge or even been detained abroad; but don't ask me how I know, please! There is one thing... might he have been thinking about moving house?'

'I don't think so! Why? Did you find estate agents' brochures or something?'

'Not brochures, no. I took the liberty of checking the internet history on Norman's computer whilst Jane was out of her office. Two local estate agents came up, sites which he'd visited before the summer break, so they were almost certainly not her searches. There were no brochures at the house. The house wasn't particularly helpful at all, as before.'

Peter's expression was forlorn.

'Peter, tell me about Norman's friends. I'm asking because last week you left him a telephone message, so did Jane. But no one else appears to have done. No, that's not quite true, there were half a dozen silent messages, possibly all from the same source. But no friends or family... does that ring true?'

'Perhaps he's with his family.'

'Have you checked that? Back in Luton?'

'Well, in a way. I got my sister – she still lives that way – to check out the phone book. There are no Flaggs in Luton any more.'

The two men thought about the problem for a moment, unproductively.

In order to break the silence, but with an air of purpose, Ken asked: 'You shared some of his upbringing. Tell me more about how you got here, how you got to where you are, politically.'

Peter raised his eyebrows, quizzically.

'OK... It's a long story, Ken! let me get us another drink before I start.'

Chapter 5: Peter's Politics

At fifteen I thought I had it all sorted; I guess Norman thought the same. Life was simple, there were goodies and baddies: the goodies were the ordinary people, the victims of the system. The baddies were the the grey, anonymous, power hungry, uncaring bureaucrats and their capitalist bosses and paymasters who saw every human interaction in terms of how it would benefit themselves. They might create wealth, by some academic definition, but they didn't distribute it fairly. They denied it to those who *really* created it and they sucked wealth out of the system, ultimately into their own mega bank accounts and tax havens.

Rather than play football on Saturdays, as a teenager I'd help my mother run Labour Party jumble sales, hardly noticing that other kids had wholly different interests. Somehow, I thought, those people outside the church hall, desperate to pick up a sweater for a couple of bob, those who could bear to wear second hand shoes, had something in common with those who were dying in the Cambodian killing fields.

My dad, who studiously avoided the jumble sales, was a towering political presence. No academic, Kennedy had told him that world hunger could be resolved in a generation, Wedgwood Benn had told him that the white heat of technology would address society's problems and Luther King had had a dream which dad knew was relevant to all. Even Ted Heath, bless his cotton socks, had admitted that there was 'an unacceptable face of capitalism', though my dad had never believed there could also be an acceptable one! All those influences were before my time but my father's politics were forever in the present day.

'Profit' was the dirtiest word in our house. Yes, my father worked for a private company which made profits first and cars after, so 'profit' put food on our plates, but dad wouldn't hear a good word for 'the system'.

He was a conscientious worker, coming home every day with dirt and grease on his hands from the swarf and the coolant of his lathe, his clothes grubby and sweaty, despite the overalls. He would clean the muck from his face but his hands were indelibly scarred. I admired him for that. But along with dirt on his hands came a chip on his shoulder: he was always moaning about something at work, always voting for industrial action for the sake of it, always complaining about the union when things didn't go his way. Working with his hands entitled him to be arrogant, that's how he saw it.

He was always criticising the Labour Party, too, but it was like a family falling out - blood's much thicker than water. His faith in Harold Wilson never wavered. Wilson was just about the only person about whom Dad said, when they disagreed, 'Perhaps Harold knows better than I do.'

He never met his hero, of course. You didn't in those days. Perhaps that was no bad thing.

Dad's most consistent passion was education. He was determined that I'd be the first Elder to go to University, a generation after 'our boys', as he called them, had returned from fighting Hitler to build a land fit for heroes.

He never talked much about his youth. Dad was too young for the second world war, but he did national service. He told me all about it, lamenting the passing of Empire. He wasn't happy that Labour, his Labour, might have got that wrong.

He never missed a trick in condemning the enemy, but he was barely more charitable about our friends. His loathing of Russia kept him well clear of the Communist Party - he was wedded to democracy, with all its flaws. The Yanks, he said, were worse; cheap values and throwaway culture. Even back immediately post-war they epitomised the waste of resources inherent in quick-buck capitalism. 'What can you expect from a country with no history?' he used to say.

So at University my political ideas were 'sorted'. I was part of a generation that would inherit the earth. I had to take responsibility for my fellow man just as Dad and his generation, collectively, had taken responsibility for me. Dad had made sure that I was well to the left, that I hated what he hated.

There was just one exception to this, as I've said: 'profit'.

Dad's views about profit had never really struck a chord with me. Today, I acknowledge the benefits of markets as I did even back in my university days. I could distinguish between corporate profits to be reinvested, creating jobs, generating the wealth to pay for services, on one hand - and the sickening nature of self-indulgent fat cats on the other. Dad couldn't see a difference between those who facilitated wealth creation and those who hoarded it. To him 'profit' was the spawn of the Devil.

We had a row about it once, I must have been about twenty. I told him to open his eyes and live in the real world. He said I had no spine. I wish he could see what Labour's done for working people in the eight years since 1997! We've had Labour representation for a century and it's only now, with a so-called moderate leadership, that we're achieving century-old goals! It turns out we only needed those politicians whose feet were on the ground, we could manage without those with their heads in the clouds.

Dad's not with us any more. He took his untainted views to the grave.

So, at university, half our movement was saying 'Nationalise the one hundred top monopolies!' and the other half were pleading 'Just hang on a minute...', so I parted company with the likes of my contemporary, Mr Norman Anthony Flagg. He was out of order, irresponsible, a hothead, or so I thought back then.

I left university in 1981, with a decent degree, slid easily into business. Worse than that, I went right to the heart of the capitalist system! My dad was ashamed; although we still talked it was rarely about politics: his prejudice, not my wish. I still had a party card, of course, which just about redeemed me in his eyes. If I'd sold my head I hadn't sold my heart, it said, though I wasn't particularly active in the Party at that time.

I learned my property craft in Tory Surrey – it gets worse, doesn't it? I was dealing with properties my dad would never have dared enter, mansions he would probably have spat at. He would've said that my business was designed around the needs of finance and profit, not around housing people.

Someone's got to do it, of course. Even in leafy Guildford there's still the first-time buyer on a modest income, anxious to get on the housing ladder in order to bring up their family in security. Of course I know why the property industry is a pariah: we make big profits from apparently not much work, simply by buying and selling. And what do we invest that cash in? Nothing, as far as most people can see.

What I was doing was a means unto an end. I moved on.

I'd met Laura at University. She just happened to be a property heiress, I didn't seek her out for that reason and that wasn't why I fell in love with her! If anything, as she grew into adulthood she found being rich a cross she had to bear.

She was an artist, she got an excellent degree and taught at a college in our early years together. Soon after we married it became clear that I could earn for both of us so if she'd rather paint and sculpt, that's what she should do. Only recently she's taken up etching and she's really very good at it; she has flair. She etches onto steel plates, which means we need to keep bottles of some pretty nasty stuff, nitric acid, in her studio, under lock and key, of course. Never had an accident with it yet, fortunately. All of her art's very… evocative. I like it. Nowadays she teaches two days a week, the rest is her time to be creative - however she sees fit!

She's a fitness freak, too: she'd go jogging every day, even back then. She encouraged me, too, so I joined a gym but when my subscription expired and I'd hardly used the damned place I didn't renew. I'll tell you what I did do, besides the golf, which you know about: I took up karate at University. I became a blue belt, would you believe? One level below brown. These hands can be deadly weapons, you know, I ought to need a licence for them! I'm pretty rusty now, of course, but for several years I was really keen.

It's amazing what you can do with a pair of hands.

So, where was I? My politics and my marriage have been my most consistent comforts over the last twenty years.

Laura's not political in the way I am, though she knows what's right. When her father died she inherited a large property portfolio, which meant that we would, with care, always be 'comfortable'. Once we had that sort of cash behind us the move from an office desk to the property front line was inevitable. I wouldn't call it speculation: there was as little risk involved as possible... I just needed to be in the right place at the right time. I was lucky. I made shed loads of money. It was easy.

I realised that with wealth, energy, youth on my side, I was in a better position to change the world than my father ever had been. With no children, the one commitment that Laura and I never got round to making, I even had time to work on it.

I started to invest in low cost housing. Low cost equals low profit, but lots of it means more profit. By taking control of the whole development, not simply trading, I could make deals which produced quality homes at affordable prices, in dynamic communities. I became a developer, building decent homes for people who really needed them. I was working with housing associations to produce a good income stream for them, quality properties which were low maintenance and low rent, for decent, ordinary people.

All the money I made was properly accounted for, all the tax paid, nothing hived off into offshore accounts or whatever. People were benefiting from – let's call it my altruistic use of capitalism. But it wasn't enough, I wanted to do more, and I'd created space and time which I could dedicate to the public arena.

The Labour Party was looking for people to fight county elections in the early nineties, as it always was. I'd kept my membership ticking over and I volunteered to stand in a middle class council seat as a paper candidate, one who wasn't expected to win. But I put in the effort leading up to the election and paid from my own pocket for decent quality election materials – a pretty original idea at the time, I can tell you! Despite my humble origins it was easier for a developer to persuade suburban voters that I was worth their trust than if I'd presented as someone more typical of the deprived council estate where I grew up.

The hard work paid off, I got elected and quickly created a profile on the council's back benches. I was resigned to spending my political career in opposition, locally, but nevertheless got re-elected, four years later. I enhanced my standing further by becoming a village primary school governor and then the board chair. The rest is history.

I've been in local government for over ten years. There have been ups and downs but I don't regret a moment. It's been frustrating – dealing with cuts under the Tories and the tight hand of central control under a Labour government – but the overall it's been in the right direction.

Back in 1995 I stumbled across something that felt very wrong. This episode… changed things, helped keep me here, made politics even more exciting: initially. I learned a few harsh lessons…

The brother of the then Tory leader of our council, John Wheatcroft, was also in the property business. Eric Wheatcroft owned several companies under different names, lots of fingers in pies, but only people actually inside the business could really see that. I discovered that whenever local councils were disposing of land assets – which was not infrequent – one or other of Wheatcroft's companies got advance notice of the council's intentions, often enabling them to acquire the land cheap.

As a councillor, if I'd bought council land surreptitiously it would've looked very wrong. Questions of insider dealing would have been raised, even if everything had been above board. This man was the brother of a councillor, working through several anonymous companies, no single one of which individually had acquired vast quantities of land from the council - but between them, they had. Without hard evidence that favours were actually being traded – names, dates, facts – I was powerless to do anything about it.

I got frustrated but Eric got greedy. Councils were selling off school playing fields in those days and when a particular one was passed to a Wheatcroft company at well below market value, I really did smell a rat. It couldn't have happened without a council officer either being involved or turning a blind eye.

It was something the District Auditor ought to know about.

So I started sniffing; within six months I'd presented the DA with a dossier linking Eric Wheatcroft, the developer, his councillor brother and a senior Estates department employee, called Mayall, to something as close to corruption as you can get. I'd picked up clues that other officers, in other councils, were doing the same thing: there was a land transfer network maximising profit for Eric Wheatcroft from former public property. This cabal was a ticking political time bomb.

Do you remember what was going on back in '95, in Parliament? 'Cash for Questions'. Tory MPs by the barrel-load, trading in brown envelopes, being exposed or entrapped by journalists. Remember the Hamilton Affair? Martin Bell in his pure white suit? Hardly a week went by without another scandal.

So… the Leader of my council's minority Labour group called me in. I'd shown him the dossier, of course, I thought he backed my investigation. Well, of course I had his support, he said… with caveats…

In short, Councillor John Wheatcroft, the Tory Leader, was prepared to put his hands up. He coughed to the Auditor for everything in late '96, was prepared to take the wrap for his brother and Mayall. But... my colleague wanted to tick the 'no publicity' box. The Leader of my group and a few other key players were prepared to go along with Wheatcroft to get him off the front line whilst keeping things quiet.

I was flabbergasted! The political weapon in our hands was armed, loaded, aimed and ready to fire in the run-up to 1997's county and general elections. And I was being asked to stand the cavalry down!

I asked why: I was told that the reputation of the whole of local government, not just of our council, was at stake. Labour didn't want more questions raised about the propriety of politicians, months before a general election that everyone assumed was ours for the taking. They had to 'get the balance right', I was told. I thought that such exposure could only do us good!

The whole political house of cards was vulnerable, that was the implication. A bit of scandal, it seems, was a good thing for us and a bad thing for the Tories; too much shit hitting the proverbial would frighten all of the horses. Am I mixing my metaphors too much? With no hint that the press had any knowledge of what the Wheatcrofts were up to, would I kindly keep quiet. Quiet? I was dumbstruck!

There were other factors, too. John Wheatcroft had received royal recognition for services to local government just months previously, after thirty-odd years in office. It was strongly hinted, because that's what they do, that the Palace would not appreciate any intimation that the establishment had erred in its judgement in awarding him a gong so recently.

Wheatcroft was seventy and newly diagnosed with prostate cancer - I didn't know that. A deal had been done between him, the Labour group leader and a few Tory councillors who were appalled at what their man had been doing. The deal didn't involve me, I was small fry, I wasn't consulted. Wheatcroft would bring forward his announcement that he was planning to step down from the council at the next election. He would go public about the cancer in order to justify stepping down as Council Leader with immediate effect.

Meanwhile, his brother would slip a quarter of a million pounds back into the council coffers by means yet to be agreed, probably by overpaying on future land purchases. The Leader of the opposition Labour group would be quietly consulted as to how that 'windfall' would be spent - we didn't get granted that sort of influence very often, I can tell you! And Mr Mayall would quietly 'retire early' at the same time.

The stink of dead fish made me sick.

On the positive side, the council would improve its audit processes to ensure better scrutiny of dealings with commercial companies in future. There would be an improved register of members' interests and a new register, of companies bidding for commercial contracts and sales. This was long before the law required all this! I was invited to chair what would be, in effect, an embryonic Standards committee.

To cap it all the District Auditor, who hadn't even acknowledged receipt of my complaint - and still hasn't, ten years on - had indicated approval of the 'new arrangements'.

I took my time to consider all this but eventually realised I had little option but to agree to everything. The '97 election was even closer and I'd already committed to fight to retain my council seat. There's a theory that when politicians throw shit at election time it's because they have some of their own to hide. So I kept my head down.

This was my all-time low in politics. The deal stank, as I said. I told no one about my worries – except my dad, who was still alive. His advice was totally pragmatic: I expected no less. He said win the election, then publish and be damned, but I couldn't do that. If I'd thought that keeping quiet was absolutely wrong I'd have gone to the press right then. I could never explain a delay retrospectively, certainly not to my own satisfaction. It was do it then or never, as far as publicity was concerned.

So I didn't do it and I've not done it since. It's a dead issue now, both Wheatcoft brothers are dead, Mayall's not around and even the DA has retired.

Pragmatism has always been an important guide for me and the Party made it clear that it was only the timing of the matter which had stymied it. An official told me, a couple of years later: 'If only we'd heard from you six months earlier we'd have done something about it.' I immediately thought: 'Now, he says!' But that soon turned to 'How did *he* know?'

I picked myself up, brushed myself off and tried to live up to my new role as a person of consequence: an 'Elder statesman' - get it?

1997's election changed the world, for me and those I represent, truly a moment of liberation. The delivery of traditional goals, justice in a modern setting, has been skilful and effective.

But you'd expect me to say all that, wouldn't you? On the whole, I do actually believe it!

Perhaps it's just the modern world, this legitimate fear of terrorism, but Brighton these days during party conferences feels sterile – excuse the tasteless metaphor – as though a bomb's hit it. 9/11 was a bullet up the backside of politics globally, not to mention the bomb at Brighton's own Grand Hotel, in 1984. Unforgivable.

Many of us in the local Party are volunteer stewards whenever the Labour Conference comes to Brighton, it's a great way to be involved in the movement. I've done it myself in the past but it's important to get younger members to volunteer. I get a visitor's pass to Conference when it's here, I've even attended as a delegate. And I'm much more at home politically now, of course, in 2005's modern Labour Party, New Labour or whatever you want to call it, compared to twenty years ago when people like the younger Norman were on the march.

It's a pity that we need such overt security at the Conference, though. Steel gates, armed officers, concrete barriers… no one's going to bring a bomb or gun inside, are they, really? But 9/11 taught us that it's not only weapons that kill people. No one's ever questioned me about taking blue belt karate hands inside the cordon…

I love these events. Thousands of us come together to debate, on the conference floor, on the fringe, in the bars, issues that really matter. Ideas that will change people's lives, philosophies to guide our national and world leaders, melding theory with practical experience and the responsibilities of leadership with the passion of the grass roots.

It takes some effort to realise that the security is there because someone wants to kill us and our leaders.

We know that not only from The Grand Hotel but from the 7/7 bombings in London just a couple of months ago. Just look at Parliament today: there are fences there too, barriers and armed guards like never before. If we value our democracy we must protect it. If that means tight security at conferences and police carrying guns to defend innocent, well-meaning people then that's fine, I say, the price is worth paying.

For democracy to survive we have to defeat the bombers both politically and organisationally. It can't be done by military means alone, the peaceniks have got that bit right, at least. But whilst we're getting there we need protection.

Look at my hands: they look so innocent. They've never been called upon to exercise deadly force.

Not yet, anyway!

Chapter 6: Nottinghamshire, May, 1984

The lines were drawn.

To the right, sixty police officers in black padded kevlar riot gear, plastic shields, helmets with visors and chin straps, batons held erect. Many of the officers were local young men who'd escaped from the pit culture to become constables; some had relatives amongst both the men who continued to work in the colliery, defying the union, and their former comrades who were out on strike. Others had been brought in from constabularies elsewhere to bolster the number of uniforms available to police the dispute. The number of officers on the front line anticipated the growth in demonstrator numbers predicted with each daily cycle.

To the left was a smaller but undefined number, mostly men, mounting a 24 hour picket which waxed and waned, peaking around the start and end of the pit shifts. Initially, these were local union members who were nominally lobbying the workplace to encourage their fellow miners to join the strike. Over the weeks they, too, had been joined by numbers of outsiders in excess of what had been either anticipated or planned. Their purpose was to use rational argument - in volume, if not cogency - to persuade working miners to join the nationwide campaign against pit closures and the defenestration of a proud and historic trade union. But if rational argument failed…

This particular week was the schools' half term holiday so some of the pickets had teenage sons with them, bolstering numbers artificially but temporarily.

Today, as on all previous days, there was a stand-off. Ten yards of open ground gaped between the two front lines. Stand-off was the new 'normal'. Off to one side a posse of reporters and photographers would continue to diminish by the day - as long as 'normal' was all there was to record. Their purpose was to see all and tell the world, but only if there was something to tell. The members of the press were positioned, on neutral ground, like umpires at a tennis court, switching their gaze from one side to the other. The strike was two months old and already some of the observers were bored; but at least they were being paid well and, for some, the alternative was snapping predictable flower shows and interminable weddings.

A fourth and final group stood thirty yards further away again: the audience. Often absent, today a larger than normal proportion of this group were again children, family members seeking to watch entertainment coloured by the lens of whichever side of the argument their menfolk had rallied to.

One of the police officers, himself born and bred in Nottinghamshire, was very experienced. At 38, he was a uniformed sergeant with ambition. The neatly trimmed, reddish moustache behind his vizor, only recently cultivated, had met with the general approval of his colleagues. His alert eyes flicked from side to side. He was known amongst his many friends as a professional, solution-orientated, community-focused individual who always talked of the police 'service', never the police 'force'. He was there to do his duty, uphold order and the rule of law, fairly and in line with his oath, ethos and practice.

But the man inside the uniform was uncomfortable. Uncomfortable in his stuffy, itchy, padded armour, uncomfortable that his helmet restricted his vision, uncomfortable that he must hold a weapon constantly in his hand for hours upon end. He was particularly uncomfortable that his uniform bore no name or shoulder number so that he could not be identified - which went against the precious principles of transparency, accountability and responsibility with which he always sought to discharge his public duty. He was uncomfortable too that he knew men on both sides of this chasm of ideas over the future of the coal industry and could understand what each had to say. He was uncomfortable that his role was to keep apart two warring sides of a community that should be, and hitherto had been, as one in its culture and social life.

Today it was almost inconceivable that such a peace could ever return.

If he was uncomfortable that this was a community tearing itself apart then the fact that others, outsiders, were involved was even more worrying to him. He wasn't just thinking of the 'flying pickets', miners from other collieries, from other parts of the country, who were seeking to persuade and inveigle fellow workers to join the protest, but uncomfortable that the dispute clearly attracted 'professional' protestors too, mercenaries from extreme political groups. Even within his own ranks there were coppers from cities who didn't understand how pit communities worked, who were a little too keen to engage physically with the situation, who could easily take perverse enjoyment from the threat of violence both upon them and by their number - in 'defensive retaliation', of course. 'Proactive protection' some of them had called it, even 'anticipatory holding action'.

All such outsiders, on all sides, were worrying him and before his eyes the demonstration was swelling as the shift change time approached. Some demonstrators were clearly not miners at all, they were young men who had never wielded a pick, young men with pale and smooth hands, probably students, who almost literally wore their hearts on their sleeves. 'Coal Not Dole' said the dominant tin badges but alongside them were CND symbols, red flags and even portraits of a bald man with a pointed beard and a hammer and sickle. He guessed it was Lenin, but the sergeant's knowledge of neither history nor iconography was sufficient to be certain.

The police had their backs to the colliery entrance. Ten yards away, but inching closer, the crowd opposite was growing noisier as the first of the working miners was due to leave the colliery, threatening a direct confrontation with the officers who stood between them and those they sought to 'persuade'. The order was given for the police cordon to move forward two yards. It was barked out, vizors were down, batons and shields were raised. The no man's land between the lines was eroded to create a passage behind the cops along which pitmen arriving to work could walk. As the first such miner approached a call of 'scab!' from the crowd was immediately echoed by another and the band - of 40 or 50 men by now - moved further towards the phalanx of police. Over the following moments a ritualised routine would be observed, well established over the the weeks of the strike. Lines would be respected and passions aired but actual physical contact between the two leading files - the demonstrators and the police - would be minimal, token. Even arrests were unlikely.

Closer again, now just ten feet apart, stood the two rows now. A minibus arrived, discharging more workers who passed behind the cordon to get into their workplace as the volume of noise grew. The tumult reached its peak as the first miners to leave the outgoing shift passed through the protected area and headed for the vehicle.

The sergeant with the moustache stood his ground, his eyes searching for anything out of the ordinary. Immediately in front of him one demonstrator was being especially loud. Requiring no megaphone he was telling all and sundry that this was not a strike about pit closures, it was action to defend the working class and an opportunity to end economic exploitation for once and for all; the action was aimed at bringing down the Thatcher Government and all it stood for, to re-establish the coal industry under workers' control. The man - with tousled dark hair, perhaps in his early twenties - gesticulated emphatically with each phrase of his fluent, well-rehearsed, prolonged diatribe. Briefly the policeman allowed himself to wonder how this analysis aligned with the fact that here in Clapstone, and probably across Nottinghamshire, there was no consensus, let alone majority feeling, that a socialist millennium was the motivating cause which these working class communities were really pursuing.

'Not my place to tell him,' thought the officer, as the shouting man in the leather jacket continued to command his attention.

Over the minutes that followed there was more shouting, the front lines grew even closer and the threat of a break in routine - actual physical confrontation - felt very real.

Suddenly, the young man with the attitude broke rank and stood alone before the line of police officers: the moustachioed one felt as though the stand-off had become a one-to-one confrontation aimed at himself. As the words were being screamed and spat in his direction the demonstrator's pointing hand was outstretched, barely a metre from the sergeant's vizor.

'And you are the agents of the state, a state that denies working class people what's rightly theirs, the fruits of their labour - you should be ashamed of yourselves!'

With each phrase the hand jabbed the thin Nottinghamshire morning air like a deranged woodpecker, an actor on speed.

'You stand by, impotent, as faceless, multinational American companies take over our coal industry, that's *our* coal industry, the industry that powers people's homes and workplaces, that creates the very wealth which is then plundered by the rich and denied to the poor! You're not neutral in this one, coppers, you're agents of the inhuman and exploitative state, that's what you are!'

'All I want is a quiet life,' thought the officer, his gaze transfixed on the face of the man, stubble-cheeked, hair lopping over his eyes, face obscured further by the pointing hand, fore-shortened arm which targeted the bridge of his own nose. 'And you, sonny boy, are advancing no further,' said the officer - but only to himself.

Then a klaxon sounded, a hooter powered by a canister of compressed air. It was the stewards' sign to the protestors that it was time to retreat, a signal also understood and agreed by the police. The initial idea of using a whistle had been abandoned as too similar to the traditional call of a police officer for assistance. Just as a crescendo had been threatened this modest wave of humanity started to subside. The young man ceased his rant and stood motionless for a moment, staring at the blank visor made impenetrable by the glare of spring sunshine.

The young man thought: 'I want to remember that pig's face'. In truth, however, he couldn't see it, not even the moustache, because of the glare on the vizor, the riot gear, the muscular contortions of his own face still rictus rigid from the shouting of his message. This was his ritual call for hope, justice and purpose, for liberation for the oppressed masses of working class people; it was, in his heart, what he was. All he would recall from the minutes of this brief confrontation was this anonymous, faceless uniform.

The officer watched the yob turn and depart, sensing no emotion save for a small sense of relief that violence had been avoided. He tried to picture the man in his mind's eye: the jacket, the hair, the stubble, the piercing, accusing eyes and the pointing finger attached to a hand that looked as though it had never done a day's manual work in its life. Only one thing distinguished the man from the identikit professional demonstrator: the top joint of the thumb of his right hand was missing.

Sergeant Ken Hemmings dismissed the image from his mind. He couldn't afford to take these things personally.

'I'll probably never see him again,' he thought, 'and that won't be a moment too soon...'

Chapter 7: Cornwall, September 2005

The long planned week in Cornwall with Amanda, his sister, was just what Ken needed. The Hemmings clan had always been close, when absolutely necessary, though they were few in number. Amanda, his younger and only sibling, was in her mid-fifties.

The agenda for the holiday was simple: they would both read newspapers and novels, stroll seafronts and byways, enjoy the weather and, when the mood took them, talk long and hard. Theme parks, pantomimes, even national treasures would be low on their agenda. Whilst each year a novel venue was deliberately chosen the pattern, the strategic approach, had developed into a rewarding process.

Ken and his sister had not been as close as some siblings manage and, without ever verbalising it, both felt it important to minimise the chance of familiarity breeding familial contempt. That was why this week of intensive contact was so enjoyable and valued: it was both predictable yet out of the ordinary at the same time.

The two had gone their own ways at an early age. Amanda's childhood sweetheart had been Roger Dorling, as debonair as a coalfield boy can get, who'd conducted his life with what passed in Notts as panache. It took her more than a decade to snap him up. Theirs was an on-and-off relationship during which time he'd enjoyed others whilst she had kept her honour just for him, or so she had let her beloved and the world believe.

Meanwhile she had risen easily through the ranks of local government administration, through different councils in or around Nottinghamshire, until she was a Borough Treasurer. Marriage to Roger, when it finally came, did not divert her from her chosen professional path and that arrangement suited him, too.

Roger had joined the army at 18, in 1968, seeing Amanda only when home on leave. She knew he served in Northern Ireland, Germany and the Far East, but he spoke little of the details and she never followed him abroad. There were (it was later revealed) occasional trips which did not get reported to her; but that mattered not to either of them as no subterfuge or disloyalty was involved. He had her arms to come to and she enjoyed the stability that even his absent presence bestowed.

Shortly after their wedding, in 1978, Roger was diagnosed with diabetes which he found difficult to control, ending his army career earlier than anticipated, in 1983.

Back on Civvy Street, Roger set up in business as a specialist in outdoor pursuits, despite a leg injury sustained in action in Londonderry, of which he never spoke. From his base in a Nottinghamshire farmhouse he and his minibuses could access the Peak

District with ease for day-long adventures. These usually involved groups of young people being sent by a well meaning or statutory organisation for some personality-forming or team-bonding experience on a river raft or a perpendicular rock face. Occasionally he would lend his facilities – at a good profit – to inspirational business gurus who wanted their followers to acquire a hard edge through night-time orienteering without a compass whilst 'discovering' compassion, co-operation or their more feminine sides.

This perfect working environment of fresh air, chosen hours, glorious landscapes and fulfilled and generous clients, was not to last. Roger's condition became chronic and it was only then, as cynical friends might have said, when he put on weight and became less mobile and attractive to women, that he turned to Amanda full time to fulfil his need for love and security. Long after giving up on her own wild oats she was there, waiting for him when he needed her.

Being late into marriage and neither wanting children each had maintained their profession. Roger continued to manage the outdoor pursuits business whilst Amanda made ever greater commitments to the proper functioning of local democracy.

Again thwarting the cynics, Roger and Amanda enjoyed 21 happy years of togetherness - more or less. However, in 1999 and with barely a moment's notice, a heart attack killed Roger whilst he was abseiling down a rock face on Curbar Edge. It was how he would have wanted to go.

At Sheila and Ken's invitation, the widow Amanda joined the couple for occasional holidays. Once Sheila, too, had died the siblings' joint annual forays became the norm. They normally opted for destinations within Britain but outside high season, places neither had previously visited, taking it in turns to choose. This particular September Ken had nominated the Eden Project in Cornwall, where the late summer sun promised to render this extraordinary modern museum of plant life a most attractive prospect.

Though Ken loved his sister he did not always profess to understand her. He respected her senior position and professional success, felt sorry that she'd enjoyed a briefer and more spasmodic experience of married life than he had and felt an occasional passionate sense of fraternal responsibility towards her. In turn she admired her brother's achievements, felt a slightly reluctant maternal feeling in his direction, despite his greater age, and sometimes felt she understood him far too well for his own good.

The first evening of this year's holiday was spent 'catching up', with Amanda anxious to hear every detail of Clive's family and the children's development. The next morning, after a lie-in and a routine breakfast for Ken, which Amanda skipped, they meandered around the narrow streets of base camp, a quiet seaside village near St Austell. As part of their pre-lunch conversation Amanda said: 'So, Ken, you're helping out with the old folks a bit, trawling the internet and sending emails left, right and centre, setting up your own Eden Project in the back garden…'

'That wasn't *quite* the impression I was trying to convey…'

'…being a grandad every now and then and quaffing a few beers at the Golf Club. What else are you doing with your well earned retirement? There must be something more, how shall I put it? More positive in your life right now?'

'I must confess that it isn't the garden. Stiffness of the fingers and a reluctance to kneel mean that I must find my fun elsewhere than amongst the F2 hybrids, I'm afraid. As a matter of fact, something has become a bit of a hobby. I'm hunting for a missing head teacher.'

'And you think he's in Cornwall? Is that why we're here?'

'No, not at all! If I knew where he was, I wouldn't be hunting.'

'So, who could be so careless as to lose their head teacher?'

Ken outlined the story of Norman Flagg: the chance meeting with Peter Elder some weeks earlier, Elder's approach to the retired policeman just as term was about to start and Ken's detective work in London and at Flagg's cottage.

'I'm no nearer finding him now than I was then. I'm baffled, to be honest.'

'This Peter Elder. I'm sure I've heard of him.'

'Possibly. He's quite active on the council conference circuit, which includes Borough Treasurers, no doubt. A good man, his heart's in the right place. He's a committed Labour person and genuinely concerned about his school – did I say he was Chair of Governors? – very aware of his responsibilities.'

'Good Lord, I wish all councillors were like that! I don't want to bite the hand that feeds me, but there are some pretty rum goings on amongst that fraternity which don't ever see the light of day, I can tell you.'

'So I gather. Peter was telling me as much. Chatham House rules?'

'Of course.' Their talk was off the record, nothing either said could be attributed.

'A story about a man called Wheatcroft.'

'Wheatcroft…?' Amanda clearly recognised the name.

'A Council leader in a property scam.'

'Ah, yes… So you know about that? The Wheatcroft story has achieved the status of 'modern myth'. Everyone in local government knows it, no one can quite put their hands on any evidence that corruption really was the reason why Wheatcroft resigned. It was about ten years ago, the chap disappeared off the face of the earth once he stepped down. Though didn't he die not long afterwards? Thought so. So, Peter Elder was behind all that, was he?'

'Apparently... but that's got nothing to do with my missing Head. Peter had no finger in the till then and he hasn't now, I'm sure. Straight as a die.'

'Have you checked the Head out on the fraud front? Something to hide?'

'Well... no, but I'm sure that if Peter had any suspicions of Flagg on that score he would have told me. Particularly after the Wheatcroft thing.'

'It might be as well to check, you know. He wouldn't be the first teacher to siphon off the PTA summer fair money on a holiday, or accidentally forget to bring back the school's new telly after selflessly testing it out at home over the long holidays.'

Ken acknowledged the phenomenon but dismissed it, though he was slightly stung by his sister pointing out that theft might be a motive for Flagg's disappearance; this was something he had indeed overlooked. Was he losing his touch or was the thought simply not credible?

'So where d'you think this man is?'

'Quite honestly? No idea. The new term's more than a week old and things are going well, as far as I can tell. It's a sign of a good Head that the Deputy – Jane Moore – has the confidence and ability to step in, don't you think?'

'I'm sure you know better than me, you've had Sheila 'on the inside'! Didn't you used to go into her school to help the kids read? My job is only to make sure the money goes to these Heads when it should, in the quantities my lords and masters have decreed. I hardly ever meet actual teachers in the course of my work.'

'I think the steady ship's a good sign. She's learned her trade from him. Everyone says that Norman Flagg was – is – a good Head, very conscientious.'

'He can't be that conscientious, if he misses the first week of term without an explanation or apology! Perhaps he's dead – have you thought of that?'

'Amanda, really! No, I don't think he is dead. Between you and me I got Clive to make a few discreet enquiries. I know that Norman Flagg hasn't been reported dead, or admitted to hospital locally or detained by a foreign power. Nor has he been issued with a driving penalty.'

'So he's taken a lover and whisked her away to the Seychelles.'

Ken pursed his lips for a moment.

'No evidence of a girlfriend.'

'Not up until the point at which he disappeared, you mean.'

'Well, that's true...'

'Did he win the Lottery?'

'Amanda...' Ken started to protest.

'I'm serious! One of our cleaners at work won last year, two million, I think! Never saw her for dust after that.'

'She wasn't a very good cleaner, then?'

'Sorry?'

'The dust?'

Amanda had grown immune to her brother's sense of humour over the years.

'She ticked the 'no publicity' box and took her six children and their families to Barbados for a blow-out holiday.'

'I haven't actually checked the Lottery... I can't believe he was a gambler.'

'Has he gone abroad and been kidnapped? It happens, you know. Travelling by himself, no family, who's to notice he's gone?'

'Isn't the whole point about kidnapping that you make a demand in exchange for the victim's return? There've been no demands.'

'Perhaps the kidnapping went wrong and he's lying in a Moroccan sand dune with a knife in his back.'

'I've no evidence he's left the country. Not through normal channels.'

'Or English Channels?'

'Touché! As I said, Clive can... check certain things for me.'

'It must be frustrating not having your hands on the levers of power any more, Ken. Having to get your son to act all surreptitious for you, clandestine enquiries. Accessing the Police Computer behind the Super's back could get him into trouble, couldn't it?'

'I really don't think he'd do anything he's not empowered to do. He's an Inspector now, you know.'

'I know. And he's a good man, I'm sure he does a great job. You can be proud of him. Come on, Ken, I'm teasing you!'

'Yes. OK.'

'All the same... it sounds odd, doesn't it?'

They had reached the end of the readily meanderable part of the beach and in unspoken agreement they made for the steps up to the promenade. A tea stall stood, paint peeling, between them and the road. Instinctively they headed for it. It was clearly going to be a hot day although it had not got there quite yet, as the climbing sun burned off the last of the morning's haze. Nevertheless, both Ken and Amanda were thankful for their warm coats, Amanda's woollen hat and Ken's trademark trilby, and they welcomed the opportunity of a hot drink.

Amanda took the two polystyrene cups to an iron table and pulled up collapsible iron chairs as Ken paid for their drinks.

As he sat down, she said 'So is Clive taking this seriously?'

'Clive?'

'This missing Head thing.'

'Well... the Head's now in breach of contract, but that's not a police matter. His family haven't reported him missing, there's no evidence that he was doing anything criminal, so there's not really anything for the police to look into.'

'Hmm... I see. Have you actually spoken to the neighbours?'

'Sorry?'

'Mr Flagg's neighbours in the village. Perhaps they've seen something. And don't you think they might have reported him missing? If it's been nearly two months? You said Peter Elder first mentioned it at the end of July.'

'Oh, God.'

'What's the matter?'

Ken sighed briefly.

'You're absolutely right. About everything. The neighbours, the lottery, the fingers in the till. I'm losing it, aren't I? I should've checked all these. Instead, off I go gallivanting to London to interview some pompous city type about a chance meeting that he may or may not have had with Flagg at a CCF function 20 years ago, which I find out didn't actually happen. I'm supposed to be a detective, aren't I? And now you come along and in the course of a quarter of an hour you list all the things I've overlooked. All the bloody obvious ones.'

'Oh, come on, Ken, I'm not getting at you! You're doing a friend a favour. It's not your responsibility to make sure the school has a Head. You say there's no suggestion he's done anything illegal, improper? It might be easier if he had. Hey, he's not been feeling up the kids, has he?'

'Not as far as I know.' Ken spoke with a resigned air even if it was clear that his sister's words had been jocular. 'But there would only have to be rumours, allegations of something like that and any Head would be out on his ear. Look, Amanda, you get a feel for these things when you've been in the police as long as I was. I bet my bottom dollar that the neighbours in the village won't be able to tell me anything.'

'But you haven't checked, Ken.'

'This isn't a police investigation. But you've got me thinking. Do you know what? I think Mr Flagg might have a second home... That's one reason I don't think the neighbours would be helpful – my guess is they don't know him very well, so they wouldn't really notice if he was away for weeks at a time.'

'Hmm… Well, that gives you something to investigate. Lots of people have second homes. Anyway, you've got a different angle to get your teeth into now. And you've been told the chap isn't dead, in hospital or in prison. I'm sure that was a relief to Peter Elder.'

'I suppose so…'

'So why worry yourself about it? Let's face it, Ken, with the best will in the world you aren't a policeman any more. You haven't been for a while. There are reasons why men of your age are no longer put at the forefront of cutting edge investigations. And you haven't got the back-up you had as a Sergeant.'

'Inspector.'

'Whatever, sorry.' She reached across the table and held her brother's hand. 'Look, you did a fantastic job when you were in the police. Everyone said so, you had lots of friends and people respected you. You even had your son following in your footsteps, you can't get a greater tribute than that. You did a great job and you should be proud of what you did. But you're not doing it now, not any more. If this councillor wants to find his Head Teacher, let him do it. Let him make the effort. Advise him, by all means, give him the benefit of your experience, whatever. What's he done to help you?'

'Well…'

'Well, there you are. Don't blame yourself just because you, a little old man acting by yourself with no resources, haven't solved the problem in just a few days. You aren't Sherlock Holmes! This isn't fiction, Ken.'

Ken did not reply but nor could he look his sister in the face.

She went on: 'You know, it seems to me that this Flagg, whatever his name is, doesn't want to be found. Something has happened in his life, something that's got nothing to do with you, with Peter Elder, maybe even nothing to do with the school. He's trying to cope with it somehow, don't you think? But when someone really doesn't want to be found you're going to have Hell's own job finding them. You might never do it. You have to accept that, Ken.'

'Yes, Amanda. You're right.'

She squeezed his hand.

'I don't want to upset you. But you don't have to do this. Let Peter Elder do his own dirty work. Hey, come on. Let's finish our cup of tea and go and buy some cockles.'

He knew she was right, she always was. She always put things into perspective. It was time for a deep breath and to shake off Peter Elder, Norman Flagg and the rest of what was not here or now. He was on holiday, after all.

'Yes, you're right, Amanda. Come on, let's go.'

They walked back along the promenade in the direction from which they had come. Their conversation was sporadic and superficial, discussing which buildings they were passing could do with a lick of paint, what the weather might do later in the day, where to have lunch. Small plastic containers of cockles and mussels were duly bought and their contents consumed with the aid of cocktail sticks, a couple of shops were browsed and, within no time, lunch was beckoning.

Plaice, chips and peas with a generous helping of tartar sauce for each of them in a seafront pub was just what the doctor ordered. At one point Ken held aloft his fork upon which the sauce had secured a dozen green peas.

'Peas in our time!' he laughed, 'like Neville Chamberlain!' Amanda condescended to smile at this annual, inevitable repetition of one of Ken's favourite bad jokes.

He was clearly feeling himself again, after the earlier discomfort.

'Tell me,' said Ken, later, 'From your experience, what sort of person becomes a councillor?'

'How do you mean? As representatives of the people they are… representative of the people, I suppose. It takes all sorts.'

'You're talking about backbenchers. What sort of person makes a career out of being a councillor?'

'A pretty lucky one. It's only in the last few years that their allowances have made it possible for some councillors not to have another substantial job, to think of making it a career. And they have to be lucky too, they depend on fickle voters – in their wards, in the nation as a whole – and on the whims of their colleagues. Once elected, that's when the trickiest bit comes, getting on with and staying in tune with your political compatriots.'

'I suppose so.'

'Local government has greasy poles like any other job. I sometimes think theirs is especially well lubricated and has razor blades embedded in it.'

'Nasty!'

'There's a story about a new councillor who says to an experienced colleague 'Isn't this fun? Standing up here in the council chamber and making a speech with the enemy arrayed there in front of you, isn't it thrilling?' And the older guy says 'Enemy? No, they're the Opposition. That's the enemy, behind you.' Internal group politics can be much more ruthless and cynical than those between parties. And it doesn't matter which party they're in, they're all the same.'

'Do you have a lot to do with councillors in your work, Amanda?'

'Not as much as you'd think, actually. Not directly. As senior officers in a council my colleagues and I usually deal with the group leaders and cabinet members rather than backbenchers. Former leaders have an odd role: they can never accept that their turn is over! Though that can be helpful because they know the officers and still talk to us. That way we know more about some of the backbenchers than they think; sometimes more than they know about themselves.'

Ken smiled. 'I thought *my* career relied on 'intelligence'.'

'I never said councillors had to be intelligent...'

'So to be successful, what does a councillor need to be? As well as lucky. And not necessarily intelligent.'

'Oh, lucky, ruthless, committed...'

'Bright? Eloquent?'

'Not necessarily, no. Having the 'common touch' helps. But being in the right place at the right time is the key to a successful career in local government.'

'Does passion help?'

'Well, it's not a prerequisite. But it depends what you mean by success, I suppose. Twenty years of representing a safe seat, with a big majority on five occasions, might be regarded as success. Yet you might never say a word in public, never scintillate on the airwaves, never write a press release. Achieve nothing. And there are conventional definitions of success too: a meteoric rise in the Party hierarchy, getting to implement a policy associated with your cause, never being off local radio. Then there's getting elected to the Party leadership or re-elected to your ward when the political tide is running against you. That's proper success.'

By any definition Peter Elder had been successful in local politics, Ken thought. He had evidence of the luck, the popularity, the commitment, the means and even the passion. Did he have the sense to get out before ignominy set in? Ruthlessness must be in the mix somewhere, he thought.

Once the food had been disposed of and enjoying a pint of rather excellent local ale, Ken's journey back from reverie was complete.

'Nevertheless, Amanda, you know there are some fascinating aspects to this case. Flagg's house looks barely lived-in. He was a raving leftie who became a pillar of the establishment. A raving leftie who'd been in the army cadets, come to that. And we have a councillor who knows a bit more about the background of our man than either he or the incomplete CV of our friend has been letting on. Add to that, a feisty deputy head who might have the politics today that Flagg had twenty years ago. Place all this in the setting of a quiet village school and it's quite a rural mystery, don't you think?'

'I see what you mean. In the same way that some people find Cluedo fun, then yes, I suppose it's fun.'

'It's not quite Colonel Mustard in the conservatory with the hammer!'

'No, indeed, but that's because there isn't actually a problem to solve here, Ken. A man has gone missing but the school goes on, you said it yourself. No one's indispensable, as my Chief Executive is constantly reminding me.'

Ken felt as though his commitment was being downplayed again, though his sister's self-deprecation helped to temper it. But instead of drawing the theme to a close, Amanda picked up an issue.

'Did you say he'd been in the army?'

'Sorry?'

'The army? This man Flagg?'

'Well, no, not as such. Not the CCF either, but the University equivalent – Officer Training Corps.'

'Oh, yes.'

'He'd have had a uniform and access to a rifle range but he didn't do much else with them, as far as I can tell. He wasn't a full member of the army, didn't go on to sign up… as far as I know. There's a bit of a hole in his CV in his early twenties… but I don't think he was ever actually in the army.'

'I was just interested, what with Roger's experience.'

'Of course.'

'I don't know if I ever told you this, but Roger went all around the world, Northern Ireland, Africa, Middle East.'

'Yes, I knew that.'

'More places than he let on. He was often there *before* their troubles started, I mean. He was sent out under cover. I don't suppose it can hurt to mention it now.'

'No, I don't suppose… We're still 'Chatham House', aren't we? Go on.'

'He was in military intelligence. Before we were married I used to think that phrase was an oxymoron. I couldn't say as much to Roger, of course.'

'And the point you're making is…?'

'Officially, Roger had a very undistinguished military career. In actual fact he was always up to derring-do, much of it off the record. I don't know that much about it, but I do know that there was a point where he was lying in bushes with his binoculars trained on Eritrean soldiers whilst officially he was somewhere else entirely. There would have been all hell to pay if he'd been caught.

'But he also spent time in Britain and Europe, tracking down soldiers who'd gone AWOL. This happened several times that I knew about, possibly there were more. He wouldn't make direct contact with them, but he'd find out where they were and report back. Mostly, he found them getting drunk somewhere – Blackpool, London, Majorca. One or two had gone to be mercenaries in Africa, fighting for the side that would pay them the most. He found those people too, and sometimes arranged for them to be... well, 'taken out of service' is the euphemism Roger used. I don't know exactly what happened, I never asked. But sometimes I don't think they returned willingly... and some never returned at all.'

'Goodness!'

'It was probably for the best. I'm sure it wasn't nice and he never gave me details. On another posting the records show that Roger was in Germany but he was actually in Sudan, doing... that sort of thing.'

'I see.'

'All this was going on whilst he was a soldier, but he didn't tell me about it until long afterwards. Of course, he wasn't the only one doing this sort of job – herding in the wandering black sheep. But some of his colleagues, the other sheepdogs, as he called them, were apparently civilians.'

'Civilians?'

'Former soldiers. It was important to use fresh blood to make the actual contact with the prodigal. If a sheepdog got exposed in a mission then it wouldn't be safe to use him in that country - or that continent, maybe - again. The professionals couldn't just stop and the sheepdogs needed their appearances and identities to be kept secret, so they pulled crack troops back out of retirement and used them as bait. So, how would an engineer, or a bank clerk, or a gym instructor explain a sudden disappearance? It might be for Queen and country, but it would all be a great secret.'

'I see what you're getting at. You think that's what's happening here?'

'Maybe...'

Could Flagg be a British agent, Ken thought, tasked to shepherd errant soldiers in hostile terrain and get them out? He could be in Afghanistan right now, or Iraq, Bosnia or Sudan, anywhere that British troops or former troops might go AWOL. And if that was the case then the considerable powers of the state, powers which he had worked with and alongside for so many years, would make absolutely certain that no amateur sleuth, no male Marple, would get anywhere near Flagg's working identity. A teacher, of all people, could easily slip away for a month every summer without being noticed... until something went wrong.

Meanwhile, there was that hole in the younger Flagg's curriculum vitae to be accounted for, the lacuna just before he committed to being a teacher, which suddenly looked very large - and possibly military. That giant hole was now brimming to overflowing with the words: 'what if'.

Sod it, he thought.

Down here in Cornwall he was enjoying sharing the sea air with his sister. Right now, that felt rather more important than playing detective games.

* * *

Alone in his bed that night, Ken heard a Cornish clock strike three. Flagg would not leave him alone. Over the next few days with Amanda he would challenge himself to stop thinking about Head Teachers, confident that, nevertheless, the ideas would ferment and mature even if he did succeed in putting them formally to one side.

He was almost looking forward to lifting the lid on the story again in a few days time and seeing what had developed. For now he would try to let it lie, and get some sleep.

* * *

One day the brother and sister visited St Ives, on another they explored Land's End. The impressive Eden Project was duly examined in detail. Amanda told Ken more about her work and how she was enjoying her new hobby, watercolours; Ken mentioned that Mrs Elder, Laura, was an artist, though Amanda hadn't heard of her. He told his sister more about Clive's ambitions for his children and some of the characters he'd met at the pensioners' functions he'd dared to attend. Each silently read a newspaper thoroughly each day and in their conversations they explored every issue and topic of common interest.

They visited museums and harbours, fish restaurants and a cinema. Going to see a film one afternoon reminded them of rain-soaked holidays as children.

On Tuesday, September 20th, Ken mentally ticked the box labelled 'Cornwall, Done' as Amanda returned to the northlands for another year.

* * *

Back in Sussex Ken felt that his batteries had been recharged.

There was a note on the mat from Peter, explaining that he and Laura had decided to take a few days off and he would be back on the Wednesday. Notes were Peter's favourite way of communicating, it appeared.

On his doormat the local weekly newspaper was also awaiting his return but there was no follow-up to the story about the missing Head.

The morning of Wednesday 21ˢᵗ Ken started with a brief phone call to Irene, secretary, receptionist, tea maker and general factotum, confirming that nothing had changed on the school front, so Ken made his way back to the village where Norman Flagg had his home. A third discreet peremptory check of the property revealed nothing new. From the dust and the presence of two bills and some junk mail on the floor by the front door he concluded that Mrs Goose had not visited since his own last visit. There were two new but blank and anonymous messages on the answering service.

He spoke frankly to the elderly spinster who lived next door: he told her that Mr Flagg had not been at his school – it had been in the paper, after all – and that the governors were concerned about him.

'Well, I think his name is Nigel and I think he's a teacher. He's quite tall and he listens to the radio in the mornings, the news programmes, I believe, when he's here.'

'Which is how often?'

'Oh, every time that he's here.'

'And how often is that?'

'My hearing isn't very good, you know.'

'But you hear his radio?'

'Only sometimes, when he's here. I suppose he must have it on quite loud.'

'So you haven't seen him for a while?'

'He's not been here for a while. Otherwise I would have heard the radio in the mornings.'

'Is it unusual for him to be away for a few weeks at a stretch?'

'Oh, no. He's often away for weeks, especially in the summer.'

A similar experience with Miss Needham's neighbour finally confirmed to Ken Hemmings that Norman Flagg's occupation of the cottage that he'd spent so much time investigating was superficial, to say the least. He was barking up the wrong tree. This was not, he was now certain, the Head Teacher's only home.

This raised certain questions, Ken mused, deciding to sample a lunch time pie and pint at what ought to have been Norman Flagg's local. Rekindling his powers of discretion he introduced himself to the barmaid as she poured his drink. There were others in the bar but Ken had chosen a spot where they would not be overheard.

After explaining that he was from the Education Authority, trying to find Mr Flagg to talk about some contractual issues, Ken asked the Geordie-woman with a dozen rings on her fingers if she knew his quarry. She showed a borderline prurient interest.

'He's been here about three years, I'd say, pet, about the same as me. I don't live here, not in the pub. I live down the road, I work here lunchtimes most days. I don't know as I'd recognise him, like.'

'He's not a 'character' in the village, then?'

'Never see him, pet. Never hear nothing about him. He's gone missing, you say? Well, as far as the village is concerned, how would we know?'

'Is the landlord at home?'

'Mr Joyce? No, not today. Oh! Ay up, pet! Is this the man that was in the paper? The Headmaster who went missing? So he's still not turned up, is that right?'

'Yes, that's it.'

'Well, I never!'

The steak pie arrived and the barmaid offered mustard. He accepted, but then she was called to the other side of the bar. Their conversation had run its course.

So, no new information. Would further interviews would reveal more, without generating unhelpful rumours? No, on reflection there seemed little point in this line of enquiry. In this village Norman Flagg was Norman Nobody.

Ken doodled in his notebook and several words emerged:

If not Flagg's primary home, where is?

20+ minutes drive from school, convenient for work over last three years.

Single man, small property.

Can a primary head afford two 'decent' properties?

Nearest supply of basic props - Brighton / Hove.

Which is exactly where the estate agents whose web pages he had seen could be found.

Thursday 22nd September

'Hello, my name's Hemmings. May I speak to the manager, please?'

The girl in the front office of Hathersage Homes looked barely old enough to have left school. She wrote his name on a pad and disappeared into a back office. Ken surveyed a nearby display: the price of houses these days was shocking!

'Hello, Mr Hemmings? I'm Valerie Boon. How can I help you?'

Ken made an instant assessment: wedding ring, over made-up, over-weight, well-dressed. Not happy. The woman was naturally suspicious of anyone wanting to see the boss, so customer contact was clearly not what this manager thought she was for.

I'll put her mind at rest, he thought, get her on my side.

'Mrs Boon, I'm so sorry to disturb you. I have a bad back: may we sit down?'

'Of course. Come with me.'

Valerie Boon's lair was separated from the rest of the open plan office by a wall with a mirror window in it. Through it she could see the rest of the office but no one out there could see her. Ken felt it was time for a cup of tea but none was offered, which he took as normal in the fast moving, high finance, live for the day world of south coast estate agencies.

'I'll come straight to the point, Mrs Boon. I'm carrying out some enquiries on behalf of the education authority, trying to find a Head Teacher who's gone absent without leave. It's a contractual matter. I think he may have taken a property in this area recently and I'm hoping you might be able to help me find him.'

'Well, of course, I would always want to assist yourself under such circumstances, but I do have a duty of confidentiality to my clients. You will appreciate that I cannot give out personal information willy nilly – even if I had it. Do you think that your gentleman has acquired a property through our good offices?'

Ken smiled. 'I honestly don't know, Mrs Boon. I only know that he did access your web site.'

'It's a good web site, don't you think? Hathersage Homes is very proud of our user-friendly customer interface. We've become the fourth most successful estate agent in the whole of Brighton and Hove since we had the web site revamped. It wasn't cheap, you know.'

'No doubt…'

'So… I'll help you if I can, subject to what I've said about discretion.'

'The man's name is Flagg, not a common name. I don't know if he was looking to purchase or to rent.'

'Well, at least he's not called Smith! That makes it easier.'

'It's Norman Anthony Flagg, with two g's. This chap's in breach of his contract, Mrs Boon, through reasons of absence. It's nothing criminal, you understand, just contractual. You may have seen the story in last week's paper. We want to make sure public money isn't being wasted. I'm telling you this as a professional person, but as a human being I want to know first of all that he's safe, he's not ill or even dying somewhere. You never know, maybe even dying in one of your rental properties…'

Valerie Boon blanched at the prospect of adverse publicity and its concomitant potential downside for her ongoing customer interface.

Ken went on: 'I'm sure you'll understand. He moved to Sussex about three years ago but seems to have changed his accommodation arrangements recently. He may be ill,

Mrs Boon, possibly a nervous breakdown. It's really in his own best interests that I find him.'

'I see… Look, let me take a look and see what I'm able to tell you. I can't promise anything.'

'Of course not. Thank you.'

She swivelled her chair around and tapped the computer keyboard. Ken waited patiently. Her fingers moved over the keys like mercury.

Valerie Boon relaxed her shoulders.

'Yes, I think I can help, Mr Hemmings.'

'Oh, good…' Play it down, thought Ken. He hadn't expected his task to be this easy.

'On 23rd April, 2003, a Mr Flagg made enquiries about several one-bedroom properties available for purchase and he took some brochures with him. I don't know which properties they were, but I can tell you that we haven't heard from Mr Flagg since then. He's neither a tenant nor a purchaser of a Hathersage Home. On that visit, yes, he did register as a user of our web site. He's no longer registered, but that doesn't mean that he can't access the public areas, of course.'

'Why would someone need to be registered on your site?'

'If they desired to keep fully acquainted with the local property and/or rental accommodation market, yes.'

'Of course.'

'Sometimes customers already have a property they intend to let and they wish to see what prices are commanded by similar properties within the preferred locale.'

'I see.'

'If he was seeking to purchase or engage in a letting situation then the site would automatically send him an email whenever a property came onto the market adjacent to his preferred locale and appropriate for his affordability criteria.'

'And he would de-register because…'

'Perhaps he found the property of his personal choice, hopefully one from Hathersage Homes.'

'And in this case?'

She glanced at the screen once more. 'I really can't say. He was on the mailing list for several months. But as I say, he's not currently a domestic tenant or registered as a real or potential purchaser.'

'And the email address he was using…'

'Mr Hemmings, I'm sorry, but there are limits!'

'I appreciate that, Mrs Boon. I may know it already, from earlier enquiries. Would it end with 'sussex.gov.uk'?'

The manageress knew her way around her database.

'As you say, I don't suppose there's any harm in confirming what you already know.'

'Thank you, Mrs Boon. You really have been very helpful.'

Outside in the street Ken assessed his new evidence.

Two significant things had been learned: Flagg had indeed been looking for a property to buy, not long after purchasing his village home. If he had followed this through, perhaps buying a property through a different agency, it was not because he was dissatisfied with his cottage; he still owned it, used it from time to time, didn't rent it out and had not disposed of it.

Why then seek a second home which was less convenient for travelling to work than the first, yet still not terribly far from either? If that was indeed what Flagg had done, it was the sort of conflation of innocent events from which the good detective might draw sensible inferences.

Could a primary school head afford to buy two properties, albeit small ones, one in rural Sussex and another in Brighton at that time? This felt unlikely. Either the second purchase had not taken place or Flagg had access to income or capital other than his teaching salary, perhaps an inheritance. An inheritance felt unlikely, though not having children would help. A military salary or retainer?

He now needed proper access to the computer on Jane Moore's desk.

With a spring in his step, Ken headed home. He would seek out Fintons, the other estate agent where he knew Flagg had established some e-contact, tomorrow.

* * *

Jane Moore opened the school door as Ken approached.

'Mr Hemmings, do come in! Nice to see you. First things first: a cup of tea. How do you take it, again?'

'Hello! Tea would be wonderful; milk, but quite strong, no sugar, please.'

This head teacher was much more relaxed and comfortable than the rookie he'd met on the second day of term. The school was quiet and neat, with a busy atmosphere.

After leaving the tea order with Irene Jane led the way to her office as she continued 'Please, come and sit down. I take it there's no news about Norman? Or have you come to offer to listen to Year 2 reading, after all?'

Ken smiled. He'd already deduced that the woman was revelling in her new responsibilities. Her outfit and manner declared both her raised status and her warm approachability, a difficult balance to achieve and an even more difficult one to fake. There was no doubt that she had the necessary skills for the job.

'Not on this occasion, Jane. May I call you Jane?' She nodded her assent and Ken was pleased to avoid the 'Ms' business. 'But you're right on the first count. No news, I'm afraid.'

'Do you know, I've barely had time to think about Norman these last couple of weeks. He was a star, really. All the records are immaculate, I know where everything is, nothing about running this school has come as a surprise. I have over two hundred happy children here and it's all down to him. I've merely picked up his baton and run with it.'

'You're very fortunate. Too many incoming Heads must find themselves inheriting a mess, I'd guess, because they're taking over from someone who's either failed, lost interest or whose ways of doing things are impenetrable.'

'I'm sure that's just about it.'

'Expecting to be handed a baton, finding you're tied up in a three-legged sack race.'

'Exactly.' She smiled her appreciation of the primary school focus of his quip.

'And Peter is being supportive, I'm sure.'

'Well... I think I may have barked at him a little too ferociously that first week - you were there! I've perhaps scared him off a little. He's doing his bit, of course, I've never doubted his commitment or professionalism – but he's not been coming into school unnecessarily, let's put it that way.'

'He's a busy man in his own right.'

'If you want something doing ask a busy person. Nevertheless, I thought I might have seen him a little more than I have, though he's never far from the other end of an email, so we keep in touch.'

'Ah, yes, an email. Jane, I do have a theory about Norman and I need your help to take it further.'

'Go on.'

'Your computer. Can you access your local authority email account remotely? From home, for example?'

'Yes, why?'

'Forgive me. It's Norman's email account I'm asking about. I don't suppose you've been accessing his account.'

'No, it hasn't been necessary, the LEA is pretty good about communication. Everything intended for the Head has been coming to me almost since day one. I did look into Norman's account at first, to see if there were any outstanding matters I needed to deal with. And I put an auto-response on it which told people that their email was being redirected to my account, as I was now the acting Head teacher.'

'So any email to do with him would be forwarded to your account?'

'Yes. A copy would be sent to my account and – '

'Did you delete very much? Of Norman's mail that was forwarded to you?'

'No, not a lot. As I said before, Norman's very professional. There was very little extraneous stuff, not directly to do with school. Even that's mostly dried up: between me and the spam filter there's almost no mail coming into Norman's inbox.'

'But you have the password to get into his emails?'

'Yes, if it hasn't expired. If you stop using the account for a while the password expires and you have to call county to re-activate the account.'

Ken thought about it. 'That shouldn't be a problem. The auto-forwarding would count as using it, so I guess that the password's still valid. Jane, I'm not especially interested in the emails that he might've been getting in the last few weeks, unless you think that something might be of interest to me? No?'

She shrugged.

'Good. But I would like to look at the archives on Norman's account. May I?'

As the Head hesitated there was a knock at the door and Irene entered with a tray.

'Two teas, no sugar, that's right, isn't it?'

'Thank you, Irene.'

'Jane, you won't forget that the man from county's coming about the windows in the infant block in fifteen minutes?'

'Thank you, Irene. I'd not forgotten.'

'The tea looks grand, Irene,' said Ken, 'Just as I like it. Thank you.'

Jane Moore appeared distracted. Irene left and closed the door behind her. Ken jumped as a piercing bell rang in the corridor outside.

'Afternoon break,' Jane explained. 'I have to go and show my face in the staff room and playground, if you don't mind. I'll only be two minutes. But… there's the computer. Mr Hemmings, I'm sure it's not good practice to let others see his emails but, under the circumstances, be my guest.'

'Thank you. I'll be discreet, I assure you. You've said that there's nothing untoward there, so I'm sure there's nothing to worry about.'

'Indeed…' but her air of confidence had waned.

'Don't let your tea go cold, Jane.'

'No.' She picked up her cup to take it with her.

'And the password is…?'

'It's... all lower case, red, underscore, flag, with just one 'g'.'

'Oh... 'red flag', eh?'

'Norman's little joke.'

She smiled briefly and left the room. Ken held himself back from rushing to the computer, to find where this new jigsaw piece fitted. He stood, exhaled, alone; then walked purposefully towards the keyboard with a premonition that something important was about to be revealed.

He sat at the Head's desk and collected his thoughts. The Red Flag pseudonym must be more than a coincidence.

At no point had he ever mentioned the revolutionary material he'd found in Norman Flagg's house to Jane Moore, but his speculation that the diary writer of Workers' Voice, perhaps over many years, had been none other than the errant Head Teacher had just received a massive vote of confidence. In the next few seconds it could be proved certain.

He typed 'red_flag' in the on-screen dialogue box and waited. Outlook revealed its innermost thoughts relatively quickly. A list of incoming messages in bold font, indicating that they were unread, filled the screen.

He clicked 'Sent items' and this confirmed that the forwarding mechanism had been activated on September 10th. Prior to that, the last message sent from this computer was to County Property Services in July and it was entitled 'Urgent repairs to infant block windows'. It sounded so dry and genuine that he didn't bother to open it, noting that the man from Property Services was probably on his way to the school at that very moment, in response to that 'urgent' request. He did not have long to work.

Back to the Inbox. As he scanned the list of incoming messages he blessed his son, without whom he would never have acquired his flair for email at his advanced age. He navigated the windows with ease.

There was no recent incoming mail; Jane's strategy had worked. Nor was there anything of any consequence from the last two weeks. Although the list in bold had initially filled the screen it didn't stretch to a second page.

Like most people, Norman Flagg had his Inbox sorted into different categories, but none of the boxes was displayed in bold so it looked like he sorted them manually. The categories were predictable: Catering, Curriculum, Governors, LEA, Personal, PTA, Staffing.

Ken clicked 'Personal'. The oldest of no more than twenty messages were three years old, going back to Flagg's early days at the school. He was obviously disciplined in not mixing business with pleasure and there was possibly another account somewhere, probably web-based. He would not be able to locate such an account without access to the proper channels. Unless Flagg had used this one to talk to that one, of course…

Jane would be back at any moment. If there was gold dust here he wanted to see it before she returned.

And there was: one incoming personal message dated June, 2003, from Finton's estate agents in Brighton, listing a dozen single bedroom flats on sale in the city at that time. Flagg might have received several such emails, from different estate agents, over a period of some months; but only this one had been retained: there must be a reason for that. One of these addresses must be that of the spot marked 'X'.

It was easy to send the list to his own account, where he could read it at leisure. He moved the cursor to the top of the screen and clicked 'Forward', typed 'kenhem@' and stopped.

No. This would leave a trail which could be traced back to him. Jane knew he was looking but not what he was looking for. She was on his side but there must be an element of 'need to know' in his enquiries. Jane did not 'need to know', and nor did Flagg if – it suddenly occurred to him – the head teacher was monitoring his email traffic remotely. This thought caused a shiver to run down Ken's spine. And what, he fleetingly wondered, if Jane was a Worker's Gauntlet co-conspirator?

So, forwarding the message was a bad idea. He clicked the 'X' in the top corner of the email he'd just created and it disappeared for ever, without trace. Clicking again on the original list he hit the 'Print' icon and hoped for the best. After the click he hoped that the printer was here in the office and not outside in Irene's den; a reassuring noise from somewhere near his feet confirmed that this was the case.

He snatched the single sheet from the printer, folded it neatly into three and placed it in his inside jacket pocket. He would read the details later. Now he had a lead to Flagg's whereabouts, and there was surely more treasure here yet to plunder.

He went back to the 'Sent items' list and was surprised how few emails were there. None was older than May 2005 nor incriminating in any way.

This explained why there was no message to tell Flagg that his mailbox was full, even though it had received no attention over the summer. When people clear out an Inbox for this reason, he knew, they often neglect to delete sent items at the same time so the 'full' problem is postponed rather than resolved.

But at the bottom of the Inbox tree he found what he was looking for, the label 'Personal Folders'. He'd only recently discovered the joy of Windows' .pst files for himself. By saving emails onto a hard drive rather than on the server, available storage space was increased almost infinitely whilst keeping the messages accessible from within Outlook.

Sure enough, the folder structure of the Inbox was duplicated in the Personal Folders. Ken sensed perspiration on his brow as he clicked again on the 'Sent' tag within it.

If the list of properties had been gold dust, this was dynamite.

At the very top of the list was an email which made Ken's blood run cold. On May 10, 2005, Flagg had written a brief message to half a dozen recipients, with a Word file attached. The message read:

'The traitor has been re-elected. What shall we do? Thoughts attached for WG, views welcome, RF'. 'RF' would be 'Red Flag', the formerly pseudonymous diarist. 'WG' would be Workers' Gauntlet, that little known magazine from the same stable.

The office door remained shut. Ken again selected 'Print'. The magazine article would only be a couple of pages at the most and the printer was pretty efficient. Printing it was worth the risk.

As an afterthought he clicked to print the covering email itself. As the printer digested he surveyed the list of recipients: Jasper, Courier, Monument, Phantom and Almanac. More pseudonyms, more covert operations, more… Moore. Jane Moore. Moore's Almanac? Now his mind really was playing tricks. It was amazing what paranoia a bit of adrenalin could generate.

Jane Moore had been gone longer than expected and her next visitor was due. Ken looked again at the list of emails saved to the hard drive whilst waiting to collect the paper from the printer.

One was from Jasper in June, to the same group of people: 'Meet OS Thursday at 7'. In the thread, Phantom had written 'Will do. P.' And Almanac had helpfully contributed 'Does Monument know OS? Map attached.' This was followed by a URL too long and complex for Ken to write down. He hit 'print' yet again and hoped for the best.

Feeling that his luck was about to run out, Ken returned to the original Outlook Inbox and breathed a sigh of relief. The last piece of paper was now in his bulging pocket. He went to Internet Explorer and clicked on 'History'. As expected, the two estate agencies were there, as he'd seen on his previous visit. They had been viewed in July but, apart from that, the internet had rarely been accessed from this computer since 6th May, when someone had accessed the BBC news page on several occasions, no doubt to scrutinise the results of the general election of the previous day. On 7th July, BBC News again had been used to monitor the story of the London bombings. Many horrified, innocent and incredulous people with a humanitarian streak would have visited that same website on that day.

As might someone who sympathised with the perpetrators.

Other than that, the little-used internet revealed no more secrets.

'Sorry I took so long.'

Ken jumped: Jane Moore had re-entered, silently.

'Anything useful?'

He furrowed his brow before stating 'Not much. Either he was disciplined, abstemious or diligent in deleting stuff, but there's virtually nothing on either the internet history or the email record that's of any interest to me.'

'All three of those adjectives would describe Norman.'

'So I don't think I need detain you any longer, Jane. I know you have a visitor coming.'

'Indeed. Well, Ken, look – if you ever do want to come in and listen to the children reading, you really would be very welcome.'

Ken smiled and picked up his trilby from the desk. 'Thank you. I will certainly bear your kind invitation in mind. I ought to go now. Things to do, people to see. People think retirement is all about slowing down and doing a bit less but, believe you me, it isn't! It's busy. Goodbye, Jane.'

'Goodbye, Ken.'

They shook hands and the old man left. As Jane Moore sat at the desk and collected her thoughts about window frames, children and the upcoming home time, she found herself doing her own detective work.

Ken Hemmings was most definitely a tea man, she remembered, rather than coffee, but in his distraction he'd left his mug untouched. And the 'no paper' light was flashing red on the printer under her desk. She was sure it hadn't been doing that earlier so, if Ken had found nothing, what had he been printing?

Chapter 8: Belfast, August 2004

Getting down from behind the wheel of the white transit van, Ray Spears made an instant assessment of the four men who stood before him in the North Belfast street. The man whose body language said 'leader' was short, in his fifties, a large belly perched above inappropriately slim hips and beneath what the TV producer understandably hesitated to describe as a 'bomber' jacket. The Leader reminded Spears of a beaver: his hands were in his jeans pockets, his hair was grey with a natural quiff, close cropped on the sides of his head, giving the impression of having just left the water after a powerful swim. His thin lips drew a firm, horizontal line. The man's air exuded confidence through home advantage. Forty years ago he would have been a teddy boy. Today it was already clear that the Beaver would be the central figure of the planned interview.

To the left was a man whom Ray instantly christened 'the Rat'. He was the same height as the Beaver but half the build. Rat was dark, unshaven, chewing, watching, more nervous. The silent type.

The third in the group was a large, round-faced boy who could be Beaver's son; perhaps 'Otter'. He had his father's eyes, a ruddy face and jeans that didn't quite fit.

The fourth and last had placed himself to one side of the group, almost semi-detached. He was the tallest, the thinnest, with a mop of dark hair, hands thrust deep in his pockets. Ray judged him to be the most educated of the group but, his gut told him, the scariest. 'Weasel' fitted him perfectly.

'Musters Peers? Hawaii, yew?' Beaver offered his hand.

Taking a moment to translate, Spears returned the compliment. 'I'm fine, thank you. And how are you?'

'Fane. And thus would be ewer varn? Ut's a fane varn.'

'It does the trick, thank you! Just let me…' He turned to the van, slapped on its side to attract attention and called 'OK, guys. We're here!'

It was August. David, the tee-shirted cameraman, descended from the passenger seat followed by the diminutive Ellen in an unseasonal leather coat. She was the sound recordist.

'Hi, everyone,' drawled David in a general greeting to the whole party. He then shook each man's hand momentarily – except for Weasel, who still stood aloof. They exchanged nods, instead. David went to the rear of the van to assess what equipment was needed for the interview, not that there was a great deal to choose from. Ellen smiled nervously at each rodent in turn. The sun was high.

'So you're Mr Riley,' asked Ray. 'Patrick?'

'Thad I om. May son, he's Patrick too, we call hum Part. He's our Youth Officer, so he is.' Spears had identified the large boy's antecedents correctly and they exchanged smiles. 'Thus is Michael Donovan, Mucky. He's our Treasurer.' Micky the Rat shook Spears' hand voicelessly, firmly. 'And thus is…' Riley the Beaver looked around. 'Jawn.' The Weasel, making no effort to approach the group, nodded again.

The film crew had been surveying the area as they drove around the housing estate over the previous few minutes. The straight street was brick lined with two-up, two-down houses. They were perfectly ordinary homes, with low-walled front gardens just large enough to park a motor bike, fridge or oil drum, three habits which were evidently fashionable in that community. This could have been any city in Britain were it not for the pale skyscrapers in the near distance, each adorned in massive gothic letters with the name of a Republican hunger striker from days gone by. The Community Centre before which they now stood was also constructed in brick but was more modern. It had clearly originally been a row of shops, but these days was more orientated to social activity than commercial, perhaps after the failure of the latter to survive. Posters in its windows asked passers-by if they were claiming the benefits or tax credits due to them, condemned racism and advertised a locality meeting.

'Than queue for coming, Musters Peers. We sometimes thunk that those over across the water don't thunk about the orn'ry people of Belfast and Northern Air Lund. Thus under view is a grey-at opportunity for us, so it is. Can I show you a rind?'

Ray appreciated the business-like approach yet found himself both gritting his teeth and smiling at the same time. His own disposition may be mature and sensible, he thought, the arty type, the media mogul in waiting, but he'd been deliberately vague in his email exchanges with the Irish. Although Ray Spears and his crew were merely postgraduate Media students the film was, nevertheless, intended to be magnificent and pull no punches. However, it had no guaranteed audience outside his tutor and immediate media circles - not yet - information the team was keen to keep to themselves for now.

'Yes… please. David and Ellen will set things up whilst we…' He swallowed. 'Yes, please.'

The three members of the chorus adjusted their footings, standing almost in formation to escort the visiting party into the Community Centre.

'What you moss remember,' Riley said, as though a recording had just been switched on, 'is that thus part of North Belfast is a Catholic area within, that's completely in sayed, a much larger Protestant community. That's way it's important that we have our centre here, where it's accessible, if you know what I mean, to the Catholic community. But having said that, you mustn't get me wrong. We proof aid services which are available to everyone, what we do is denominationally blaned, if you know what I mean. Protestants are welcome here, so they are, and welcoming them as individuals, as fellow citizens, is a very important part of what we're here to dee.'

In at the deep end, thought Ray.

'And does this work? Do the Protestants come?'

'Oh, yes.' End of story. 'Now, thus building, as you can see, was bulled as shorps. It was actually bulled using European Structural Fond money, it was important to get the privet sector involved in the social infrastructure, if you know what I mean. Bark in those dais, people had to walk round certain streets rather than along them, a Roman Catholic wouldn't walk down a Protestant street if you know what I mean. Putting the shops into the community meant that the people in these streets could purchase their victuals without leaving the community, without having to walk in fear.'

And didn't that strengthen the divide? thought Ray. Riley anticipated the question.

'But the shops aren't here now, as you can see. Just the launderette, that's the only one of the original businesses that remains. That's because things are easier now since the Troubles ended, since the Good Frayday Agreement. People are travelling more and shopping elsewhere. Now even when the privet sector was here, the small supermarket, the dray cleaners, the others, they didn't bay the property. They wouldn't take that rusk. It was us, the community centre, our organisation: we owned the property, thanks to ESF, as I said. When it was bulled we had the community offices upstairs, as you'll see, but now we run it all, so we do.'

They were still standing in the street, a street which Spears noted was eerily quiet. The tour had not yet begun.

'Let's go on. Hey, Party, go upstairs and put the kettle on for a cup of tea for our guests.'

Riley's son left the group instantly and entered the centre without demur, through a single unmarked door with reinforced glass in its window. Across the road was an empty school – it being August – surrounded by high steel fences with razor wire along the top.

'This part was the beg shop but now it's a crèche. Let's go on.'

Riley knocked on the door and a small, pale, red haired woman with a baby in her arms opened it.

'It's you, Patrick. We were expecting you, come in. And is this your guest from London?'

'It is. Musters Peers, this is Aileen. She runs the crèche here, so she does.'

The two remaining men in the party followed them in and Micky locked the door behind them. Although clearly in accord with crèche security, Ray did not find the action comforting.

There were five rooms full of children on Aileen's tour. Some wore body-length aprons to protect against paint, water and what appeared to be mud; some wore conventional plastic bibs to protect against yoghurt or jam; some were without bibs, sleeping on mattresses on the floor or crawling, walking, dancing, playing. They were listening to stories, talking to minders, being comforted or crying. The women – and one young man – who attended them were also be-bibbed in sensible green overalls and they were working twenty to the dozen.

Micky had stopped to talk to some of the women en route but had now rejoined the party. The silent John, the Weasel, had followed Riley and Spears at a respectable distance throughout.

A few minutes later, astonished by the energy of the place, Spears was led by Riley and the 'guards' out and around the building to the rear. They climbed an external staircase to find themselves in a chair-lined first floor foyer.

'A doctor comes here for consultations on Thursdays, so he does. That's whey there are cheers in the corridors. But here is our parade and joy.'

Through double doors Ray could see a site familiar in mainland communities: a modern computer suite. Almost every one of the 20 stations was occupied, mostly by women. A male tutor was attending to a student at the front. The group stood in the doorway as a couple of the women acknowledged Patrick.

Around the walls were posters promoting the European Computer Driving Licence, further education, anti-racism, benefit take-up and, most powerfully, condemnation of domestic violence.

'Oh, ut's a problem.' Riley had noticed that his guest had paused to read the poster which urged women not to keep silent when faced with an abusive partner. 'It's the way working class society works, Catholic and Protestant tee, come to that. Women traditionally don't stand up to domestic violence, they don't even talk about it amongst themselves. They suffered in silence for tee long, so they did. You can imagine, unemployed for fifteen years maybe, frustrated and feeling as though you and your tape are not getting a fair deal in society. So you come home from the pub one night after maybe one too many paints of the brine stuff and she says 'where've you been?' So you just give her one and make her nose bleed. And the next day everything is back to normal, so the next time it happens, well, that's normal tee.'

It was almost as though Riley was addressing the room.

'And at's got to storp, so it has.'

Ray was surprised at the passion with which this middle aged, white, working class Catholic male spoke on a topic which, in his experience, was the province of young, educated, middle class women conversing at safe dinner parties.

'I suppose,' he said, 'the more you draw attention to it…'

'The statistics, Musters Peers. They showed a beg raise in domestic violence since the Good Frayday Agreement and that's good! Don't get me wrong: there's no more of it about now than there was before, hopefully less, but women are reporting it more, that's way the statistics are op. More confident she is, see in the past she says she'll report hum and he huts her harder, so he does. There are more convictions, and that's the truth. And that's a good thing tee. Nye the figures show the reality is coming dine and I believe that thus is genuine. And that's good, tee.'

The connection between domestic violence and the Good Friday Agreement was obscure to Ray; perhaps the Agreement was simply a convenient milestone in time against which all things could be measured. He remembered the excitement of it being signed, only a few years earlier. It marked the end of the Troubles, which his own mother had survived in streets like these for so many years.

Riley brought his face up close to Ray's and half-whispered: 'Most of us in this community have been there, Musters Peers. So we have. We know what we're talking abite.'

The Londoner knew intuitively that this was true. The violence that was hidden by the words made a chill run up his spine.

It was a salutary moment. Riley nodded to Micky who opened the door and led the group back out into the corridor, whilst Weasel brought up the rear.

'And these are our offices. We employ eight people here in the Community Centre and we ron the Community newspaper from here, tee. And thus is our mating room.'

They entered a large, stark room almost filled with about ten plastic-topped tables, bunched together to form a boardroom table, and a more than appropriate number of chairs. Around the walls more posters, on now familiar themes, hung in various states of disrepair.

Ray pointed at a poster. 'I wasn't expecting so much emphasis on anti-racism. Isn't this a very 'white' community?'

'Maybe that's way. Maybe coloured people don't feel welcome here. Sure and aren't there more black people in Dublin these days? It's not because we're Airsh that they aren't here.'

Ray shrugged his shoulders: Belfast still had other burdens, besides racism, that might deter settlers.

Almost as soon as they had seated themselves Patty reappeared, placing a tray of steaming plastic teacups in front of them. Ray, the film maker, aware that he had contributed little to the conversation, felt somewhat over-awed. No matter: his host continued to talk about what Ray wanted to hear, the background to the piece. Micky, Patty and John (Rat, Otter and Weasel) sat around the table where they were joined by David and Ellen, fresh from setting up their filming equipment downstairs.

The red-haired girl entered, left a plate of cheap biscuits on the table in front of Riley, silently and without a sideways glance, and left.

The film would be the jewel in Ray Spears' cinematic crown. He had turned to film-making relatively late in life, in his later twenties, following a degree in English Language and a short career on the administrative side of publishing. He'd already learned that the video camera could open doors that the single lens reflex or spiral-bound notebook alone could not, and that the advent of digital made everything cheaper and more convenient.

Ray Spears' mother had grown up in Belfast but had left the province, conveniently through marriage, at the start of 'the Troubles'. After much planning, her British-born son was now spending a week in Northern Ireland, or Ulster as her Protestant family still called it, starting here in North Belfast. He was not just making a film and seeking professional excellence but also trying to learn about his roots.

'So… this was originally a Community Centre for Catholics?'

'Ay wouldn't say that. Our doors have never been closed to Protestants or Loyalists and there's a Protestant on the management committee. Certainly they use our services and they're welcome. But you read our newsletter, the one you saw them rating in the office next door, you'll find it's not sectarian, so it isn't. Even the advertisements, they help to finance it, there are Protestant businesses advertising there.'

'Great.'

'In the past, yes, when we were set up it was with the purpose of letting Catholic and Republican people get access to help and services which weren't available to them by other means. Lake benefit advice, homelessness support, access to counselling. That's an issue in a place like thus. Do you know, on thus estate the use of tranquillisers - legal use, on prescription - is four tames the national average for the United Kingdom? And this is during better tames for us! Think what it was lake for ordinary people during the Troubles.'

Ray shook his head.

'My waif is on tranquillisers, has been for ten years nye,' said Micky, his first significant contribution in an encounter which was already approaching thirty minutes. Patrick Riley had held the fort, Patty had made the tea and John, the Weasel, had watched, listened, scrutinised every word. It was as though he, too, was an observer.

John's five o'clock shadow made him look lean and hard. He wore his dark hair in a conventional if unkempt manner; his tall stature apart he wouldn't stand out in a crowd. Ray wondered what sort of a man this was. His brief had told him to expect a group of active members of the Community Association. Whereas Patrick was clearly 'the man', Patty was loyal and Micky had shown signs of being involved, John remained so far an enigma; 'active' was not an obvious word for him.

'We strave for normality here, so we dee,' said Patrick. 'But after forty years we don't know what it me-ans, so we do our best. And things have changed, they've improved, we have Britain to thank for that, and the Taoiseach. We have the economic investment nye because people have recognised that we're a community, lats of communities, and we can walk together. They don't have the discrimination nye, in the jobs, or even in the po-lice - now that was a good idea, so it was, to tackle that.'

'The schools?' Ray ventured to add two words to the conversation.

'Well that's a difficult one. You have Catholic and Protestant schools in England, don't ye? But you're rate, we have to tell our children that communities pull together or they day. We don't want our children growing up the way that Patty here grew up, may boy. It wasn't may fault then, as his father I didn't know any better, none of us did. Now take Mucky here, where did you go last year, Mucky?'

'Bosnia, Patrick.'

'Bosnia. And what did you do there? You took what, sixteen? Twenty?'

'Sixteen, Patrick.'

'He took sixteen young kids, teenagers, to Bosnia. Catholics and Protestants, is that right?'

'That's right, Patrick.'

'Yes. A mixed group, going to look at how people live there, meeting young people like themselves. And way? What for? I'll tell you what for.'

He pointing to a country far away, through the window.

'Thus is what will happen if you don't learn to love together. Thus, what they could see around them in Bosnia, in 2004, thus is a divided society and we've had our share of that. Prejudice. People killing each other. If you don't play together as children you end up shooting each other as adults. People who live in the same street, you can tell the children what it was lake in the past in Belfast but it's not lake that any more, so you have to take them somewhere where you can see it today. Give a man a fesh and he will eat for a day. Teach him how to fesh and he will eat for lafe.'

It was almost a platitude, but it was well meant.

'If it was as simple as that…'

'Exactly! And whilst we are making progress, there're still problems here in Northern Air Lund. We're not shooting each other any more, but… I don't know how much you know about all this.'

'Tell me.'

Patrick folded his arms.

'There's stull crame and there's stull organised crame. And there are stull the gangs, and whilst they're not shooting the other sade any more they are helping people shoot up, if you get my drift. Some of these Loyalist gangs you know, they have given up the bullet and the balm but they are now into drug dealing and all that. And protection. Extortion. They're crummy nails, so they are, sample as that. That's way you need good community associations, they bring openness and transparency and that's the best way to fate the undergrind. But look, it's 2005 and wave had 35 years and things have changed and we haven't got it rate yet. But we're train.'

Ray wished he was recording this.

Micky joined in, his higher voice not achieving the gravity of the Chairman's.

'Now take me, I'm a Republican and everyone around here knows that. I'm not saying I hate Loyalists, but I used to say that, though. I've grown up. All of us have grown up since the Troubles, that's all behind us nye. But they can't keep undermining it, we can't let them. We can keep the bad men out of our community and we do that, as Patrick says, by being open in the way we support our community, in the way our community helps itself.'

Patrick took the lead once more. 'People won't turn to the bad boys if they can turn to their neighbours, is what Mucky is train to see. That's what our community association is all abite.'

He went on:

'We need devolved government back, we do. We have a Member of Parliament for round here, he's DUP. Now, as people, when you get to know them, they're all rate, you know what I mean? But he's train to represent a big area, mostly Protestant. Who represents us? That's whey we need local government, just lake you have over there on the mainland. We managed to get a Sinn Fein man elected here for the Assembly, so we did, and he's being paid to do the job. He comes here and holds his advace surgeries, so he does, but he's got no chamber to set in. No one asks him to vote on behalf of the people he represents. That's not rate. That's not representation nye, is it?'

'We need to get our unemployment down, it's still sixteen percent around here, did you know that? And that's after years of economic growth. We have had years of money put in, we have, mostly from Europe, they've done a lot for us. But we haven't got there yet. And I'll tell you what else, and it's a real problem rind here. Down at the Tine Hall here in Belfast, they've got a thing about former detainees, they won't support projects which benefit former detainees, they won't support projects which involve former detainees helping themselves or their communities.'

'They *say* they won't,' clarified Micky.

'That's rate. It's their policy.'

'Former detainees', thought Ray. That was a euphemism if ever he'd heard one. Hunger strikers, dirty protests, excrement on the walls of cells. Bobby Sands, whose name was huge on one of the skyscrapers visible through the first floor window. Ray's mother had called them murderers and thugs.

'Do you know, on this estate, this area rind here, seven ite of every ten men on this estate have served tame?'

Ray was incredulous; he sensed his colleagues shiver. 'Seven out of ten?' he repeated.

'Seven. Ite of ten.'

There were four Irish men in the room. Statistically, three of them were, possibly, murderers. A second chill ran down the English spines.

Patty spoke: 'The Tine Hall doesn't do what it says, though.'

'Being in prison doesn't mean you're a criminal,' Micky added. 'It includes political prisoners, people detained without trial, men convicted by kangaroo courts in the past.'

Patrick, the Beaver, took up the theme again. 'All that's tree. But in a place lake this they have no choice but to fund us. Where seven ite of ten men have been detained at some time if you carried that policy through it would mean that really we should get no public funding at all for community development. Of course we get the funding, you can see it, and funding community associations like us is really cost effective. We're part of the Peace Process, so we are.'

This made sense to Ray, even if it challenged his family prejudices.

There was, for the first time since they had met the Irishmen, a short silence.

'Do you mind if I ask…'

'Go ahead,' said Patrick Riley, guessing correctly what was to come. 'All ire visitors dee.'

'Are any of you… former detainees?'

'You mean 'have any of you culled anybody?' That's what you mean, isn't it?'

The Irishmen looked at Ray in a practiced manner. Ellen and David, evidently more nervous than Ray, averted their eyes; their body language placed them several miles away from that stark room. Time froze: the moments that followed passed very slowly.

'Yes. I shot a Brutish soldier,' said Micky. 'I'm not pride of it. Not nye. I served eight years in prison before the amnesty.'

Ray digested the information.

'Patty?'

'They found a device in Patty's hice in 1998,' said the boy's father. 'They couldn't pun it on him but they kept him in prison for six months while they trayed.'

A device. It felt as though half the conversation was being carried out in code. 'Device' was another euphemism, a means of killing people. A bomb. This was frightening. Although Ray was sweating, journalistic integrity forced him to address the Leader.

'Patrick: what about you?'

'I saw myself as a soldier in the Republican cause. Yes, I served tame for murder, I culled a Loyalist in a fate. It wasn't a fair fate: I had a knafe and he didn't. He'd come into a pub where he'd no rate to be, not at that time, but things have changed now, lake I said. I argued self defence at my trial but they didn't believe me. They were rate not to, so they were. I deserved to go to prison, I know that nye. I wanted to scare him, not cull him, but the knafe got caught in his collar and slupped – unto his thro-at. You could say I've paid my dees to society.'

There was sincerity and a marked lack of excitement in the laid back Irishman's voice.

'But I nye know that what I was convicted for... was a cowardly act. There were other thungs too, which they never caught me for, thungs I'm not going to tell you again on the fillum, so don't ask me tee. Very many years ago I pulled the trigger a few times and pressed the button more than once: twice, actually. I know it was wrong and in my heart I knew it then, tee, but that's the way we were brought up. All that's behind me nye. Everything I said to you carlier is tree. But sometimes you need to have been there in order to know what it is you're leaving behind. You have to learn lessons the hard way.'

Patrick had everyone's wrapt attention.

'We must never again ally people to learn what we learned, in the way that we learned it. There has to be a better wee: through using our experience in a positive wee, we hope the children of Belfast will learn it in a way of pace.'

Taken at face value, this was the most positive and credible sentiment Ray had heard all morning. Yet only slightly reassured, he mulled over the context of what he was hearing. One of the gang – correction, the committee – had not yet spoken. Each of the speakers had been more ominous than the last, so what had John got to reveal?

'And you, John. Have you ever killed anybody?'

This time silence preceded the reply. John, tousled hair, tall, seated, ordinary, had not been introduced as having any responsibility within the organisation and nor had he engaged in the conversation in any way. Broody, calm, slightly ominous, he had not taken his eyes off the film maker throughout the exchanges in the committee room. He stroked his chin with his right hand, as though his answer required careful thought. It was not the hand of one who'd spent too much time on manual work. Ray spotted something that might add to the macho countenance: John's thumb nail was missing.

His life story was summed up in two threatening baritone words: 'Not yet.'

The atmosphere was Antarctic, so metaphorically cold that Ray could hardly draw his breath or focus his eyes.

Outside, the August sun was shining.

The conversation was over.

David and Ellen at last raised their gaze from the table.

The Irishmen's tea cups were empty; the British contingent's were hardly touched.

Above Ray's head a small piece of sticky substance charged with securing a poster onto the painted wall gave up the ghost. The top right hand corner of the poster trickled down the wall before geometry and physics halted its fall barely a long second later.

In a broken voice, David said to the film director: 'Shall we do the interview now, Ray?'

'Good idea,' Ray replied, quietly. 'Thanks for the tea, guys.'

A few minutes later, out in the street, both Micky and John had disappeared. David had previously established exactly where to stand his camera tripod, and was now aligning it with Ray and Patrick to good effect. Ellen, cans on her ears, had adjusted her sound levels to perfection as she prepared to record the interview. Her microphone was shielded from the wind by a fluffy cover the size and texture of a small rabbit. Patty held his father's jacket and Patrick coughed to clear his throat. He pushed back his shoulders and stretched his mouth and cheeks to aid annunciation in preparation for speaking on video tape. This was not the first time he'd been on the record.

The film maker himself, however, was distracted.

The interview that followed with Patrick Riley, a community leader from North Belfast, was mechanical and dry; it was not one of Ray's best. Patrick knew what he was doing and said what he needed to say, in a manner which was to the point and an accent which was endearing. If the film was going to work, and this interview was crucial, it would be Patrick, not Ray, who'd made it happen.

Something that Ray had heard that morning had jarred, something which didn't sound right, but he couldn't immediately put his finger on it.

After ten minutes on the record the interview was 'in the can'. Ray said 'thank you' and 'goodbye' to the Rileys and Patrick turned away, taking his jacket back from his son and putting it on. Job done, the Irish bade the team farewell and walked back to the community centre, whilst David and Ellen reloaded the equipment into the rear of the van.

It was a perfectly ordinary, white transit van. Some might regard it as a fine van: a 'fane varn', no less.

'Hawaii yew', Riley had said.

'Musters Peers'.

'Fillum'.

'Not yet'.

Those two crisp, short words had contained one clear, short 'o' and one 'e', similarly.

Neither word had contained anything resembling an Irish diphthong.

In all his studies of 'the Troubles' or talking with his Irish family Ray had never heard such a construction from a native of Northern Ireland. Having studied linguistics back in the day he could draw but one conclusion. The man with the missing thumbnail, 'John', was not Irish. He was English. Ray concluded that the man hadn't spent more than five minutes living alongside the Belfast accent which had been Ray's mother's own.

John had been asked if he'd ever killed anyone, at a time when former soldiers of revolution had become mainstream and all mainstream parties were committed to peace and democracy, eschewing the way of both bullet and bomb.

'Not yet', the Englishman had said.

Not yet.

If not yet, when?

What, wondered Ray, shivering again, was that all about?

Chapter 9: Sussex, September 2005

Ken Hemmings walked calmly to his car and left the school premises.

In the interests of road safety he fought to subdue his rising adrenalin levels and completed half his brief journey homewards before he found a convenient and safe place to stop.

He fumbled the papers from his jacket pocket and spread them across his lap. The email showed the existence of a cell, but a cell of what? The aliases must be there to protect somebody from something, but who, and from what? The attached document was only two sides long but would demand careful reading. On scanning its vituperative content he detected self-indulgence, self-importance, a shallow shield of bravado and venom. Such 'all mouth and no trousers' characters used to be known in some parts of the police as 'Spartists' – for reasons Ken had never understood – but, against his better judgment, he preferred the epithet which was more common in his own former nick: 'wankers'.

He read it again, more carefully. Under the heading 'Suggested second lead for next edition,' it read:

The New Labour Project is in tatters after a bruising 2005 general election for Blair. Throughout the country working people, clearly confused as to where to put their crosses, thanks to Parliament's quaint and outdated voting system, delivered a small majority for Saint Tony as the least worst option.

For too long we have failed to provide the working class with a decent alternative to conventional Labour. Now they have rejected Blair's attempt to ride two horses at once. The stallion of social justice and the carthorse of private profit have inevitably diverged in their journeys.

Now he has come unstuck. He has one foot in the stirrup of each mount and, as they charge headlong at different speeds, in different directions, one is reminded of nothing less graphic than the ancient and terminal punishment of quartering.

The screams of the ruptured Premier can be heard throughout the debates on identity cards, the abolition of the historic right to jury trials and, most of all, in his proposals for so-called anti-terror legislation. Behind the bland façade is the goal of preventing ordinary people from rising up and taking what is rightly theirs, through the legitimate use of force, if necessary. For too long we have had to bow to the hegemony of bourgeois democracy and the platitudes of the so-called wider Labour movement.

After two further paragraphs of purple diatribe it concluded:

Those of us who have lived with the cause of the people in our blood; who believe in the international solidarity of the oppressed; or who are convinced that Workers' Gauntlet represents a just, essential and achievable programme, know something else, too: that some of our comrades will perish as they take forward our common commitment to the cause.

The only ones who fail in this struggle will be those who die in vain.

And the time to act is now.

After a couple of carriage returns were the words 'What do you think? RF.'

Red Flag, or Norman Flagg, or the Head teacher, whatever persona was the most appropriate, was clearly taking the piss. Or he was deliberately playing games. Or he was mad. Some combination of such explanations must describe the truth, Ken surmised: no one rises to the level of Inspector in Her Majesty's Constabulary without developing psychological skills. It was just possible, for the sake of completion, that the author of the rant was posing a serious threat to national security, but really! Such an idea was an insult to the intelligence.

What on earth did 'people's justice' mean? He remembered where he'd been on 9/11 and on the day of the four London bombs just a few weeks ago. Was this what Flagg was getting at? Surely, you don't get to be a responsible and admired head teacher with those sort of views? Not that Ken had ever met anyone, socially, who had 'those sort of views,' as far as he knew, so how did he know? Perhaps Flagg had not even written it, even if it was amongst his 'Sent items'. Perhaps it was something the Head had found on the internet, something he'd wanted to share with a group of friends who would be entertained by its rich and gory prose.

The second document was the printed email from 'Almanac' which was intended to help 'Monument' to find the 'OS'. The links, later to be typed in to his own internet search engine, would almost certainly reveal a road map of the Brighton sea front and confirm what Clive had happened to mention over a pint, shortly after 7/7, that Brighton's Old Ship Hotel was a potential den of revolutionary activism.

Ken complimented himself on his patience as he turned his attention to the third document: the list of properties sent by Fintons, estate agent.

This was more like it! Of the three documents this was the most likely to deliver results in his search for the missing teacher. He would bet anyone who would listen that Flagg was domiciled at one of these addresses at that very moment. They all looked to be in central Brighton, which could be easily checked within minutes of getting home. The date on top of the print-out was, conveniently for Ken's hypothesis, some weeks after Flagg had signed up to the Hathersage Homes' email register. It would be amazing if the discovery of one or another of these properties had not prompted Flagg to terminate that search.

None of this implied that the teacher was just sitting in his new front room, reading the paper and waiting to be found, of course. 'Coming, ready or not!' this was not.

On the other hand... did any of this justify the conclusion that Flagg had actually obtained a home? The list may simply have confirmed to the Head that he could not, in fact, run two homes on his salary. Or perhaps Flagg had himself been using the list to find someone else. Did Flagg's 'prey' live at one of these addresses? Perhaps he had a 'weekend girl' with whom he shared steamy liaisons at a secret abode? The absence of any sort of sex life in Flagg's curriculum vitae was an omission which had not previously occurred to Ken.

There was only one way to find out the truth, thought Ken, flexing his door-knocking fingers.

* * *

No sooner had Ken Hemmings arrived home than his telephone rang. He placed his trilby on the hall table and lifted the phone to hear a familiar voice.

'Dad?'

'Clive! What can I do for you?'

'Glad I caught you. I wanted to check about lunch on Sunday: are you still up for it? I mean, can you make dinner instead? I'll be off duty from about four o'clock, I was supposed to finish at twelve but my shift's been extended, so to be on the safe side let's say six. Is that all right?'

'I suppose so. I can't think that my diary has anything more important in it.'

'Right, good. Sunday's the first day of Labour's Conference, hence the changing shifts. We're expecting rumpus.'

'Really? Who from?'

'Oh, you know. Strikers, pro-hunt activists, animal rights, you name it. The usual rent-a-mob. So, that's sorted, then.'

'My hectic social life will have to be put on hold,' Ken laughed. 'That will be fine.'

'Great! We'll see you about six and you can tell us all about Aunt Amanda.'

'She's in fine fettle, as usual. And I'll bring you up to date with my quest for the Holy Grail.'

'Pardon?'

'The latest posting in my search for Mr Flagg.'

'Oh, you mean... a flag post?'

'Yes, Clive. Something like that.'

'So he's not turned up yet?'

'Not a peep. The school's getting along fine, but there are some interesting developments. Have you got a minute now?'

'Literally a minute, yes. I've got a meeting in five, so... yes, go on. What 'developments'?'

'I have had come into my possession an email. It suggests, among other possible interpretations, that our friend's adolescent fervour for matters revolutionary has not diminished.'

'Really?'

'Indeed. He appears to have told a small group of anonymous friends that Comrade Blair is a bit of a bad lot and something has to be done about it.'

'An email, you say?'

Clive's carefree demeanour was evaporating.

'Yes, it was written last May, in the wake of the election, to a group of people with untraceable email addresses who were expecting to meet up at 'OS', in Brighton.'

'That could be the Old Ship.'

'That was my guess, too.'

'On the seafront. All sorts book rooms to have meetings there, especially at this time of year.'

'For the Conference.'

'Exactly.'

'But this was last May, Clive.'

'Yes, you said... Look, just out of interest, can you forward the email to me, Dad?'

'Are you interested in missing persons at last?'

'Well, no... but I might recognise some of the aliases.'

'That's a thought. But I can't. I've only got a paper copy of the email. I'll bring it with me on Sunday.'

'Right. Sent in May, you said?'

'The tenth. Just after the election.'

Clive seemed to relax. The matter was clearly not urgent, though it did encourage him to speculate about the attachment's content and the significance of the list of pseudonymous names.

After a few moments of idle family banter Clive made his excuses and ended the call, its filial purpose achieved.

'I'll see you on Sunday, Dad. Our house, at six.'

'I'll be there.'

Ken made himself a cup of tea and settled down at the table with his newspaper and a Brighton A to Z. The Sudoku would have to wait: with a yellow felt-tipped marker he identified the six streets on the map.

Friday 23rd September

Ken was finding it difficult to get back into the domestic routine following his break. However, as there was no one to wash his clothes, do the shopping or even iron the odd shirt in front of daytime television for him, this was what he found himself doing. The excitement of the chase would have to wait. Perhaps on Saturday he would follow up his 'leads', the addresses of the Brighton properties.

Peter was due to visit that evening. Rather than sit and drink Ken's whisky, this time the councillor had offered to take the older man out for dinner. Thinking that it was about time he got a bit of recognition for the hours he'd dedicated to finding Elder's missing minion, Ken had accepted the invitation with alacrity.

Just as he was preparing for his host and chauffeur to meet him at the gate, the telephone rang.

'Dad? It's me again.'

'Clive? Aren't you at work?'

'Yes, but… I need to change the arrangements for this weekend again.'

'I see…'

There was something distracted about his son's voice, as though his mind was on other things.

'Could you… how does Saturday lunchtime fit? Instead?'

'Well, I suppose…'

The nail-grinding search for Flagg would have to be postponed. No matter.

'Yes, I could do that. Look, I'm happy to cook - why don't I? I'd enjoy that.'

It would be a rare opportunity to rekindle his legendary hospitality skills.

'Thanks… so we'll come over to you then, is that all right?.'

'That sounds wonderful.'

'See you at twelve tomorrow. Is that OK? Thanks.'

The telephone line was dead before pleasantries could escape or banter be released.

* * *

By the time the two men reached The Coach and Horses in a nearby village Ken had brought Peter completely up to date with all of the salient information which might, by any stretch, be deemed 'evidence'. The fact that the tale was so short served to remind him how little they really had to go on. Elder, twitchy from the start, was starting to relax by the time they sat down, pints of ale before them, to survey the menu.

'Did you see what it said outside?' asked Ken. 'I get disturbed by terms like 'gastropub'; makes me feel like I'm entering a giant mollusc.'

'What?' Elder was not completely listening.

'Gastropub?'

'Oh, yes! Yes, I see, very good.'

'It's a twenty-first century word, I suppose. Did you ever hear it used back in the twentieth?'

'I think, maybe in London.'

'Ah.'

Peter would know that better than I, thought Ken. He was the cosmopolitan type, whereas I moved from being a Midlander to senile Sussex by the sea and missed out on the high life completely.

Peter came back from ordering their steaks at the bar and was clearly thinking hard. The conversation did not immediately burst into life.

'Penny for them?' asked Ken.

'I'm sorry, Ken. It's just... I really hoped that we'd have found him by now.'

'You're worried that something bad has happened.'

'No, it's not that... I just want this whole thing to be over. At the beginning of the month I was genuinely concerned for Norman, worried like a friend, wanting to be sure he wasn't in any danger, had come to no harm. Then the Chair of Governors in me took over and my concern gave way to anger. You learn to control your emotions in politics, or at least control how they appear, but after a couple of weeks I was fuming: how could he do this to the school, to me? That's what I wanted to know. It wasn't fair on Jane, me, the children... Then that bloody newspaper, poking its nose in. And after that I came to – I don't know – just resent him, totally. I want to know what's happened, but frankly if what you find is that he fell under a bus two months ago well, hard shit, but that's the way it has to be and I'll cry no more tears over it.'

'I don't think there was a bus.'

'No...'

'Experience tells me that the sequence of emotions you've just described does happen in families when a member goes missing. It doesn't stop the genuine warmth when the person is found - and the grief is equally genuine when the corpse turns up.'

'Yes, I'm sure. Sorry.'

'You do appear to have gone through the emotional gamut quite quickly though, Peter.'

'Oh, I put that down to Jane.'

'Oh? How?'

'She's just been... so good. I haven't had to worry about the school at all, she's handled it all so well. That's given me time to... experience my emotions, I suppose.'

'You weren't that impressed about her handling of the Debbie Pearce incident, Peter.'

'Oh, that was what, her second or third day in charge? You can't have everything, she'd never had to handle anything like that before. I thought at the time that Norman would have handled it better if he'd been there, but -'

'Precisely!'

'What?'

'If he'd been there! If he'd been there, there wouldn't have been a problem – there'd be no missing Head, nothing for Debbie Pearce to have got on her high horse about.'

'Well, that's true... Anyway, apart from that – let's put it down to a learning experience – Jane's been wonderful. A real credit to the school – and to Norman's own example.'

'Have you... I mean, has he got a job to come back to?'

'You know, Ken, even in these circumstances it's almost bloody impossible to sack a teacher. He's now been suspended without pay but that's all we can do. We will be able to formally terminate his contract - eventually. Until that far off day Jane will remain only 'acting' Head.'

'Yes, teaching was always a secure job. I remember Sheila telling me how difficult it was to get rid of a teacher on grounds of competence. A gross misdemeanour equivalent to – how did she say it? – being discovered *in flagrante delicto* with the Head teacher's 12-year old daughter, on the stage, in front of a speech day audience, on the day the school first team forfeited the rugby finals! That sort of thing was the minimum requirement for getting a teacher sacked, she said.'

Peter smiled. 'When I was at school an incompetent chemistry teacher caused an explosion which blew out all the windows in the laboratory, caused several minor injuries and put two boys in hospital.'

'Goodness!'

'No serious injuries, fortunately.'

'And what happened to him, Peter? Did he lose his job?'

'Eventually.'

'How d'you mean?'

'He's now Director of Education in a London Borough.'

'Goodness…'

'He climbed the greasy pole, all right.'

'Is that a good thing? That sort of job security?'

Peter thought for a moment.

'In some ways, yes. Security of tenure is certainly what my friends in the trade union movement have always wanted. Perhaps they're a little more enthusiastic and dogmatic about it than I might be.'

'Is that the New Labour thing again?'

'How do you mean?'

'Security of tenure is in the producer's interest rather than that of the consumer.'

'Well, as Chairman of the Board, as it were, I'm a producer. And not being able to get incompetents out of the system is not in my interest! But I know what you mean. Yes, some people would claim this state of affairs as a victory for working people.'

'Some people – like Norman?'

'In the past. But even he couldn't defend dereliction of duty on this scale, this past month – could he?'

It was a rhetorical question which served as a curtain-raiser for a steaming meal, delivered by a round and matronly barmaid.

Mustard was applied to the sizzling steaks and the two men took ravenously to the task in hand.

'So what you're saying, Peter,' said Ken after a couple of mouthfuls, 'is that if Norman showed up tomorrow he would still have a job to come back to?'

'Well, it wouldn't be quite that simple. He's been suspended and it's not up to him to decide when the suspension is lifted. It's not my call, either. When a Head's involved it's the Education Authority's decision. I can't believe that if he showed up tonight they'd let him go straight back to work on Monday – he's clearly in breach of contract, after all.'

'Hmm…'

'I have a meeting with the Director on Monday, with my vice chair.'

After a few quiet and healthy mouthfuls, Ken asked 'Do you think Norman's off on some political mission?'

After a fraction of a pause, during which he momentarily raised his eyebrows, Peter replied 'Good heavens, no. I've told you, he isn't active politically. Hasn't been since he came down to Sussex, at least. I'm sure he got all that infantile disorder stuff out of his system years ago.'

'You sound very sure. You say he's very professional, but is he so professional that if he was engaged in political activity he wouldn't let that influence his conduct at work? Or wouldn't even let on when talking privately, socially, to his Chair of Governors?'

'You know Norman and I have 'a past', Ken. He knows he needn't hide 'political thoughts' from me, of all people!'

'Unless they were the sort of thoughts that he knew would be anathema to you. It'd make no sense for him to discuss things with you that were guaranteed to wind you up, even revolt you, would it?'

'No, Ken, I can't believe that.'

'That's it? You can't believe it?'

'Are you going to have a pudding?'

The interview was over.

Saturday, 24th September

Clive, Chris, Troy and Sable arrived promptly for their Saturday lunch. They parked the car across the quiet lane and Sable ran up the path to the cottage yelling 'Grandad!' at the top of her voice. It's as though she hasn't seen me for a year, Ken thought, amazed at the six-year old's capacity for pure and unconditional love, as she threw her arms around his thighs, pushed her head against his hip.

Troy was more circumspect: 'Hello, Grandad Ken,' he said respectfully, distancing himself with dignity from his sister's overt emotion. Ken went through the ritual of shaking the boy's hand.

'Hello, Ken,' said Christine, 'Hang your coats up, children.' She kissed her father in law on the cheek. Her flesh was cool, he thought, as she went past him into the hallway: it was chilly for late September.

'Good to see you, Dad,' said Clive, following his family into the house before moving his father's trilby to clear a space on the hall sideboard for the basket of children's toys he was carrying.

'The 'old faithful', eh?' He made a grotesque smile for the children and put the trilby on top of his own head. It was too small for him, which made Sable laugh.

'Daddy, don't be silly!' Troy admonished his father, embarrassed.

'Da-ad!' scolded Sable, coming into line with her brother but still laughing. Ken enjoyed it when his son played the fool, though it was quite rare these days. High ranking police officers were serious people and the cliché that they were never off duty was true, even when arriving at their father's house for a family Saturday lunch.

'Come on, now, children!' said the grandfather. 'Guess who's got some pop in the fridge!'

'Yippee!' yelled Sable, clapping her hands.

Troy pulled a face: 'pop' was an uncool word, one that only grandads would ever use. But fizzy drinks were acceptable, so the disdain was brief and he followed his grandfather, sister and mother in the direction of refreshment.

Clive was now alone in the hallway, holding the trilby in his hand, a serious look on his face.

* * *

Cooking a weekend family lunch had once been routine for Ken. He'd bought the roast, prepared it and put it in the oven. He'd peeled the potatoes, par-boiled them, as Sheila had taught him, before dousing them in oil and putting them under the pork; made sure there were peas in the freezer, unwrapped the cling film from the broccoli. Christine, bearer of a home made trifle, would finish off.

The meal went like clockwork. Ken and Christine performed their culinary magic and they all ate as if it was their first meal for a week. Afterwards Ken read a fairy story to Sable, Troy was deep in a book he'd brought to read himself and Clive was skimming through Ken's *Times*.

'This is a lovely place, Ken,' said Christine. She didn't visit the cottage as often as her husband did, this weekend ritual usually taking place in her own home. But on his territory she had no distractions and her attention was at Ken's disposal. Seeing the two chatting effortlessly about domestic and housekeeping issues was good to see, thought Clive.

Later, the two men found themselves in the garden admiring Ken's late roses.

Inevitably the talk came round to missing head teachers and Ken brought his son up to speed.

'So, I'm going on a hunt tomorrow!'

'Dad...'

'I'm not going over the top, I'm just going for a little stroll around Brighton.'

'I don't think it's healthy, this... this obsession.'

'Obsession? Clive, I've just had the best holiday sunning it in Cornwall with my sister! I can pick this thing up and put it down again, really. According to Peter the school is running pretty normally – without Norman Flagg, of course – and every avenue we've explored has led, well, nowhere. It's all over.'

'Apart from your walk...'

'I don't like loose ends. And... yes, it'll all be over tomorrow.'

Clive smiled in capitulation.

'I'm pleased. You can... get on with your life then.'

'You've got a busy day tomorrow, yourself.'

'You're not kidding! The pilgrimage of the faithful has already started but tomorrow things go into top gear. All the Labour big-wigs will be there by the afternoon and there's no police leave for fifty miles around for the next five days.'

Ken smiled. 'Police operations... It takes me back...'

The rest of the afternoon went according to plan and his son's family, sated, prepared to take their leave. The children showed little sign of exhaustion despite a menu which had included Sable shouting at her brother, Troy shouting at the television and Chris spilling red wine on the (fortunately, tiled) kitchen floor.

They collected their coats and stepped out into a dull late afternoon, kissing and waving their goodbyes.

As he shepherded his flock Clive accidentally knocked the familiar trilby onto the floor. He picked it up, dusted it off and carefully placed it back on the sideboard where his father wouldn't miss it.

Chapter 10: Palestine, August 2005

From the passenger windows of the minibus the observer found himself wondering what all the fuss was about. There was simply nothing here. The terrain was arid, boulder-strewn, infertile; it looked like the surface of the moon. Only occasionally did sparse groves of olive, in more or less organised rows, give any suggestion that the soil, in the countryside south of Jerusalem, had any life in it at all.

In the distance yet more scorched hills told the same story. On top of some of those hills, however, there was evidence of habitation: a fence, a cluster of caravans, a shed or more substantial but nevertheless makeshift buildings.

The so-called settlements, unofficial islands of Israeli occupation.

And thereby hung a tale.

* * *

On the previous evening the group had been deliberately organised to arrive on separate flights into Tel Aviv airport where Jan, a tall, blond Dane with a tidy beard, had welcomed them. From there they'd headed on the motorway towards Jerusalem in a rattling minibus, with its Israeli plates and Palestinian driver, in the dark.

It was August, 2005 and the bus proceeded breathlessly. Jan surveyed his silent and awestruck team members, his recruits. All except himself were new to the country. Four were blond, one brown-haired. Three were male, two female. Four were young, in their twenties, but one was significantly older, maybe even a generation older than the youngest. Tomorrow the newcomers would have their first experience of the West Bank, known globally as Israeli Occupied Palestinian Territory.

'Hey, guys,' Jan's voice punctured the darkness above the roar of the engine, breaking the ice. 'Let me do the formal bit. Thank you all for coming. As you know, you've been chosen from many applicants who volunteered to spend a month with POEM, the Palestinian Occupation Expedition Monitoring organisation. Our group was founded in Sweden in the 1970s - which is why you'll be issued with blue and yellow armbands to wear during your stay. Please wear the armbands at all times – not necessarily in bed or the shower, of course. You will find it helpful.'

There was a quiet, nervous, respectful chuckle.

'As you know, we'll spend our first night together at the Jerusalem Hotel, near Damascus Gate, one of the entrances to the historic Old Town. That part of Jerusalem is the home of three of the most important holy sites from the world's religions.'

This much, at least, the volunteers already knew.

'Do you know them? This is the first time in Palestine for all of you, I think?'
Nods of assent.

'I'm not testing! I'm talking about the Noble Sanctuary, Al-Haram al-Sharif. Here you'll find the Dome on the Rock, the third holiest shrine in Islam, next to the Al Aqsa mosque, which has come to symbolise so much of the tension in the history of this area. On the other side is the Western Wall, the Wailing Wall, a holy site of the Jewish people with, of course, the Church of the Holy Sepulchre, said to be the site of Jesus Christ crucifixion, five minutes walk away. We'll bring you back to Jerusalem from time to time and you'll have opportunity of a bit of soul tourism.'

The audience smiled in the dark. Jan's discourse, in almost perfect English, was interrupted as the minibus was obliged to pause at a routine road block on the Israeli motorway. At that time of night there was no queue so the delay was minimal. Guards, young men and women, conscript soldiers, inspected the driver's papers. They were not interested in the bus' cargo as its Israeli licence plates conferred a presumption of innocence. They were just doing their job.

Two more, similar interruptions pushed their journey time of 45 minutes to well over the hour.

Once at the hotel, the five volunteers had time to find their feet. After taking a few minutes to settle into their rooms and unpack they naturally gravitated to the hotel bar, which was outside, beneath a plastic awning, where they ordered beers. It was 10 p.m.

POEM volunteers on their first night were not normally gregarious, but the ice was broken when one of the girls wondered in an Irish accent how it was that some of Palestinians in the bar were smoking from hookahs at the table, having assumed that the the pipes were fuelled with hashish. The Englishman, the older man, told her that it was more likely to be apple flavoured tobacco. Each member of the group formally introduced themselves to the others.

Jan the Dane, 30 years old, had lived in Ramallah for six years. A divorced pacifist and one of POEM's three permanent representatives in the West Bank, his job was to train each new batch of volunteers who arrived to work with the organisation every few weeks. POEM's role was simply to observe the actions of Israeli troops and settlers and report on them, via a convoluted route, back to the United Nations. They were not, under any circumstances, allowed to intervene.

Normally his charges were younger people, students who spent their vacations in this way in Bethlehem, Tulkarm, East Jerusalem or – as with this group – Hebron. Tonight's trainees were a diverse group of slightly older strangers. The youngest was Ella, a 24-year old Dutch postgraduate student of international politics at Haarlem, tough and avowedly pro-Palestinian, committed to a six week stretch. Paul, also Dutch, from Groningen, was 26; he wore a cheesecloth shirt and his hair in a pony tail. Back home he was an unemployed graduate who wanted to do 'something different', so his parents had paid for his trip: they thought it would do him good. Niamh was from Ireland and vegetarian. Born into a reformed Jewish family, her parents had rejected the Occupation, Israel and Judaism, in that order, over the course of her 28 years. Believing hers was a sheltered life, she'd come to find out what 'it' was all about.

Piet was another Dane, another postgraduate student who was planning to stretch his academic studies indefinitely. He was writing a thesis on conflict prevention - four weeks with POEM looked like good value for money. Jamal, their local driver, had joined them but remained silent throughout.

Tony was the odd one out. By some way the oldest of the party, he had a slim, fit body and dark hair. On the face of it, Jan thought, Tony was the closest to deserving the epithet 'conflict tourist', as cynics had been known to describe POEM and its work. Some even used the phrase 'conflict porn'. Tony had first attracted Ella's attention when, back at Tel Aviv airport, he'd successfully declined having an Israeli entry stamp applied to his British passport: 'It can make it tricky entering an Arab country in the future if you've got an Israeli stamp in it,' he explained, and Ella had followed suit. She was impressed; he seemed to be a sympathetic and interesting man.

The following morning the traffic was heavy as the minibus left Jerusalem and headed south towards its destination, Hebron. Under 'normal' circumstances the 30km journey should take less than 40 minutes, Jan explained, but nothing here was 'normal'. In the harsh light of day the devastated natural environment and the ubiquity of the Israeli military were each as obvious as the other. The atmosphere in the scratched and grey, unmarked vehicle was apprehensive and subdued. Each volunteer – Ella, Niamh, Tony, Piet and Paul – was aware of the size and gravity of their task and grateful that two days of training still lay between themselves and active service on the streets without a guide.

The minibus stopped in a queue which stretched as far as the next bend and beyond.

'But we're in middle of nowhere,' said Piet.

'Road block,' said Jan. 'You got off lightly last night. This is the real thing, it's the only road into Hebron from the north. I guess that this will be... forty minutes wait from where we are now? It's going to get hot. Think yourself lucky; it's still morning, you're all fit and this vehicle is air conditioned. Most Palestinians – lookout their plates, most of these cars around us are Palestinian – have to do this every day. It can get a lot worse than this.'

Jan rubbed his chin. He was used to such delays but they still sorely tried his patience.

'Think if you had to queue here for a couple of hours, in hotter temperatures than this, with children in the car. And you get to the barrier at five o'clock and guess what? The gate is closed until the next day.'

'Some of those lorries are carrying food!' cried Ella. 'You're saying they can't guarantee to get the food into the city that day if they arrive in the afternoon?'

'That's right.'

'What's the road block for? On whose authority are the soldiers here?' asked Piet.

'No authority, no reason. They're an occupying force, they don't need authority, or that's what they say when you talk to them. The road blocks are illegal but there's no one here to enforce international law.'

'But why?'

'There are over 600 permanent Israeli military road blocks in the West Bank alone. This is one. On some days there may be 300 flying road blocks, temporary ones, also. When they decide to put one up a military jeep just stops, turns around, side on, to block the road, then the soldiers point their guns at the cars and they inspect people's papers in every vehicle. If they don't like something the car will be searched, the people too, maybe arrested. Most who are arrested are released a few hours later, no charge; the arrests are arbitrary, not part of a legal process. It's all about generating fear and exerting control.'

Niamh joined in the conversation.

'What if someone's ill? Do they let ambulances through?'

'Ambulances? This is third world, Niamh. But no, very often no, they don't. It depends on the commander at the road block - or at the gate in the wall, like in the Bethlehem area.'

The minibus was inching forwards.

'What have they got to gain from this?'

'Who?'

'The Israelis.'

'Not a lot. But it's like water on a stone. It's little acts of oppression together help to subdue a nation. I'm sorry, I can't be very objective about this.'

The Dane took a deep breath.

'You have to remember that Palestine is a nation without a state, it has no army, its economy - I think this is English word, ramshackle? It is without many features of government that we Europeans take for granted. There's an internationally defined border but it's not respected. There's a fucking great wall going down the western border of their country and a tenth of their land - ten per cent - is on the wrong side of the Wall. Much good land and water sources are in that ten per cent that has been stolen. To the east there's the Jordan Valley which might as well be part of Israel, economically. It's very fertile, relative to the rest of this country, but they control it, not the Palestinians. And criss-crossing the whole place – remember, the West Bank is smaller than the Netherlands – there's a network of good roads, which cars with Palestinian plates cannot use. We don't think of them as roads, they're like iron bars. It's not just the soldiers, even the geography is used to oppress.'

Ella said 'But international law...'

'The international law sucks. They go through the motions. Even the Israeli courts go through the motions, they changed the route of the Wall in a few places, it's not as bad as Ariel Sharon wanted it to be, but it's still a fucking Wall. There's an illegal occupation by the Israeli army, an illegal wall, illegal arrests and extraditions and judicial executions without trial.'

Piet intervened 'Look, guys, I might be, er, naive but don't we supposed to have solution? Two state solution? You know, like, Road Map?'

Jan replied 'We have a process. It's better than nothing, but not really going anywhere.'

The minibus spluttered as it jumped forwards twenty metres and then stopped again.

There was silence.

'What are we going to do in Hebron?' asked Niamh.

'We have lunch!' Jan smiled. 'After that a seminar. You get to meet someone from the local Governor's office and a Palestinian NGO. They tell you a bit about Hebron, its history and what is happening now. We have a Powerpoint presentation about the way the Israeli settlement policy works, you will be shocked.

'Then we go for a walk in the Old Town and you will be shocked again. You will see turnstiles, road blocks, empty shops. Economic separation. Just wait.'

Tony simply listened.

He knew the theory but wanted to see all this for himself.

Now here he was in the West Bank, an ambition fulfilled.

Around where he sat in the immobile minibus he could see so much evidence of personal oppression. The arbitrary road blocks, economic brute force, the epitome of the abuse of power by a state against the people. Everything he could see, and anticipated seeing, convinced him in every fibre of his being that he was right, that the principles which defined and empowered his activist soul were the correct ones.

The situation here, where it was just all so fucking obvious, was merely an extension, a distillation, of what could be seen every day in London, Washington, Frankfurt or Hong Kong. Capitalism was the means by which the state oppressed the masses; and the state itself was the antithesis of what co-operative human society could and should be.

He had a four day growth of beard.

Using a thumb with no nail he stroked the dark stubble on his top lip.

* * *

When they finally got to Hebron, two hours behind schedule, lunch consisted of tasty humous, warm pitta and a variety of finely chopped salads, followed by a choice of several dishes of lamb or chicken. The promised Powerpoint presentation, in a featureless, cell-like office whose thick, white walls protected against the desiccating sunshine, was itself dry - though the audience was attentive, not wanting to miss a detail. Some of the younger ones took notes. The minor politicians who lectured and answered questions were humourless but passionate: an occupational hazard.

In due course the minibus took the team to a makeshift car park on a featureless street corner where the party descended. Two Palestinians from the building where lunch had been provided had travelled with them and a third now joined, Ali, immediately assuming a leadership role. The second, the most taciturn, was young Mahmoud, who later told them he was no muslim but an Armenian Christian, as many Palestinians were. The third, whose name wasn't given, wore a dark green polo neck jumper under a brown jacket, inappropriately warm clothing under what was by now the afternoon sun.

'We go down into the Old Town,' Ali said, without introduction, 'Follow me.'

The westerners, each now wearing their bright blue and yellow arm bands with differing degrees of self consciousness, did as they were told.

They turned a corner where the narrow road between the buildings was blocked by a solid steel fence. The centre panel opened as they approached and behind it was a deserted street which led directly down into the old market, or Souk.

Most of the shops here were empty and boarded up. In the few that were trading modest quantities of brightly coloured vegetables were piled high – aubergines, tomatoes, sweet potatoes. Children stood guard, ready to trade with anyone who might pass, with little confidence that their wares would sell.

'Follow,' the man said again.

As they approached the turnstiles the team suffered a collective intake of breath. There was no way around the building, yet the tunnel underneath it, before them, was almost blocked by a forest of steel bars. This was like entering a prison, not a market.

The group was filtered to the right: the first robust turnstile was two metres high with horizontal bars just ten centimetres apart up its entire height. Only one person could pass through the gate at a time, with room for them to carry nothing more than a shopping bag. This was followed by an airport-style scanning gate. At the far end of the floodlit tunnel, six metres on, an Israeli soldier, snub-nosed machine gun in readiness, was visible and those negotiating the tunnel were now within his scrutiny.

A further turnstile, no less imposing than the first, led to fresh air where another soldier, a boy in full combat uniform, including helmet, carrying a very large machine gun, was watching them.

Turning back to see where she'd come from, Niamh said: 'Jesus! Look at the way out! If you want to leave this place carrying the kitchen sink there's just so much room! But not coming in....'

'Not very welcoming, is it?' asked Jan. 'It's designed for one way traffic. Palestinians who leave this area are not encouraged to return.'

'Is it all like this?' asked Ella.

'In the Old Town, yes. You've seen nothing yet.'

30 metres downhill from the checkpoint Jan pulled the group together. But it was Ali, the older man who'd recently joined the group, who spoke. Behind him the next check point was already visible at close quarters, a tower populated by several soldiers, standing in the centre of what ought to have been a busy road junction, clad in inappropriate camouflage netting.

'There are soldiers on every corner in the Old Town, as you can see. Israeli soldiers. Remember, Hebron has *never* been part of Israel. We not even close to any actual or suggested border or even close to the Wall. It is Palestinian town, the people born here are Palestinians. You see that building down there, the tall one? The ground floor is medical centre. It's Palestinian one, that's where our mothers take their babies. Or it was.'

'What d'you mean?'

'When we get down there you will see. It is now army post, Israeli army post.'

'Where do the mothers and children go now?' asked Ella.

'Of course, they don't care. One day the children cannot get to their medical centre because of road blocks, then the next day there is no medical centre here any more, so what's difference? There are concrete blocks across street, razor wire on pavements. Wait and see.'

At the bottom of the short hill the road junction could barely have been negotiated by cars, had there been any, since the Israeli watchtower had been constructed on top of the very junction. Three soldiers attended it, one at the top of the tower, two in the street facing different ways, their backs dutifully to the tower. Niamh took out a digital camera from her bag: Jan placed his hand on it immediately.

'Be discreet. Use carefully, don't provoke. I'll explain policy on cameras later. You will have another opportunity.'

She put it away. As they got nearer to the soldiers in their dark green combat uniforms, tight metallic helmets and heavy armour and weapons, it was clear to the group that most of the conscript Israeli soldiers were little more than boys.

'They're all so young,' Ella said, 'God, they make me feel old! What do they know? What can they know?'

'They're bastards,' muttered Paul.

'And they're listening,' cautioned the Dane.

The party turned right when they reached the junction and squeezed through a concrete-lined corridor to the side of the watchtower. Two hundred yards further on was a ground level equivalent of the watch post where three more young boys, looking no more than fifteen years old, in Israeli uniforms were touting powerful rifles. Half way down the road Ali called them together and resumed his commentary.

The man in the green polo neck and Mahmoud listened as attentively as the westerners.

'As we told you, and you saw in the presentation, there were six small Israeli settlements here in Hebron, six small areas where Israeli settlers came in and took over. They were stable for many years, they were small, they were not much trouble to most of us. They kept themselves apart, though some of our young brothers sometimes attacked them with stones, angry that they had no right to be there.'

'So that's why all these houses have wire mesh at the windows,' said Ella.

'No, these are not settlers' houses, these are Palestinian homes. If our young people go into the settler area to throw stones they get caught, or beaten, or taken away. Arrested, even taken to court in Israel - something else illegal under international law. But if the settlers' children throw stones at our windows the soldiers protect them.'

'What about the police? The Palestinian police?' asked Paul.

'Can you see any? No. We have police, you will see them in Ramallah, but they are not allowed near the settler area.'

'What? But this is your country!' insisted Dutch Ella, her pale skin flushing with anger.

'Tell us about it,' said Jan, ruefully. 'Ali, continue.'

'They are using fences, check points, razor wire, concrete blocks. Slowly they are joining those six settlements together so the settlers can walk freely between them.'

Jan took up the narrative: 'You see up there on the hill? That's a settlement. They start with a handful of caravans, always on a hilltop. They're replaced by something more permanent, then an army post moves in to look after them. Then a fence appears around the settlement – many metres away, bigger if it's in a country area. Then in the country area a road is built, for settlers' use only, guarded by fences along both sides. Palestinians cannot use it, the soldiers make sure of that. That's not a bad deal for a settlement that's supposed to be illegal even in Israeli law, not a bad return on your taxes, is it? In the city they move the local people away, close down their shops, help them to relocate.'

'They help them?' asked Ella. 'How?'

'They point a rifle at them. That helps them move.'

'The bastards,' said Paul.

'It is – what do they call it, ethnic cleansing? Like in Serbia?' said Piet.

'But without killing them,' said Ella.

'True...' said Jan, 'not here in West Bank. Gaza is different...'

Niamh stood and shook, silently. What was she doing here?

Ella wondered aloud 'Why would they leave Israel to come and live in these settlements?'

Ali responded 'They don't. Very few settlers are Israeli. Many are Russian Jews, some are American Fundamentalist Christians. Most Israelis they can afford to live in nicer places than this.'

Tony watched them all, taking in every reaction, every element of the environment, and he listened.

Jan had to exert some control. He could not afford to have his team's emotions spoil their monitoring mission.

'Yes, it's frightening. But the people have to live with it. There's no change on the horizon for them. Our job is to watch, to listen, report. The international community has a right to objective information and that's all we do, collect information. Data. We just tell it like it is, we can have no opinion on it – in public. But to see it like it is we need to live amongst it. The soldiers know what these arm bands mean, most of them respect us. What I mean is, they will moderate their behaviour when they see the arm band, and we're not the only monitors. There are lots of other groups here in West Bank, international organisations, watching. I hate to think what would happen if they thought that the world was not watching. But watching is all we can do.'

'I don't know what I was expecting,' said Niamh, visibly moved, her gaze fixed on the floor.

'Let's move on,' said Jan. 'So that's a settlement, up there on the hill. At the bottom of this street is another. They are in process of joining them together, by excluding anyone who lives in between.'

A group of children in colourful clothes on a low roof stopped their play to watch the strangers with the distinctive bands around their arms walk down the street. They saw six with pale faces and three Palestinian friends. There was no laughter from the children, no smiles. Not yet world weary, their faces nevertheless described permanent apprehension.

Ella turned her head upwards and smiled at the children; they would not have seen many with blond curls such as she had, before. Like nocturnal spiders in a beam of light they scuttled away.

Thus, for a moment, the attention of most of the group was distracted.

'Halt! You go no further!'

The soldier was barely one metre sixty, thought Paul, and had never yet needed to shave; a pipsqueak. But what happens now?

His gun is pointing at me, thought Niamh, and held her breath.

Piet looked to his right. Two other soldiers had emerged from behind what looked like a coffee bar, made from sandbags.

Their guns were also pointing in the group's direction, ominously.

Ella felt her blood start to boil. This whole thing was making her angry and this was only the latest moment in a serious of sobering and saddening moments of elucidation. And it was still only day one.

Tony's pulse, on the other hand, barely wavered in his silent body.

Jan assumed the role of spokesman. He'd been to this place before, many times, although last time there had been no block on this road. He pointed to his armband.

'We're international observers, please let us pass.'

'No!'

'Is this road closed now?'

'Why you bring here them?' The Hebrew-speaking soldier's clumsy speech showed his command of English to be less than that of Ali or Mahmoud.

'Why are you stopping us passing?'

'This our country!'

'No it isn't!' Niamh could not help shouting. She put her hand over her mouth as though to prevent further unfortunate challenges.

'We Isra-eli soldier. We here protect Isra-eli peoples.'

None of the Palestinians had stepped forward to challenge the youth, nor did they appear likely to do so.

There was a palpable stand-off.

After a moment of pointing his gun vaguely in Jan's direction the leading soldier had a word in Hebrew with his colleagues.

Jan stepped forward: 'Soldier – I want to talk to your commanding officer,' he stated.

The soldier ignored him and continued his muttering. Eventually he turned to Jan.

'OK. You pass. Not the Arabs.'

He gestured with his gun at Ali, Mahmoud and the man in the green jumper. The experienced Jan had come across this pattern of behaviour before, but not on this particular street: why was today different from every previous day?

Sunshine grated on the road and the skins of the observers. There was dust in the dry air.

'They are Palestinian people. Why do you not let Palestinians through? This didn't happen last time I was here.'

'Twenty thousand people die on September eleven,' was the automatic, matter of fact response.

Tony, at last, felt his hackles rise. For one thing, that figure was simply untrue, the figure was less than three thousand, for another... but he knew it was not worth arguing. Jan would have reminded him, in any case, that arguing was not why the mission was there.

Patience, thought Tony. Patience.

Jan, too, felt anger and it was only by monumental effort that he controlled himself. His skin was used to these atmospheric conditions so it wasn't the heat that was causing it to creep so.

The other observers were numbed into a surreal silence, an air of fatal anticipation.

Jan spoke to his team rather than to the soldier.

'It seems we can go no further. I mean, we will go no further if we cannot all go together.'

As one the group turned, to head back the way they had come.

A few moments later, the situation defused, Ali again assumed the role of tourist guide, continuing his spiel as though nothing had happened.

'You see mosque up there, on hill, the other side of the tunnel we came through? The people who live here, many of them attend that mosque. It used to be a five minute walk up the hill, just here, this way. But now – because of security – it takes more than half an hour. They must walk all way around the Old Town.'

As the guided tour continued in a subdued vein Ali pointed out where shops had once been, spoke of food shortages, gave more examples of the settlers being set above the law at the expense of local Palestinians.

Eventually they returned to the minibus, where Niamh and Ella were the first to board, followed by Piet and Paul. None would admit openly to the relief which they felt in its sanctuary.

As Tony prepared to follow, the man in the green pullover gently touched his elbow to hold him back.

He spoke, for the first time, in clandestine fashion: 'I think you friend Mr Aqbar? In Luton, England?'

'That's me.'

The man nodded.

Tony had expected an approach to be made soon and it was no surprise that it came from the man with no name, who now spoke quietly to Jan in Arabic. The Dane nodded. Jan now climbed aboard the bus and Ali shut the door behind him leaving Tony and the unnamed Palestinian on the street.

Inside the bus, as the driver fired the ignition and Jan announced: 'We will drive now to where we stay for the night. Tony has a friend here in Hebron, he will join us later, in time for dinner. It's now past five o'clock so we would not be allowed to leave Hebron today, even if we wanted to. The gate will be closed.'

Paul, Ella, Niamh and Piet did not hear the gate actually slam: but they could feel it.

* * *

'Come with me.'

'I wondered when –'

'No talk. Please. Follow.'

The man in the green polo neck led Tony on a brisk walk back into the Souk but they then left it in a new direction. They were heading further into the Old Town.

At the side of a large and once proud building was a discreet entrance. Inside the door two large men wearing suits, moustaches and Arab headdresses stood as they entered, then relaxed as they recognised the young man.

The man led Tony down some stairs and through a narrow underground corridor, lit by two exposed but dim light bulbs, one at each end. They were connected by ancient electric wiring hanging from the ceiling.

At the far end a heavy wooden door barred their way; the younger man knocked twice.

'Can I ask your name?' asked Tony, aware that they were now in a secret and secure place.

'Yes, you can ask,' he replied, in a perfect English accent. 'You don't need to know.'

The door opened. Inside, another doorman scrutinised the two carefully and indicated that they should sit on two wooden seats. He disappeared through a second door and the two sat in silence.

The room was little more than a cave with doorways off and white-painted walls, and it had the same basic lighting as the corridor, though more of it. Before Tony could scrutinise or speculate further the second door reopened and a smart man of about Tony's own age – early forties – entered.

'Anthony! What a pleasure!'

The well dressed man who entered had a shaven head and western garb, his black moustache had been trimmed almost out of existence. He was armed with a large, moist grin. Taking the Englishman by the shoulders he kissed him firmly on each cheek.

The man in green left his seat and stood discreetly by the doorway. Behind the host a young woman had entered. At least, from her body shape, size and posture she looked young to Tony: a white scarf, a niqab, hid her whole face other than her eyes whilst a black robe covered the rest of her, including her feet.

The man led the conversation: 'My honourable father Aqbar, may Allah bless him, has told me so much about you! I am Asif. This is Suli, she is a very important person, as you will see.'

He turned to the escort: 'Khaled, bring us tea. Tony, please, take a seat.'

There were only two chairs. Even though the escort, Khaled, now left the room there was nowhere for Suli to sit. She knelt on a mat as the two men took the chairs.

'I am so honoured to see you, it is indeed great privilege! Welcome to Palestine! Have you had a good journey from England?'

They engaged in small talk, a talent which the fluent Asif had either learned from his father or inherited through his Arab genes; it was honed to perfection.

Tony had not seen Aqbar, Asif's father, for some years although throughout his adult life he'd occasionally exchanged letters with his former neighbour. Aqbar, who worked at the same Luton car factory as Tony's own father, had been an inspiration to the young man in his schoolboy days. He had given the eighteen year-old Tony one-to-one seminars to help sate the boy's passion for global politics, in a style which generated both attention to detail and everlasting loyalty. Asif explained that Aqbar, now over 70 years old, was not in the best of health, confirming what the old man had written to Tony a few weeks earlier.

'I fear,' Asif said when Tony questioned him further, 'that my father is not very well. He is an old man. But my father is happy: he knows that it will not be long before Allah, may his great name be praised, relieves him of the responsibility of this world and welcomes him into heaven. That will be a very proud moment for my father and myself. I hope I, too, will earn a place in heaven as a reward for my conduct in life, as my father surely has.'

Tony smiled courteously: heaven was a concept which he had always found difficult, whether it be that of his Muslim mentor of so many years or the vision of the more oleaginous Christians to whom he'd been obliged to kowtow from time to time in his public life in English schools.

When Khaled returned they sipped mint tea, sweet and sticky, from delicate glass cups.

What had bound Tony to Aqbar for so long was the older man's ability to cut the crap and see to the heart of an issue or an argument. His wisdom, his grasp of situations and Tony's common understandings with his teacher had kept the two men's relationship so very positive over decades, despite frequent gaps of several years between meetings. Now, here, was Aqbar's son, Asif, in his element, fighting the fight with the same passion that had forever glowed in his father's heart.

Aqbar had once told Anthony – the name by which he knew him – that it would never be safe for him to return to his own native part of the Arab world as he was a wanted man with a death sentence hanging over his head. As some of those doing the wanting were from Mossad it made no sense to risk returning to anywhere in the Middle East. For that same reason Asif, about whom Tony had heard much but had never previously met, lived his life in the shadows.

The conversation continued to centre around the old man. Asif was proud that his father commanded such respect from this Englishman, who clearly had all the characteristics of a fellow warrior, something which was almost unheard of amongst his race. Throughout these exchanges Suli sat, silent, attentive.

The men spoke at length of history, of conviction and of bravery; of imperialism, of treachery, of liberty and of heroic and selfless struggle.

After more than an hour, Asif told his guest more about the third party in the room.

'Suli comes from Tulkarm. Her cousin was fortunate enough to be chosen to deliver an Act of God in Netanya, three years ago, and he went to heaven. He was a hero and his family is justified in their pride in him. Suli will show to the world how proud is her family of their hero.'

Tony recalled reading of the Netanya market bomb of 2002, one of Hamas' most deadly attacks on Israeli civilians during the second intifada. To some the victims were parents, grandparents. To Tony they were unfortunate, yes, but they were collateral damage in a greater war.

'What you mean is that she...'

'She will bring the terror of Allah, may his name be praised, to the heathen of Israel and the oppressors of the Palestinian people.'

'But... there's a cease fire, isn't there? Isn't Hamas party to it?'

'Who said anything about Hamas? Or Fatah? My friend, you said yourself that when someone is involved in politics and they know what is right thing to do, they must do it. Is that not what my father has taught us both? He was in politics. You are in politics. I am in politics. Suli is in politics: she will commit herself to a political act.'

Tony hesitated.

'So... will she... will she carry a bomb? Plant it or, or... '

He found it difficult to say the words 'die with it', though the idea of the action itself did not phase him.

'She will walk down a street in Netanya. She will go to where there are people, Israeli people, the oppressor. She will smile and she will go to take her place with Allah, may his name be praised, in heaven.'

Tony could sense Suli's modesty from behind her niqab as her eyes avoided his gaze. He realised that despite her hour of silence she had understood every word.

'You speak English?' he said directly to the young woman.

Suli glanced to Asif for approval before she replied. He nodded.

'Yes, I teach English,' she said.

'My fellow teacher..!' He smiled at his comrade. Though he could see only her eyes between the folds of her white scarf he sensed she was returning his smile. He also felt her confidence, her responsibility - and her pride.

'And when do you expect to...?'

'I do not know, sir.'

'And how will you – '

'My friend,' Asif interrupted, 'no arrangements have yet been made. All that has been decided is that Suli's wish, to find her way to heaven alongside her cousin as a hero of our people in struggle, will be granted.'

There was a further moment of silence.

Asif smiled again at his guest.

'My friend,' he said again, getting to his feet, 'you also have a job to do. The European observers of the occupation are relying on you for assistance. You have a most valuable task to perform. You need to go now to rejoin your colleagues.'

'I'm going to be here in Hebron for four weeks. Will we meet again, Asif?'

'Maybe. Maybe not. But when the time comes you will know what you have to do, my friend.'

The two men exchanged smiles, embraced and shook hands warmly.

As he turned, Suli caught his gaze; he knew she was smiling again and he smiled back, briefly.

Within moments Tony found himself back in the street. A nondescript cream-coloured car was waiting with its engine running. The man in the green pullover reappeared, opened a rear door and ushered him in.

There was a grey haze around the deep tangerine of the low sun.

The dust in the air was glittering as the driver took Tony away.

He took a deep breath: it was raw, warm and ominous in the distinctive Mediterranean dusk.

* * *

Tony rejoined his colleagues for dinner but revealed nothing, now or later, about his diversion. By nine the group had adjourned to the bar but by ten, professing emotional exhaustion, most had retired to their rooms. This left only Ella - well into her third red wine - and Tony, enjoying a long and patient beer, on the sofas under the stars.

Ella needed someone to talk to, to dump her emotions upon, and Tony's quiet but encouraging engagement filled the bill: his maturity must surely bring with it worldly wisdom. Ella was committed to the cause of Palestine and POEM and knew exactly what to expect from the experience ahead of her, in theory, her sister having made the trip a year earlier. Nevertheless she'd been taken aback by the depth of feeling she'd experienced all afternoon. So the two talked of global politics and the straitjacket of convention, of Ella's background and her hopes for the world. There was a tight spring in her soul that had become knotted, as though her mental spine had developed a kink that needed straightening. The Dutch woman needed to be unwound. She knew exactly what she was doing when, after an hour, she stood up before Tony, said 'I'm going to bed', then held out her hand.

The gesture was not a handshake of equals but of a parent reaching out for a child.

The sex that followed was just what both needed: it was raw, passionate and silent, sweaty, desperate and to the point. It was shared, not inflicted, intense and not prolonged. Not a word was spoken until the end: Ella, on top, rigid, now collapsed, rolled off him and onto her back like a rag doll.

'Fuck,' she said, aloud, her eyes closed.

A minute later she was asleep; Tony dressed and returned to his room.

They had been strangers at the start and they were strangers still now, which was how it should be.

Throughout the following weeks they neither repeated nor ever referred to the event.

The emotional chiropractics had done its job.

Chapter 11: Brighton, September 2005

On that Sunday morning a fine drizzle wafted around the Brighton seafront. It was neither one thing nor another, thought Ken. Enough to disappoint, insufficient to cleanse. Enough to dampen his trilby but not to drive him back to the car to retrieve his umbrella.

Ken Hemmings stood on the promenade and surveyed the scene. Close to him, across the road and in front of the Hotel Metropole, the iron ring of a security fence stood confident and defiant. Chain link barriers, football-ground-style, full-height turnstiles and concrete cuboid boulders combined to dissuade the uninvited from the largest political event of the year, which would commence in just a few hours.

Ken's hat and beige macintosh protected him from the worst of the blustery wind, which had unseasonal bite engrained in its dampness. Other people were gathered on the promenade, people hoping to exert influence on the powers that be, people who had generally not come so well prepared for the elements as Ken. To the east a modest crowd with placards had assembled, preparing to campaign for their pensions to be protected. There were only a few of them now but later there would undoubtedly be more noise, bustle, protest, variety. So far the presence and impact of dissent was limited. The Conference would start in three hours time.

Through a turnstile in the cordon a favoured few were already passing, but only in a trickle. Later in the day, as Peter Elder had described, queues of the faithful and the not quite so faithful, masses of Labour Party members, supporters and hangers on, journalists and lobbyists, would be assembling, awaiting their turn to pass through interminable security checks.

Tight and oppressive security was a sign of the times, a necessary evil, thought Ken, but a lesser evil than headline-grabbing violence and disruption. Democracy was supposed to be open, transparent, accessible.

Another sign of the times was the renewed facia of the towering edifice of the Grand Hotel, next door to the Brighton Centre, fenced almost beyond public gaze, distanced from the outside world. For a moment Ken saw not the Victorian shades of red brick, acres of glass and delicate filigree ironwork but, superimposed upon it, a grainy television image of a pile of dust, bricks and warped metal in the night, flashing blue lights, the nation sharing a common bond of horror and empathy in which political differences were as nothing. From amongst that 1984 rubble was carried Norman Tebbit, the scourge of the working man, dug out in the early hours. His wife, Margaret, who'd been in that hotel room with him as the bomb went off, would also live but she would never walk again.

No one who had been a police officer back then would ever forget that night; Ken's feelings about it were almost as though he'd been there in Brighton himself, though he'd been 200 miles away. Every police officer and every democrat would forever recall the words of the IRA statement that followed the event:

'Remember, we only have to be lucky once. You will have to be lucky always.'

Few threats had ever rung so true.

By a twist of fate the bombers' principal target, Margaret Thatcher, had escaped death by a matter of feet. Seconds before the bomb had reduced the front of the hotel to dust she'd been standing in a vulnerable room, her husband Denis safe in bed elsewhere in the suite. She must have seen the wall of the room disappear in an instant of cataclysmic, seismic thunder as terrorists sought to bury her and her memory.

Others, relatively minor players on the political scene, had not been lucky and five lives had been lost. What would some people not do to rid the world of their political enemies? Ken shuddered.

In an act of defiance the Grand Hotel had been rebuilt, as new, following the example of the Royal Palace in Warsaw, after the second world war, and the Alcazar at Toledo, destroyed in the Spanish Civil War. Was it really over twenty years since The Grand had been bombed? It wasn't clear, from what Ken could see before him, how today's restored facade differed, if at all, from that of the moment before the IRA changed the face of both the building and of British public life.

If one of Ken Hemmings' more outrageous hunches were to prove to be correct, today could be as significant as the twelfth of October, 1984, came so close to having been.

Unless he could stop it.

And yet it remained, simply, a hunch.

Beyond the two conference hotels, the Metropole and the Grand, nestled the Brighton Centre. Within those walls Tony Blair, supported by ministerial colleagues, would spend five days setting out to his Party his plans for continuing in government, granted by the public in May, a few months earlier. Peter Elder would be amongst that loyal throng, eagerly anticipating the package of ideas which he believed would kick start a national flow of political adrenalin. This new era, an unprecedented third term for Labour, would start in earnest for Peter on the Tuesday afternoon, he'd said, when the Prime Minister would not simply address the conference directly but also the nation and the world.

The threat of terrorism would, no doubt, be high on the week's political agenda, still urgent following the suicide attacks on London of July 7th and the abortive attempt to emulate them, two weeks later. The PM would be asking the nation to make sacrifices – through identity cards, anti-terrorism legislation and the continuing military campaigns in Iraq and Afghanistan – to stand up to that odious practice of taking human life at random which was at the heart of the use of terror to destabilise democracy.

The politically neutral former policeman could appreciate both the gravity of Blair's task and the size of the mountain the politicians must climb. The drip, drip of terrorist activity itself – whether at a night club in Bali, on a train in Madrid or through the televised horror of 9/11 – served to keep the issue on the media agenda. No doubt each new event prompted public opinion to tolerate restrictions on their freedoms which would previously have been considered unthinkable.

Democratic justice and terrorism shared one frightening value in common, Ken mused: both sought to punish the guilty. In one case, due process was the tool, transparency, evidence and a trial in which the accused were scrutinised in public and invited to justify their actions within the law. The other featured summary execution without trial, by self-appointed champions of an arbitrary cause. Being who you were was crime enough in some eyes, it appeared, individuals often being the innocent victims of clashes between differing ideologies. The desire to eradicate opposing thought was anathema to democrats and yet it seemed that the more that the world's conventional leaders – political, cultural and religious – were protected and isolated from attack, the more the perpetrators of terror were likely to kill victims further away from those positions of responsibility.

Whilst the wind was whipping and swirling more vigorously the drizzle had subsided. Ken was thankful for his faithful hat, that moulded felt security blanket, which was keeping his head warm and his brain thereby alert.

Inspector Hemmings knew what he had to do.

Beyond the main entrance to the Centre queues were starting to grow, though it was still early. Demonstrators, advocates, partisans and fanatics, sectarians and those committed to the wider cause vied with each other for the damp attention of the early arrivals.

Ken left the promenade, crossed the sea front road and stood on its corner with West Street. He looked up the road, which climbed inland towards the town centre, in the direction of the real world. To his left the cocoon of the conference centre awaited four thousand delegates and as many witnesses. Today, however imperfectly, they would embody the common values of western democracy and engagement.

He crossed the road again, a lane at a time, using the Pelican crossing in a proper and respectful manner, to the sanctuary of the eastern pavement of West Street and made his calculations.

The building he was seeking was pale yellow. On the ground floor was an amusement arcade whilst the best that could be said of the upper storeys was that they were nondescript. And shabby.

He concentrated his mind. He'd learned to focus effectively in his police career but it was years since he'd last had to employ that skill in such an ominously urgent manner, if ever.

The pavement was conventional, geometric, its cracked slabs challenging his passion for neatness. The pervading smell, despite the weather, was of frying oil, of fish and chips.

He came to a halt outside the amusement arcade...

Inside, electronic 'games' enticed, tempted, squeaked, jangled, jingled, commanded, lured and successfully seduced. They might guarantee a 70 per cent return, by law, but when the punter has won that several times over the guarantee is barely worth having. One-armed bandits and penny dreadfuls were things of the past: today's rows of cherries and pears were now merely flashing, transient images lacking the solid permanence of those heavy, randomly rotating wheels of a past era, the mechanical slot machines of Ken's youth. Today's video games were clever, high tech, high earning and too often obscene in their glorification of violence. Trainee assassins could do worse than develop their target skills by picking up a weapon which fired nothing more than a beam of light. They could practice and measure their success by the number of images of faceless men they blasted into crumpled digital heaps through the wonders of technology.

From pavement level, Ken looked up.

The yellow paint was peeling from the walls above the arcade. The westerly facing windows of the upper floors were mildly bowed, perhaps in passing homage to some Dickensian myth. From his low vantage point all the rooms appeared dark. At this time in the middle of a Sunday, however, any impression that they were unoccupied might be misleading. Several units of low cost living accommodation were located on the upper floors.

Ken turned again. Across the road was a modern, functional hotel. Next door to that was a short passage leading to a rear entrance to the Brighton Centre, cordoned off to prevent unauthorised access to the Labour Conference.

He turned again and walked a few yards, back towards the sea front. There was an alley between two buildings and he turned left into it without hesitation. The narrow way ran through to what might be described as a service road, providing vehicular access to the rear of half a dozen properties - including the one he'd now identified as his target.

Now Ken stood in a narrow *cul de sac* behind the amusement arcade: it was deserted. Around him garages and lock-ups lined up in different states of repair and in different modes of use. To the right of one was a further narrow alley which led to the rear of the yellow-fronted building. This in turn met an outside door, above which the wall was almost featureless. This rear, eastern façade of the building did not afford residents the same access to daylight as its west-facing counterpart and was in significantly worse repair.

The apartment he was seeking, flat 4, was third on Ken's purloined list of six that the estate agent had emailed to Flagg; but it was the only one within spitting distance of a potential target of any political significance - the conference centre. It was the right place to start.

The door was robust and wooden. A panel to the left bore three ancient bell pushes which, Ken assessed, were unlikely to be in working order. No matter, he wasn't planning to ring in any case. If this outer door were locked then things could get difficult but, probably despite the best efforts of the no doubt absentee landlord it was, thankfully, not.

Only the turn of a handle and a tentative push was needed to move the door, which swung open silently. The passage beyond was in darkness.

It was now or never for Ken.

Walking stealthily, barely breathing, listening hard, he found a further door at the end of the passage. He could make out a number '1' in black paint in the small amount of light that came from a stairwell immediately adjacent to the door, to the left. Ken put his ear to the wood: behind the door he could discern the insistent tinkles and electronic melodies that the modern world allowed to pass as tunes; this was a rear access, presumably for staff, to the amusement arcade.

As he got used to the restricted light he saw that a small window on each flight illuminated the stairwell during daylight hours. Years of practice allowed Ken to climb the two flights of stairs cat-like, almost silently, even at his age. Within moments, which seemed like hours, he was standing outside the door he'd been expecting to find, bearing a plastic numeral '4' hanging askew from a single nail. There was only one door on the ground floor, two on the first and two here at the top of the stairs. Whatever happened next would attract no witnesses.

Given the information he'd gathered and tested, assimilated and analysed, his inferences and deductions had generated a narrow range of feasible conclusions to the mystery. Most suggested that his quarry might never be seen in Sussex again, had probably already left. There could still be an innocent explanation, something short of a Bolshevik plot, though these insalubrious surroundings were surely incompatible the flat being used for the third possibility, a love nest. On the other hand, if his feeling was right...

So here he was, a sixty-year old man playing at spies, feeling slightly absurd and definitely out of place. Adding to this, it occurred to Ken that he was still wearing his hat and coat, even indoors. That would never do... not normally. He removed his coat and hung it neatly over his arm but left the comforting hat in place.

He studied the detail of the door: it was conventional, wooden, not a brilliant fit, a very ordinary, interior, cheap sort of door. If absolutely necessary it would, no doubt, succumb to moderate persuasion. If no one was at home then that was a decision he'd have to take, but at this moment the case for forcing an entry was not proven.

To the left of the door frame was a small metal holder where a name card could be placed to identify the occupant of the flat. It was empty.

He removed his trilby to put his ear to the door for a few seconds. There was no discernible noise from within the flat. Perhaps it was empty, after all? Ken now felt it would not be vacant, could not be, if his hunch were to have any veracity at all. But that hunch was all he had to go on, a hunch he had shared with neither Peter nor Clive, his closest confidants. He put the hat back on - not that he was cold, or needed protection, but to keep both of his hands free for... whatever he might need them to do next.

There was nothing to be gained by waiting.

He checked his watch: it was no longer morning.

He adjusted his trilby in a workmanlike manner.

Pulled his collar forward to allow his jacket to hang better.

Knocked twice with his knuckles, business-like, and waited.

After a mental count of five the door opened. Two inches.

The face of a tall man peered through the crack but said nothing. He had dark hair and a high forehead. In his mid-forties, he hadn't shaved for a while.

Although Ken had only ever seen one picture of Flagg, this was his man.

'Is it Mr Flagg? Norman Flagg?'

After a pause the teacher said 'Yes?'

'My name's Ken Hemmings. I'm a friend of Peter Elder. May I come in?'

The man flashed a glance back down the empty stairs.

'Of course.'

The game was up. Flagg must have realised that any denial of his identity was fruitless. Fifteen, love, Ken thought.

Flagg walked a few steps backwards to allow the door to open into a small room. His hands were empty. Ken closed the door behind him. He appreciated the certainty of knowing that he was unaccompanied, even if Flagg might not yet be reassured. Drawing attention to the fact was not a good idea.

'What can I do for you, Mr Hemmings?' asked the teacher.

'Peter was worried about you.'

'I'm sure he was. So... who are you, exactly?'

Ken smiled and made to relax. He took off his hat and held it with both hands.

'My name's Ken, as I said. I retired to Sussex a couple of years ago. My wife was a teacher - a primary school Head, like you. I live in the village and Peter thought I might... have the time and interest to try to find you. It's a good school you run there. By the way, Jane said to say that she's doing fine.'

'Good.' He spoke quietly.

This was going well, though it was important to avoid being condescending.

Flagg was wearing casual trousers, an open neck shirt and – surprisingly – outdoor shoes.

'So, what shall I tell him?'

'Peter?'

'Yes.'

The man appeared distracted, lost in thought. This was not the confident and determined character Ken had expected to find. He was ponderous, slow, his attention was elsewhere. The room was not 'comfortable', it was 'basic'; sparsely furnished, not particularly light. It was not the right atmosphere for conversation - or social interaction of any kind. It felt damp.

No reply was forthcoming.

'Well, Mr Flagg? May we perhaps... sit down and talk?'

There was another moment of thought. Flagg appeared to have made a decision. Politely, professionally, he looked Ken in the eyes and said 'Of course. Why don't you... come through? After you.'

Ken smiled. This was working out so much easier than he'd expected, so much less threatening than it might have been. Everything was going according to plan. The primary objective - locating the wanderer - had been achieved and lines of communication had been established. He might even be reporting a successful result to his friend in the Golf Club bar that very evening.

Flagg smiled professionally, stood back, opened the next door and gestured to invite Ken to lead the way into a larger room at the front of the flat, which must be overlooking West Street itself, out to the west.

This room was bigger and much brighter. The clouds must have cleared, as long shafts of sunlight –

Ken staggered forwards as he fell to the floor, pushed violently from behind. He'd tripped and stumbled hard - the hard leather of an outdoor shoe had curled around his ankle like a question mark whilst a hand had shoved the small of his back into inevitable topple and precipitation. With no time to put out his hands to break his fall he descended rapidly, violently, clumsily to the floor. A wooden stool caught him briefly and uncomfortably on the left collar bone then his chin made firm contact with the floor, with a carpet that was far too rough – like a pig's beard – for comfort. He'd avoided biting his tongue, miraculously, but screwed up his face in a grimace.

The faithful trilby had fallen from his hands and had rolled away, across the floor. It settled in the corner of the room, a good yard beyond his reach.

All these observations tore through his mind in the micro-seconds of his descent, its ending and its aftermath, distracting him from a startling and powerful image which had blasted his visual cortex, an image of which his conscious mind had, as yet, managed to make no sense. Before his brain could allocate time for proper assessment of the image and consideration of its implications a further sequence of events, post-fall, had already started.

Ken found a second to wonder what the hell a man of his age was doing on a floor like this. His knees were scraped and stinging, elbow and collar bone bruised, chin throbbing, then he found himself being wrenched to his knees and having his arms pulled roughly behind his back. After a moment's manhandling he was manoeuvred to lie against a hard, uncomfortable chair and then pushed to the ground once more. A familiar feeling of cold metal now circled his wrists.

Now Flagg left him alone.

Two things became clear to Ken within moments.

Both of his hands were behind his back, his wrists now threaded under the arms of a rather splendid, high-backed Windsor chair. The handcuffs attached him to it most effectively, he was immobilised as though in the stocks. Trussed to this cumbersome item of furniture, he was unable to either stand or lie comfortably. As he assessed what was happening to him, processing his newly captive status, the image which he couldn't properly identify a moment earlier now became startlingly clear.

It was a large, clean, shining, long-barrelled gun, mounted on a robust tripod. It was pointing through the window in a downwards trajectory. Although the vista from the window consisted solely of rooftops, from where Ken lay, he calculated that the gun's sight was focussed on the private, discreet, side entrance to the Brighton Conference Centre, the entrance opposite which he had stood only a matter of minutes ago.

Ken was getting his breath back and his heart rate was coming down, at last, though he was still nowhere close to his normal physiological function.

'I'm... sure all that wasn't necessary, Norman.'

The teacher spoke firmly, without emotion: 'Oh, but *I'm* sure it was, Ken.'

Ken was still slightly breathless: the wind had been knocked out of him both literally and metaphorically.

'Are you by yourself? Hmm. Don't bother answering.'

Ken really did feel 'by himself'. Alone, in a dangerous place. Very alone.

By now Flagg was seated on a tall stool across on the other side of the room. His seat was close to the left side of the window, in the ideal position for firing this undoubtedly powerful and lethal machine. From his limited experience of firearms, Ken identified the weapon as a high powered hunting rifle, probably intended for deer, elk or moose. He noted that it lacked the external cartridge that would have given it the multi-shot capacity of a semi-automatic weapon. It was unlikely that it was designed to fire a single bullet, however; six or ten, manually fired, would be its likely capacity.

Flagg now stared out of the window, giving every impression of wishing to ignore his visitor. Accordingly the men sat in silence whilst each considered the implications of their new, unanticipated, situation.

Flagg gave no indication of concern or perturbation. He stared passively through the window, down towards the street, paying no attention to his captive. Ken, bruised and dishevelled, wished he could appear as cool as his captor. Where was the legendary Hemmings sangfroid? Over the silent minutes that followed he regained a modicum of composure.

The room had few items of furniture. From where the teacher sat a kettle, mug, biscuit tin and box of tea bags on a table were within easy reach. On the floor was a pile of sandwich wrappers and three bulging supermarket bags. The would-be assassin was prepared for the long haul.

After several minutes, which felt more like half an hour, Ken spoke.

'So, what's it all about, Norman?'

After a brief pause Flagg spoke calmly. 'I want to remove the Prime Minister.'

The understated comment was clear enough for Ken. Flagg was staring out of the window. He barely blinked. Keep him talking, thought Ken, that was the advice police gave to those dealing with hostage-takers.

Keep them talking. But don't say 'Have you tried voting Tory?'

'May I ask... why you want to do that?'

'I have my reasons.'

Talk. Engage. Don't push... Not yet.

'Have you... had this planned for long?'

'You're sounding like a policeman, Mr Hemmings.'

The gunman spoke confidently and without emotion and still his attention was not diverted. There was no need to reward him by acknowledging that particular truth.

'I'm a pensioner.'

Flagg smiled. 'Well, yes. I'd guessed that.'

'Do you want to know about the school? What's happening there? I think Jane – she's doing a great job, did I say? – is feeling a little bit let down. In the lurch, if you know what I mean.'

'I'm sure she is. Yes, I'm sorry about that. But Jane's not my number one priority right now.'

'No... I don't suppose she is.'

Flagg reached out for a biscuit without averting his gaze from the road. He took out a custard cream, Ken noted, and ate it in two bites. Ken realised that he was better able to recognise a biscuit type than the genre of weapon in front of him. It was clever of him to pick the biscuit without looking, thought Ken, but he might have offered one to me, too. What had he got to lose? What if I'd preferred a jammy dodger? Would Flagg have searched one out for him? Perhaps custard creams were all that there were; either that, or Norman was non-discriminatory when it came to biscuits.

The conversation was suspended for some minutes.

As he was clearly going to be here for a while, Ken's thoughts eventually moved towards a cup of tea. On reflection, he supposed that this would be out of the question - not least as both his hands were restrained behind his back and he could see no way of getting up from the floor unaided.

'So, what time are you expecting Blair?' he asked.

'I don't know, exactly. But I do know two things. One's the nature of security: each day he'll arrive at a different time, by a different route. He won't be planning to be in the conference much before Tuesday, but he'll want to be seen on the platform at least once during each session. The other thing I know is about the Labour Party Conference. It's organised chaos. Nothing will happen exactly as planned. Things change. So I shall just watch. And wait.'

'How d'you know he'll use this entrance?'

'He did last time, two years ago. If I haven't got him towards the end of the conference, I'll get one of the others instead.'

That sounded ominous.

'But it would be best if I killed Blair.'

The chill was more than metaphorical; Ken recalled that it had something to do with adrenalin causing blood to be diverted away from the skin. The same hormone caused the hairs on his arm to stand on end.

Ken wanted to ask 'Best for whom?' But he couldn't bring himself to voice the words, eliciting, no doubt, either a macabre or trite revolutionary response.

After a few moments Ken realised that there were things he should have been thinking about but had not: what do I do when I get out of here? What do I tell the police so they can arrest this man? How can I stop this madness? But now, he realised, he'd no reason to believe that he would ever be in a position to report these events…

Now, *that* was chilling.

Ken had no answers. He returned to an earlier strategy, to keep the subject talking.

'My late wife was a teacher.'

No response.

'She worked in primary schools, like you. She gave it her whole life, Norman. Do you prefer being called Norman, by the way? Or Anthony?'

No reply.

'You've done a good job at the school. The staff clearly hold you in very high regard. Peter does, too. There's a good atmosphere there. It's… smashing. All your making, I believe.'

Flagg half-flinched as though he'd identified a possible target – but no. Ken repeated to himself Flagg's strategy that, as it was the first day of the Conference and Blair was the principal target, he would not kill a lesser target unless and until the first couple of days had proved fruitless. This could be a long wait.

Keep them talking, Ken thought. Try again.

'You've known Peter Elder a long time.'

Flagg grunted assent.

'He's a good man. Don't you agree?'

'That's not the point. I'm sure he's found the last few weeks has been destabilising, and the school, but they can cope. As you said, Jane's good. My absence is a small price to pay for enabling a major act of liberation to take place. Something that's going to change the world.'

'It will change the world, all right. But why do you say 'liberation'? I don't understand.'

'That's my only reason for... doing what I'm doing.'

'It doesn't sound very liberating for Mr Blair. Or for you, for that matter. Do you expect to get away with this?'

'It's not individual people that matter. I mean, yes, people do matter, that's what it's all about. But individuals are expendable in the cause of the greater good. I've always believed that.'

'Since the days of the Young Socialists in Luton?'

'Well, you have been talking to Peter, haven't you?'

This was accompanied by the nearest thing to a smile Flagg had yet produced. It was nostalgic, as though remembering the dead.

The moment was temporary.

'How will killing Blair help?'

'Nothing worthwhile in human history has ever been achieved without sacrifice. Human life – collective human life – requires that. Oppressors and dictators must be removed before they become entrenched. In the old days, popular uprising made so much happen, crowds acted together as one organic being, knowing that any part of that collaborative entity is expendable, if necessary, for the survival of the many. You can see this throughout nature. It's the way ant societies work. Do you think the protestors at Peterloo thought they'd all survive when they saw the soldiers charge the crowd? Of course not. Or the International Brigade, in Spain? The Amritsar protestors?'

'I'm not sure I know that one.'

'Thirteenth of April, 1919, the Punjab. Thousands sat down in silent protest, a satyagraha, demonstrating against the criminal British occupation of India. The occupying forces decided to remove the protestors by shooting them, Colonel Reginald Dyer gave the order. Hundreds were killed, slaughtered in cold blood, but thousands survived to fight the cause of liberation and independence, energised by the sacrifices of their comrades.'

For the first time, Flagg was 'on a roll'.

'I've been there, I've been to Jallianwala Bagh garden, where it happened, seen the mural, the people's art, seen how - many years later - the eyes of General Dyer had been scratched out by the fingernails of the oppressed - another expression of 'people's art'. Even the picture is hated for the story it tells.'

'1919? So independence for India came, what? Thirty years later.'

'Thirty years of struggle is but the blink of an eye in human history. There are many more examples.'

'You're doing this to avenge the actions of the British military, almost 100 years ago? You're doing all this on behalf of the people of India? Do they know you're doing this for them?'

'Don't be stupid. It's not as simple as that. This is about fighting oppression all over the world, wherever and whenever it's necessary, in the cause of liberation.'

'So... who exactly are you trying to liberate? And how will killing Blair help?'

'He's an oppressor, leading a top-down, centralised system. That's the difference... Popular liberation movements are invigorated by sacrifice whilst dictators are destroyed by it.'

The voice was matter of fact, casual but clear. The attention, however, continued to be focussed elsewhere.

'So you're the agent of a popular movement?'

'Part of an informal worldwide movement. There are no leaders, no followers, just a collective.'

'But you're authorised to act on their behalf, are you?'

'Authorisation implies the granting of permission. That's a top-down action. That's not how we work.'

'And this 'we' - how many are there of you?'

'That's not the point. I've got responsibilities, obligations to work for the collective good.'

Ken could not equate the collective good with the assassination of a democratically elected Prime Minister. Keep them talking, don't challenge them directly. If Flagg was representing Workers' Gauntlet it was possible that today could be the first of many such situations.

'Are you talking about... Al Qaeda?'

The teacher laughed. 'No.'

This answer was prompt and unequivocal. From everything he knew of Flagg, Ken took this answer to be credible and probably true.

'This idea of the common good... does that explain your teaching career?'

'Of course. I could never work for private business, for the singular motive of profit. I reached that conclusion when I was a teenager, never wavered. Socialism was my creed, my guiding principle from my earliest conscious days. It seemed to me that collective action, collective good, collective responsibility was the starting position and it would take a damn good argument to justify any alternative.'

Flagg's loquaciousness surprised Ken, though once more his knowledge of the 'handbook' on dealing with hostage situations told him that this was a positive development. Flagg went on:

'I came to understand that life involves compromise and politics is the art of the possible. Provision by a benevolent state can be, in many respects, a first step towards the optimum operation of a collective, bottom-up process. We haven't evolved a genuine state-level people's government yet, but we will. The idea of mankind being organised in a non-hierarchical form is still a young one.'

Throughout the speech he'd not once looked at his one-man audience. It was as though Flagg was talking on autopilot.

A crackle of droplets against the window told Ken that the wind had got up and that the threatened heavier rain had commenced.

'Education is a tool of liberation, Mr Hemmings. The next generation of cadres needs to know the true history of the struggle for human liberation. Of course, they won't get that from schools – not even with people like me in positions of influence. I'm not a proselytiser, an evangelist. I'm a facilitator. But what children can get from school is tools with which they can learn. I mean the ability to think, to argue, to behave rationally, to question everything they're told by the establishment.'

It crossed Ken's mind that these were the very qualities that would undermine any society based on an imperfect creed, including the one Flagg was describing. Perhaps the imperfections of democracy were its greatest strengths, its protection against abuse.

'If I can help them acquire those qualities, abilities, capacities, then I can assist them to reach levels of political maturity, as a generation, more quickly and more effectively than their predecessors. That's political evolution, which has been my goal... up to now.'

Ken suggested, positively, 'To which you've dedicated twenty years of your life as a teacher. That's quite an investment.'

'Yes, it's been a total commitment. I'd like to think that every child that's been through my schools has come out better equipped to understand the world, more aware of their responsibilities to their fellow human beings than they would've been without me.'

'And by becoming a Head Teacher you extended that influence to the whole school, not just those in your direct charge.'

'Exactly.'

'And to reach that stage you needed to a 'good' teacher, a 'good' manager, a 'good thing' in every sense of the word. You needed to operate as an effective part of the system, even though it's a system of which you disapprove...'

'That's about it. We all have to make sacrifices.'

'That really is commitment. Or 'was'. I don't suppose you'll be going back to the classroom... after this.'

'I don't really expect to survive 'this', as you call it, at all.'

Ken felt another chill. The fright and flight hormones were working overtime.

If Flagg did not survive there was a strong chance that Ken would not come through it, either, he now reasoned. He imagined the scenario: a blaze of gunfire, a fallen leader, a defiant scream and perhaps a triggered bomb, the ultimate self sacrificial gesture.

It would not pay to ask what fate Flagg had in mind for him.

Flagg glanced up the street from his second floor vantage point, then back to what Ken assumed was the pavement across the road.

Ken went on 'So, Norman: you've made the investment. You've helped equip your share of the next generation with the skills they'll need to fight the war for liberation. You've twenty more years of that in you, you're widely recognised for doing a good job. It's a long struggle, as you say. So where does Mr Blair fit in?'

'The People's Struggle has no room for Self Appointed Heroes.' The capitalisation was plain to hear. 'Those who set themselves above others are automatically suspect in their motives. When, in the name of 'democracy', they ally themselves with the most repressive regimes the world's ever known they betray themselves. The future of the world, the fulfilment of mankind's mission, can get back on track once that man and his like are gone.'

Ken distantly remembered the reporting of a speech by Tony Blair after his landslide election victory in 1997: wasn't it 'We are the servants now'? That was the phrase. It was the sentiment that had convinced Ken, and many thousands like him, that Blair's New Labour experiment ought to be given a chance to work. He'd voted Labour in 1997 for the first time in his life.

'By 'repressive regimes' I suppose you mean America? Capitalist countries generally?'

'Of course, but not exclusively. Saudi Arabia is as bad, North Korea - other peoples headed by dictators will have to take their future into their own hands in their own way.'

'Countries like...?'

'Burma. China. Russia. Nepal. Zimbabwe. Palestine.'

'Goodness! So which countries are on the right track, then?'

'It's actually wrong to see the world in terms of nations. Ultimately, the cause of mankind is universal.'

'So Blair's mistake was setting up his stall next door to Bush.'

'That's too simplistic. Once he became Prime Minister his path was pre-determined, right up until today.'

Ken recalled the magazines and pamphlets he had found in the teacher's home.

'So Blair's chosen the same path as Jack Kennedy? Young, charismatic, popular, able to bring about change, deliver hope? But isn't that what the British people wanted in 1997, the Americans in 1961?'

'A Christian, a slave to the market, the triumph of spin over substance! But yes, you're right, that's the sadness of it. And that's why he deserves the same fate as Kennedy.'

Yet another moment of chill passed up Ken's spine. He was sharing the room with the ghost of Lee Harvey Oswald. This building was the Texas school book repository in Deeley Plaza, Dallas, though they were on the second, not the sixth, floor. It took a moment for the idea to sink in, to bring his heart rate back, once again, to something like normal. The man was serious.

'So why now, Norman? Is it Iraq? Is this your protest against the western invasion of a sovereign country? Is it that capitalism and its associated military might – wasn't it Eisenhower who called it 'the military industrial complex'? – assuming the right to assert its influence with force?'

'Putting aside the idea of 'a sovereign country', which I don't accept as a valid concept, then 'no'. I don't oppose what happened in Iraq. Saddam Hussein was no friend of the people. He subjugated them, carried out summary and arbitrary executions, kept them in poverty, used chemical weapons against the Marsh Arabs, refused to share the huge wealth of the assets which truly belonged to the people.'

'But you're contemplating a summary execution now!'

Flagg's answer was prompt and emphatic.

'No, I'm contemplating an act of liberation: Saddam Hussein played with people's lives. He ordered a whole gaol of prisoners to be executed on one day not because it was the right thing to do – I have a real problem with the concept of prison, anyway – but because the whim took him. That's not a step towards liberation! He exercised power which was not his to use, he was irresponsible, actively working against the interests of the people. Those soldiers who found the tyrant cowering in that hole, like a dog, 14th December 2003, they were the ones who failed the people – by not executing him there and then. He should have fallen that day as surely as his statue toppled eight months earlier. No, when dictators fall out amongst themselves the consequences are not always in the best interests of the people.'

Ken wondered if that was a quote from somewhere he should recognise. He told himself to keep calm and he succeeded, but he had to keep his captor intellectually engaged. The words that followed did not carry the venom and frustration that he was feeling at the younger man's arrogance.

He spoke calmly.

'So what gives you, Norman Flagg, the right to make these judgements?'

At last Flagg turned from the street and looked Ken in the eye.

'The judgement will not be mine: it will be the judgement of history.'

The two men stared at each other for a second which lasted an age. Then Flagg turned his eyes once more to the street and resumed his vigil.

Had not Tony Blair himself once talked of the hand of history being upon his shoulder? That had been a reference to the Good Friday Agreement in Northern Ireland, a truly epoch-making, positive political act in anyone's book. Had that occasion not been the antithesis of violence, a real force for good?

Undoubtedly Ken felt he was right to have adopted this tactic of engagement – given that he should never have allowed himself to get into this hopeless situation in the first place. He doubted whether he had the time or skill to persuade the terrorist to abort his mission. It wasn't as though either of the men had got an alternative plan. Even if Flagg were to surrender today, his life would never be the same again.

Was Flagg a terrorist? Yes. Anyone who contemplated influencing public or government opinion through acts designed to initiate fear and terror was a terrorist.

He had to keep the man talking.

'So you kill Mr Blair. What happens then?'

'It will all be out of my hands.'

Too right it will, thought the policeman.

'Hasn't he… achieved some good things? For the people? Don't you think? Look at all that extra money that's gone into schools, they reduced your class sizes, didn't they? More teachers, school assistants, computers. Some got new schools. All that must mean something to you, of all people.'

'It is no more than children deserve, it's their right! They still need more, much more. By ingratiating himself with schools, teachers, parents, he can claim he has a mandate to continue the capitalist subjugation of working people and the imperialist nature of world politics.

'Anyway, where's the money going? Timetables, curricula, classes of 30 being taught by second income earners who just want to go home at four o'clock, this isn't investing in education as a tool of liberation! This is oppression of children just as much as the capitalist economy makes wage slaves of their parents.'

'But that doesn't describe *your* school, does it? Yours is a good school, you've liberated the children, you said it yourself... doing a good job.'

For the first time some emotion crept into Flagg's voice as he spoke through lightly clenched teeth.

'And I have sweated blood to make it so, working within the constraints I was obliged to accept.'

So it was as simple as that, thought Ken. The man did not have his sympathy. He was wary of spending too much time analysing what he was hearing, for that was not his purpose. The process of distraction – to which Flagg had by no means reacted suspiciously or resentfully – was intended to do just that: divert the agent's concentration from the matter in hand. He was never going to win an intellectual argument on merit with this man, even if he'd been ten times brainier than the tired and retired old Plod he now felt himself to be.

There were, however, echoes here of Jane Moore's reply to his similar question of a few weeks earlier. She too had emphasised the focus on children's needs above those of society – and certainly of teachers. She had acknowledged the extra emphasis on spending in schools and education in general which the Labour government had established but had gone out of her way to avoid fawning over her political masters for their wisdom and generosity. 'God knows it's better than under the Tories,' she'd said, 'but it's not the be all and end all.'

He wondered again whether Jane was the 'Almanac' of the Workers' Gauntlet collective, but decided not to ask. He did not want to disclose knowledge of a possible broader conspiracy, say anything that might anger or upset his captor. He could not allow Flagg to think he might have shared such information! But he would tell Clive of his concern, if and when he - better still, they - came out of this alive.

He wondered if Flagg might have developed differently if parents like Debbie Pearce had said 'thank you' more often. Gratitude was not the touchstone of either politics or education. How many times in his years in the police service had people thanked Ken himself? He could count on the fingers of one hand the occasions he'd heard those words used spontaneously, sincerely and appropriately by a member of the public; on reflection, perhaps he'd heard them only twice. In over thirty years.

Yet there remained a yawning gulf between a culture which struggles to show gratitude, which was explicable if not fair, and a desire to kill those who had brought about a situation for which one might, under more rational circumstances, have been grateful. If he succeeded in doing nothing else before he died, Ken thought, in the chilling knowledge that this eventuality may prove to be not too far away, he'd like to understand how this threat had come about.

How many other Norman Anthony Flaggs were out there?

Anthony, as he'd once been called, had enjoyed all the opportunities of the working class boy made good: a comprehensive education, a passage to University and – undoubtedly – a brain that had been given every encouragement to flourish. The seventies had been a time in which class barriers in Britain had fallen, post-war austerity had been over and amazing new careers had been presented at the feet of young people of his age. More university places, more jobs and the highest levels of aspiration of any generation ever before in history had been absorbed by Flagg and those like him. And he'd spat it back in the face of liberal society.

Perhaps that was the point.

At that very same time, in the sixties and seventies, the Vietnam war had alienated a generation of young people, Americans in particular, more than any event before it or possibly since. This was not because it was a most scandalous political event, an abuse of drafted cannon-fodder, or even because it represented the might of the rich bearing down on the poor of underdeveloped and repressed South East Asia, for none of these things were new or unique.

It was more likely because in the late sixties and early seventies images of that war were being beamed into homes across the world on a daily basis. In World War Two people were fed only a sanitised version, days after each event, but no more; folk could read what was happening now in their newspapers, see moving colour images of war, with their own eyes, in their own front rooms, for the very first time.

Technology, which became the deciding factor of every military conflict which followed Vietnam, had brought about new levels of transparency and accountability which worked to undermine public confidence in the perpetrators of war, to their tangible detriment. Truth was always the first casualty of war and never had been this more clear than now, as far as the increasingly sceptical western public was concerned. Through *Apocalypse Now* and *The Deer Hunter* devastating contemporary events had been portrayed in popular, credible fiction, not to mention technicolor, in ways that had never been possible so immediately before. The trend in cinema was to glorify violence: severed limbs, still twitching, were ten-a-penny on the silver screen and it was not only bureaucrats who were portrayed as faceless. This meant that viewers could be informed not just of the statistical facts but of the horrible reality behind them, too.

All this was happening well before the never-ending day of twenty-four-hour rolling news and the new phenomenon of social media had even dawned.

Yet it was not war alone which had disturbed the young Flagg. He was living proof that the age of the mercenary, men prepared to take up weapons for a cause, was not dead. It was the politics behind war, and this too – in Ken's eyes – could often not withstand the scrutiny which new media had now made possible.

These musings were taking up time, time that Ken could not spare. There was no clock in the room and his wristwatch was inaccessible. He'd been stationary sufficiently long now to have aching thighs, knees and shoulders but he had little concept of how many minutes or hours he'd been in the flat or how long it would be until... until something happened.

He thought again of Anthony Flagg, as he had been in his University days. The polemic, the ranting, the certainty which Peter had described earlier now fitted into a clear pattern. So too, bizarrely, did Flagg's previously puzzling involvement with the army. He had actively sought training with guns, experienced living rough, engaged with military strategy, all experiences which he would deploy in what had once been the future but which had suddenly become today: Sunday, 25th September, 2005.

No doubt the weapon in front of him now was carefully selected for the job in hand and had been acquired surreptitiously.

It all made a sort of sense: a thirty year operation was reaching its climax. A plan where the outcome and duration could only have been postulated in the last few years, perhaps only for the three years in which Flagg had been living in Sussex, so close to the regular biennial venue for the Labour Party Conference. Perhaps today was precisely the reason why the teacher had come to live in the county in the first place: to prepare, to scrutinise, to fine-tune his plans...

Almost on cue to fill the silence, another squall of windy rain rattled the window.

Ken looked up.

The gun was a truly magnificent machine.

In a different context, perhaps a museum, Ken would have admired its craftsmanship, its delicacy, the power it oozed from every joint and limb. It was well greased and cared for, possibly new. It was definitely a long range hunting rifle with a limited repeat facility. Apart from being great for hunting from a significant distance, it had all the features required of a classic sniper's weapon. It was mounted on a heavy tripod and aimed into the street; at almost every moment Flagg's trigger finger was less than a second away from where it needed to be.

'Tell me about the gun. Where did you get it?'

'It wasn't difficult. I assembled it here. Over several weeks, earlier this year. It's a Russian design, a Mosim-Nagent bolt action, if you must know. This particular one was actually made in Finland and it's quite old.'

'I thought it looked new!'

'It's well looked after. The basic design is over a hundred years old, this one's probably thirty.'

'So you brought it into this flat piece by piece, long before the police raised their pre-conference security operation.'

'Exactly, though I'd acquired it when I lived in London. The police are much more interested in the conference site than in anything that might overlook it. They've given me no hassle at all up here.'

'You purchased the gun on the internet?'

'I made the initial contact with the person who was selling it there, yes.'

'Probably not through E-bay.'

'No, not E-bay.'

'You've had this flat for what, a couple of years?'

Flagg flashed a rare but emotion-free glance at his captive. 'You've been doing some homework.'

Ken had indeed, but to admit as much could alert his captor to a possible – yet regrettably non-existent – plan to use the pensioner as bait to flush out and apprehend the would-be assassin.

'Not really. It was little more than a guess. You've been living in the area for three years, and your house – you'll have guessed that Peter was going to go to some lengths, however unofficially, to try to find you – but your house in the village has the air of a second home about it. Doesn't feel lived in, know what I mean? You seem to have almost as many possessions here as you do there! This is where you live now, isn't it? Your home?'

Although even this home was sparse, Ken thought. Flagg was clearly used to living on basics, as one would expect from an undercover agent in the field.

'I didn't want to draw attention to my presence here; the best way to do that is to be out in the open, become familiar to people locally, part of the street furniture, melt into the background. Not be someone who's just in this neighbourhood for this particular week.'

Ken smiled. 'So you've spent your weekends here for the past two years, getting yourself seen and engaging with what local community there is in this part of Brighton. Drinking in the pubs, breakfast in the café up the road, I'll bet. Very clever, very patient, if you don't mind me saying.'

Flagg appeared to relish the compliment modestly, without looking directly at his inquisitor. He nodded. Ken continued: 'A Head teacher not only has more influence over the way children are educated than a classroom teacher does, he also has a high degree of professional mobility. Is that why you chose your particular career path?'

'You make it sound as though I've always had today's outcome in mind! Well, I haven't. I was doing a good job in the East End, working with some of the most deprived communities in the country, giving a real chance in life to those kids growing up like I did, living in places ignored by the 'benevolence of capitalism'. Bethnal Green hadn't experienced the brave new world of the Blair Project in the late 1990s - and nor, with their high levels of immigrant children, children of asylum seekers, abject poverty, were they ever likely to, either. Capitalism needs an underclass, the system can't survive without it, and those children were the underclass. Blair and his cronies were never in the business of challenging the heart of capitalism.'

'Well, perhaps that's true, but -'

'Me and my colleagues were working our rocks off every day, every night, through every school holiday to give them the first step up the ladder. To teach them English for their convenience, give them skills, linguistic confidence, show them respect. People who are given no respect won't show it to others. Throughout our industrial and post-industrial history the working class and the underclass have rarely been granted that minimal human kindness, that's how I read it.'

Ken wondered whether the 'colleagues' were professional or political. The East End was the home of the Workers' Gauntlet, he recalled, of Arthur Birch. Again, to hint that he had some knowledge of the cabal, or of Birch himself, would be unwise.

At least the man was talking again, and that was good.

'When I realised what I had to do I knew I'd got to step up the ladder. Going from Deputy to Head gave me more flexibility, more control over my life, more access, made me better available to fulfil my political destiny. And guess what? Your friend, Peter, emerged right on cue and gave me that chance.'

Another brief glance showed Flagg to be smiling. What did he mean? Was Peter part of this conspiracy?

'So you knew that it was Peter's school before you applied there?'

'Oh, yes. I applied in early 2002. I looked on the internet for schools within sixty miles of Brighton which had vacancies - his stood out a mile. Perfect location, perfect situation, the opportunity to be wonderfully anonymous. They sent me the application form and the school details, and there on the headed paper it said: 'Chair of Governors: Peter Elder.' Now, Peter isn't one – never was – for hiding his light under a bushel. It wasn't difficult to work out that this was my childhood and University comrade. So I wrote to him - '

'You wrote to him?' Ken was surprised. 'Before you were appointed?'

'Didn't he tell you that? A courtesy letter, addressed to him 'personal: care of the school'. I told him that I'd be applying but that I wasn't seeking special favours. I didn't want him to realise who I was only on the day of the interview. In that situation it would've been understandable if he'd reacted by covering his honourable back and feeling he had to refuse me the job. Insider dealing, nepotism, he'd want to avoid such accusations. I knew that I was good enough to be appointed on merit and I didn't want to miss the chance, so I asked him for a fair crack of the whip. It was just too good to miss.'

'I didn't know you'd written to him. He didn't tell me.'

'I had no reply to my letter so I didn't mention it at the interview. But he was evidently not surprised to see me, so I was pretty sure he'd got the message. Actually, I think he said he actually told the interview panel that he knew me - to protect himself, so that he couldn't later be accused of favouritism.'

'Even though it'd been twenty years...'

'Yes, back in my Labour Party days, before I knew any better. Everyone assumes that if you knew someone once, especially in politics, you not only have blood ties which last for ever but think the same way as them. Don't they?'

'So you really hadn't seen him for twenty years, since University?'

Flagg craned his neck to see further out of the window, his face totally hidden for a moment. His reply was enigmatic:

'Is that what he told you? Then that must be right.'

Ken was disturbed by this ambiguity and the clipped finality of the statement. There was no gallery here for Flagg to play to, so he was either being mischievous in his reply – which appeared to be out of character – or he was hiding something. Either way, resolving that conundrum could wait until the Golf Club this evening or... or otherwise.

Ken changed tack.

'Do you have family, Norman?'

'If you mean wife and kids, no, never. It wouldn't have been fair to them. I needed my time, my money, my energy for my work.'

And they would have been a security risk, thought Ken.

Flagg went on: 'Being a teacher gave me time and money. Energy is something I've never lacked.'

'And what form has your 'work' taken over the years?'

Flagg was puzzled: 'Teaching, as you know. You said your wife was a teacher.'

'She was, yes. No, I meant your... 'political' work, if I can call it that.'

'For many years I had no 'political work'. Yes, I was reading, thinking, occasionally writing for one journal or another, usually short pieces, often anonymously. When I started teaching the Thatcher regime would drum you out of the classroom for political incorrectness, given half a chance. That was the way of the Tories, if you weren't 'one of us' – isn't that the way she saw it? Anyway, I was dedicated to my teaching and I didn't want to lose what was a great job.'

'No one's ever suggested that you were ever anything but professional. An excellent teacher, by all accounts.'

'Professional? Thank you.'

The humility sounded genuine.

'So what changed? What set you on course for today?'

For the first time Flagg fell silent in response to a question. He glanced at his feet and up again at the street before turning to the prostrate Ken Hemmings, manacled to a chair.

'Nine-eleven.'

'The Twin Towers...? You said you had nothing to do with Al Qaeda.'

'I don't. 9/11 was my fortieth birthday, September the eleventh, two thousand and one. My coming of age. It was like it was a message, especially for me: 'This is what you have to do'. Not exactly a message, I'm not claiming divine intervention, more... an inspiration.'

There was another pause, in which it seemed Norman was re-living the moment. Two commercial aircraft, full of people, en route from Boston to Los Angeles, were deliberately flown into each of the twin towers of the global trade centre, twenty minutes apart, on a busy New York morning. A third hijacked plane crashed into the Pentagon, and a fourth came down in a Pennsylvania field, missing its presumed target of Washington, DC. The suicide hijackers had been Muslim extremists, the world was told, agents of Osama bin Laden and Al Qaeda.

Amongst almost three thousand dead were people of every religion and none, every political viewpoint, every sense of values and every colour of skin.

It was not only for Norman Anthony Flagg that the world had changed forever on that day, thought Ken. The war in Afghanistan and the removal of the Taliban by military force had been a direct consequence, justifiably or otherwise, and the incident would forever be regarded also as a precursor to the 2003 War Against Terror which had targeted Iraq. How different things might have been for the world, thought Ken, had Bush senior completed the Gulf War of 1991 more clinically and removed Saddam Hussein from power at that time.

A world had developed since then in which conventional wars were no longer fought between states and their armies. They happened within states against movements of people who were prepared to kill for their political, moral and religious convictions, who represented more or less popular causes and fought against more or less competent, more or less powerful regimes of different levels of legitimacy in more or less stable countries. It was a world in which the pawns were fighting each other as the rooks and knights directed, with Kings and Queens engaging only rarely, only when it suited them, whilst all the time the royalty decided the very rules upon which each war was fought.

In the Middle East, Somalia, Sudan and Darfur, in Burma, Nepal, Sri Lanka, along African borders and the cocaine trails of the Andes the war was fought. More people have died in battle since the Second World War than did during it.

In places like Ethiopia and the Horn of Africa starvation and drought were the enemies, their attacks made more potent by the way the rich were abusing the global climate. Failing states punished their own through lack of will, desire or capacity to do otherwise. In the Balkans and Sierra Leone rape and pillage became 'normal' weapons of social control. Trade injustice, the mother of missed opportunities, ensured that the world's pecking order could not change.

Yes, thought Ken, it was indeed an unfair world.

Although, he had to admit, the world had occasionally experienced moments where narrow shafts of sunlight exposed a silver lining: the world was at last talking about its problems, its economy, its trade, its climate, and fewer blatant wars were being fought today between countries than had been the case for 50 years. The talk was of rescuing failing states before they collapsed and in some instances – in Northern Ireland, the Balkans and Rwanda, the site of the planet's biggest ever act of genocide – the very worst of human behaviour had been consigned to the history books.

There were reasons to be, if not cheerful, at least hopeful. He kept coming back to the fact that progress could and must be achieved without resorting to murdering the leaders of the democratic world.

Ken resumed the conversation in hushed tones, almost out of deference for the dead of the Twin Towers and beyond.

'That event stung everyone, Norman. I remember it very well, we all do. Everyone knows where they were on that day, it's the sort of memory that clings. We get just one or two in a lifetime. There was Kennedy, of course, in '63. John Lennon, 1981. Elvis Presley - was it '77? August, anyway. Though Elvis wasn't murdered, of course. Hundreds of innocent people died on 9/11. For most of the world it inspired people to organise *against* terrorism, not to become terrorists. But for you? What exactly did it do for you?'

'I saw the second crash live on television. Yes, many people were moved one way or another and you're right, not many will have responded in the way that I had to. But I'm not a terrorist.'

'No? So you're a 'freedom fighter', then?'

'I see no need for such labels.'

'Now look, I know the riddle 'What's the difference between a terrorist and a freedom fighter?' You know the answer? It's 'Ten years of history.' Mandela. Begin. Gerry Adams and Martin McGuinness. Others… I agree, it's an academic difference and no, I agree again, you don't have to have a label. But a terrorist uses terror, fear, to seek to persuade, doesn't he? So doesn't that make you a terrorist? Really?'

'My target doesn't know I'm here. I've issued no threats, no demands. I'm not using the threat of terror for political ends. No one has been terrorised by me.'

'Not yet! But won't your action today terrorise people?'

'It will scandalise them, momentarily. But because they'll soon realise that if they don't claim to be a leader, a leader selling out the working class to boot, selling out the exploited masses of the whole world, then they've got nothing to fear from me or those who think like me. Assuming I'm ever in a position to represent a threat again to anyone which, frankly, I doubt I will be.'

There was a moment of quiet contemplation. What goes for you goes for me too, thought Ken, in that last respect.

The moment continued. Then:

'Norman, are you telling me that you really are a 'sleeper'? If not Al Qaeda, then who do you represent?'

'No, Mr Hemmings!' Flagg laughed and broke his trance. He re-arranged himself on his chair and after a two-second scrutiny of the troubled pensioner, resumed his watch on the street. It did not stop him talking.

'I wouldn't know an Al Qaeda agent if he jumped out of the street in front of me, that really is a ridiculous suggestion. Al Qaeda operatives have a religious purpose, don't they? I don't. I'm a practical man. But a sleeper? Yes, I suppose I am. I suppose it's like this: what was – how shall I say? – 'beautiful' about 9/11 is the fact that not only did it happen on the symbolic occasion of my fortieth birthday, they say 'life begins at forty', don't they? But it was carried out by a small group of individuals who decided to change the world. They went out and they did just that. They knew that the world was in a bad way, that things weren't as they should be, they just knew it!'

He went on 'Two philosophical points here. I forget the quote, but it's from an American scientist. Something like 'Never doubt that a small group of thoughtful, committed citizens can change the world; indeed, it's the only thing that ever has'. That's so true! And The Butterfly's Wing, do you know that theory? We can learn from physics. The beating of a butterfly's wing in the southern hemisphere can influence the progress of storms and weather patterns even in northern latitudes. Those guys planned together for 9/11 and they did something about it. No bombs, no guns, nothing, just commitment and imagination. Boy, did that butterfly fly!'

'A jumbo jet's more like an albatross than a butterfly.'

'Whatever… It was a small incident with big, unpredictable, unrepeatable consequences.'

'And was it a good thing that they did it?'

'That's not the question, Ken. Let me give you a different analogy: you're playing with dice, right? You throw them. You get a crap result, a one and a two, perhaps, when you need double six' - Flagg raised his fist and mimed the throwing of dice - 'so you need to throw them again, in the hope that something better will come up. By that I mean something better for the world, not something just for me. It might be an act of chance – I understand the mathematics of probability – but unless you actually throw the damn things you'll never know!'

'So you admit you're throwing dice here? You don't know the consequences.'

Ignoring the intervention, Flagg continued.

'Now you only get the chance to really throw those dice, when doing it can potentially change the world, once in a lifetime. And the worse the deal you had before, the more you want to throw better next time, do you see? It might not be a double six, but if the world is starting on double one then whatever you throw cannot possibly be worse than what you've got now. If you have the chance but don't then throw them, you'll go to your grave wondering if you'd actually had that double six in your grasp: you'd spend the rest of your life kicking yourself – if only you had let them roll!'

He turned to Ken and addressed him eye to eye.

'And I don't want that regret on my conscience.'

Ken pondered. Was that traditional emblem of revolution, the clenched fist, not so much a gesture of aggression but the preparatory stage to dice being rolled? Flagg looked away once more.

'So you're saying that what those people did on September the eleventh was just throw the dice. That was all?'

'That's about it! And now it's my turn.'

Ken was momentarily stunned by the clarity of Flagg's case. Over recent weeks he'd discussed ideology and the art of politics more than at any other time in his life, thanks to Peter Elder. But what he was hearing now was not the politics of hope, which had inspired Elder to give a decade of public service, but that of hopelessness.

'Al Qaeda just rolled the dice...?'

'Don't keep asking me about Al Qaeda, Ken! I don't know. I've no connection with them. It is more than possible that I've met people who do know them, but not deliberately. I don't know if those guys who took over those planes were part of any organisation, nor the July seventh guys in London. Possibly they were, possibly not. I read the newspapers, they don't know. Possibly they were all individual freelancers who came together to toss their dice collectively.'

Tossers was indeed the word, thought Ken. No, this was too easy. He was no intellectual, he knew, but the whole thing just couldn't be as simple and straightforward as this appeared to be. What he was hearing was the ultimate expression of power without responsibility.

'But didn't Al Qaeda claim responsibility for September eleventh?'

'So what? It was in their interests to claim responsibility, it increased their profile, their political impact. The guys on the planes are hardly in a position to confirm or deny it, are they?'

'So you're not in contact with any other self-appointed 'liberation' organisation? You're a freelance operator?'

Flagg turned to his inquisitor once more.

'Ken: think about it. We've been talking about chance. Let's talk some more about chance. If the guy I'm looking for walks into the cross wires on that telescopic sight some time today, all hell will break loose. That's not chance, that's certainty. What that hell consists of, how it's expressed, that's chance. I'm only going to get one opportunity to do what I'm going to do and I can't afford to leave it to chance. I have to have certainty – or, at the very least, a high probability that I'm going to be successful in changing the world, liberating the human spirit, helping it find a new and more natural equilibrium. Let's just consider two elements of that hell, that hell which is about to break loose: my death – and your death.'

Ken, chastened, stiffened as far as his bonds allowed, as the chill that had previously run down his spine now ran up it again. So that was what it felt like: nothing in his police career had prepared him for that... thrill? There was really no other word. A callous, stinging, taser thrill.

'Ken Hemmings, listen to me. If I die first in the fracas that follows my action then there's a chance you might survive. Be sure that the police will respond to me and they will respond violently – there's no more dangerous body than a gang of police who've been made to look foolish; you ask that Brazilian guy who tried to get on a tube train two days after July seventh, just a few weeks ago. Jean Charles De Menezes.' Then, mockingly: 'Oh, I forgot: you can't. He's dead.'

This was no time to admit to his own professional calling, thought Ken. At least as a frail old pensioner he might not be suspected as an interloper.

'It might be kinder to you,' Norman went on, more calmly, 'as a parting gesture, if I made sure that your death was clean and dignified.'

Ken could sense that being shot at point blank range whilst lying on the floor cuffed to a Windsor chair might be clean but it offered little in the way of dignity. Flagg's analysis had credibility yet he was taking this threat calmly, he thought. Then he realised that any posse of police that would be deployed within moments of a major political assassination attempt in Brighton would almost certainly include his own son, Inspector Clive Hemmings of the Sussex Constabulary. Clive had said that he'd be on duty today.

'I'm not planning to do that, by the way. As things stand it's not my intention to kill you.'

That was some relief. But could there be worse to come, something worse than instant death?

'Ken, if I'm going to die today, the victim of either a police bullet or my own hand, then I think I want you to be around to tell my story afterwards. It's only if I survive, which I think is unlikely, if I decide to put my escape plan into operation, that your survival might be a threat to me.'

'A variation on the theme of the suicide bomber.'

'Exactly! Suicide's certainly an option, I've got no fear about that, but it's not my first choice. It would be far better than spending years incarcerated in a capitalist jail. I think I said, I don't approve of the concept of prison. People only offend when their society, their environment, forces them to do so. It's not right to deprive them of liberty, the last quality of civilisation.'

'That sounds like anarchy.'

'It's not far off.'

'Are you an anarchist?'

'I wouldn't say so. There are too many rules involved in being an anarchist.'

'You were saying, Norman. I asked if you had ever had contact with Al Qaeda you said 'no' – or any other organisation with a comparable *modus operandi*?'

Flagg stood and walked right up to the window, turning his back fully on Ken Hemmings for a moment, for the first time. He scrutinised the street below then deliberately strode over to his captive.

He reached down to seize the lapels of Ken's jacket, one in each hand, and rolled him over to face him as far as the manacles and the heavy chair allowed. It was not a threatening gesture, it was gentle. He ran his fingers carefully down behind each lapel. He felt inside Ken's inside pockets, removed a wallet, studied it briefly and threw it to the floor. He patted the seated man's trouser pockets peremptorily.

'You're not wired. I didn't think you would be, but I thought I'd better check.'

The would-be assassin resumed his vantage point on the stool by the gun and looked again at the street as he spoke.

'You know,' he said, 'things keep happening on my birthday. Significant things, on significant birthdays. My parents didn't exert much control over me as a teenager. Two elderly relatives died whilst I was in the sixth form and both left money in trust for me, so that I could go to University. My parents were very open minded, they didn't mind not having control, they knew that I was serious, that I wanted to study and travel, too. They were of the school of thought that said 'I want my child to have all the opportunities that I never had' and they said that travel broadened the mind. These were people who'd grown up in the shadow of war, left-leaning people, active in politics, grateful of my political support even if they appeared to take it for granted. Fancy having a son who was not only interested in your politics but who showed all the signs of being passionate about it! It was unheard of for people of my age *not* to rebel against their parents, at least briefly, as a teenager. Yet there I was.'

Ken recalled that neither he, nor Clive, had rebelled against their parents in that way, either. Perhaps we were the deviants.

'Anyway, all this meant that I could see the world. I could do all the things that my parents never did, almost as though I was doing it on their behalf, for them.

'The first visit was to Spain, to engage my mind with the Spanish Civil War... I went to Toledo whilst I was still at school, for Christ's sake. People do it all the time these days but it wasn't normal back then, as you'll recall... yes, I was a rebel! A rebel not only *with* a cause but a rebel with the full backing of his parents.

'I knew the stories: my grandad, Wilf, had told me about the International Brigades. Jack Jones was there, from the Transport Union, Ernest Hemingway, Laurie Lee. George Orwell too. I'd read Homage to Catalonia, I could have been a fucking graduate in Spanish Civil War Studies at 17 years old. Even today, I don't suppose our so-called 'liberal' education establishment would allow 17-year olds to get that deep into anything that political. But you know what I mean. I'd delayed going there whilst Franco was still alive - my grandad would've disowned me if I'd set foot on Fascist soil while the bastard was still breathing!

'Two things happened in Spain. First, I realised that real fascism was still alive and well in the so-called 'civilised' world. You only have to read the plaques on the wall at the Alcazar, the castle destroyed by the civil war and rebuilt by Franco. Don't bother with what they say - just look at who they're from... Reading those tributes to the Generalissimo really turned my guts, it was all I could do to stop retching. It frightened me.

'At 17 I'd chosen a few labels to describe myself and 'socialist' was one. It wasn't just that some people *weren't* socialists that upset me, I understood that; and that some people would fight against socialism, I knew that, too. It was that forty years after the Civil War there were people in Britain, America, France, Western Europe who held Franco and his thugs up as heroes. It just stunned me.

'And then I witnessed a bomb going off. My schoolboy vanity thought they were trying to bomb me! I was walking down a street in Santander when a car exploded a few yards from me, putting me in hospital. Now they were real fascists, in the guise of Cantabrian Nationalism. My second life-changing experience within a week, an experience that committed me to the cause I believe in and brought me here to Brighton today, training a gun on a door across the street: all the time haunted by this!'

He turned to face Ken and gave a thumbs-up gesture with his right hand, wrist twisted, mouth set tight. Ken saw the angry man's point straight away: the scarred and shortened thumb had no nail.

'A constant reminder, every waking hour, of every day, I see this!'

His voice grew louder as his explanation developed: 'This is what those feeble excuses for fascist terrorists did to me! This is all they could do. In their trophy cabinet in Santander, those sons of the fucking Nationalists who won that bloody civil war, they have the thumbnail of a teenage boy, who just happened to be passing when their fucking bomb went off! Did the tip of my thumb secure a state for the Cantabrians? No! Did it release their colleagues from slavery, or imprisonment? Did it change things one iota? Did it buggery!'

By now he was raving, but also, seemingly, under control:

'Or did it alert the world to the injustices that were happening in Spain during the transition to democracy, highlighting that classic western dilemma that with democracy comes uncertainty? Did it highlight the fact that uncertainty prompted a desire in some people then, and even now, to return to the stability that totalitarian dictatorship represents? Maybe...

'Did it cause international conferences to be convened, debates to take place in the Security Council or blue-helmeted peacekeepers to be deployed on the streets of Madrid? Did it fuck!'

The expostulations – urgent, but retained at a volume which would attract no attention from outside the flat – appeared to have temporarily exhausted Flagg. He sat once more, regained his composure, cleared his throat and sipped from a can.

Meanwhile, outside the window little of significance appeared to have happened.

At last Ken had seen evidence of the anger that must motivate all who step outside the rules to support their cause. This passion had been fermenting inside the man for thirty years; today was possibly one of the very few occasions that he'd ever expressed himself in this manner to another person.

Flagg was back at the window, seated, speaking again, mumbling, his mind focussed on the street outside.

'I'm sorry, Norman, I didn't catch that.'

'I said: my experience in Santander made me vow that when the time came I would make a better job of it.'

'And that time has come?'

'That's right.'

There was silence again. With his hands still immobilised and watch still hidden Ken had completely lost track of the time. The sunlight was now entering the window from above the Conference Centre, a significantly more westerly direction than when he'd entered the room. He must have been here about two hours. At that moment a distant church clock struck three times: it had been even longer than he'd thought.

For several minutes the silence persisted. Ken yearned for a cup of tea, a longing made worse by the sight of the kettle, the tea bags and the mug on the table behind the gun. And the biscuits. Over those minutes, as his adrenalin levels subsided from the ceiling to something just above normal, he also realised that he needed the toilet and was feeling uncomfortable. He decided, on balance, against making a scene. It was best not to present any difficulty to his captor. If needs be, the old man and his prostate would pee in his trousers, he thought, rather than challenge Flagg by seeking to have his handcuffs removed or have a would-be murderer unzip his fly for him.

Outside a rapid and repeated 'fleck, fleck, fleck' indicated that a helicopter was passing over the street. Flagg leaned forward and craned his neck to see it.

Ken noted that the rain was now coming down steadily.

As the noise subsided he said 'They're checking the route. It's routine. It won't be long now.'

The helicopter flew away like a bee seeking fresh nectar.

After several more moments Ken felt, for the first time, the temptation to be bored. Engagement, he reminded himself, engagement.

'Excuse me, Norman' he ventured, 'I didn't quite follow. I asked you about Al Qaeda and you replied that significant things happen on your birthday. But I don't see how those two things fit with the story you told about Spain. Was the bomb... on your birthday?'

'No, it wasn't. It was in July, start of the school holiday. My injuries didn't even get me a day off school.'

Ken chuckled. He hoped it sounded sympathetic,

'I was very bright at school. I did Sociology, French and Russian at 'A' level. There are a lot of immigrant communities in Luton, more so now than back then in the seventies, but it was significant. I met a lot of people who'd escaped from persecution in their home countries. Many of them came to the Labour Party for understanding and advice, even if there was little that we could give in the way of help.

'I met a man in Luton who became very important to me, my friend over many years, my political teacher. He's... dead now. He was a Muslim, with family roots in several countries. His name was Aqbar. He told me stories about the Muslim people. He also spoke Russian, he'd spent some time living there, went to University there. He was the only Russian-speaker I met during the whole time I was studying the language, apart from my teacher, so I started going to his house for Russian conversation. It was great for my studies. Aqbar even told me some of his stories in Russian, my understanding became that good.

'The stories included the history of Iraq, for example. People aren't aware that British imperialism is to blame for what's been going on there recently. It may have been the Americans courting Saddam in the seventies, backing him in wars against Iran throughout the 80s, but it was the British who set the scene. Think about it: you draw an international boundary such that there are significant portions of the population from three different and incompatible 'tribes', Sunni Muslims, Shi-ite Muslims and Kurds, such that none are in a majority. The outcome is either anarchy or a dictator who will, in effect, divide and rule, by treating each group equally - equally badly.

'So Aqbar told me that story. He also told me of Britain's abject failure to resolve the Palestine question, in 1948. He'd lived in Hebron for a while, his son lives there now, but he left during the six-day war in '67 when Israel stole the West Bank and Gaza. Now *that* was a story, and it's not over yet...

'In October 1979 I joined a few older friends from Luton to chill out in India for a few weeks. It was all the rage at that time. As I said, my parents didn't mind, they encouraged me. I visited Amritsar, as I said earlier. At one point we visited an ashram: that peace and love crap didn't really appeal to me, it was my friends' idea. After a few days I was bored but the guys wanted to stay on. The idea of setting out on my own didn't really appeal to me. I hadn't done as well as I'd hoped at 'A' level – sailed through the Russian, wasn't so hot on the others – and I'd got in to East of England through clearing. However, I'd delayed going there by a year so was in no hurry to get home.'

This confirmed Peter Elder's story.

'I remembered that Aqbar had friends in Kabul and I'd found that I could switch flights to get a stopover in Afghanistan on my way home. I phoned Aqbar in Luton, told him what I wanted to do. He said he'd help but I heard nothing more from him – there were no mobile phones in those days, so communication wasn't easy.

'Got to Kabul and a bus took the passengers from the airport to the hotel, armed guards everywhere. The manager shook everyone by the hand and said 'hello'. He explained about the curfew and gave some cock and bull story that the blonds shouldn't leave the hotel at all - because of the danger of Mujaheddin snipers thinking they were Russian and shooting them. I think he reckoned he'd sell more beer if no one left the hotel.

'Anyway, I'm not blond. Aqbar hadn't been in touch. I'd nowhere else to go and it was getting dark by the time we arrived so I decided to stay indoors, anyway. Not all the hotel staff spoke English but my Russian helped me get by. The nominal government of

Afghanistan at that time was very pro-Russian but there was some… instability. The manager was murdered by the Russians a few weeks later.'

Flagg allowed himself a chuckle of recollection.

'I've just remembered! There was an American guy, talked non-stop, latched on to me like a fucking limpet. He thought I could speak Pushtu!' He smiled, for the first time. 'Because I'd spoken to a waiter in Russian! What a wanker.'

The smile disappeared.

'Halfway through the meal the waiter told me I had a visitor. The man's name was Ahady, said he was a friend of Aqbar. That was good enough for me. I spent four days as the honoured guest of the Mujaheddin, people committed to winning back their country from Russian influence. They were pariahs in the British press at that time, but they were right and I learned a lot. On my last night in Kabul Ahady let me go out with a sniper squad. We bagged a Russian soldier. A few weeks later the Russians invaded.'

There was a silence.

'So did you…?'

'No. I've never killed anyone. Not until today. That doesn't mean I don't know how to use a gun. My first training was there, in Kabul, that week. Then I took the rather unusual decision to join the army training unit at University.'

Another piece of the jigsaw.

'After a few days I flew back to England not very much later than I'd expected to.'

'Afghanistan's a mess now, isn't it?'

'Oh, yes. It went sour, as things often do. They got rid of the Russians in the end, but it took years. The Taliban were a disappointment, worse in many ways. There's a saying, isn't there, 'my enemy's enemy is my friend'? It's not true. Friends are fewer and further between than that. That whole episode made me think that it's the getting there that's the aim, the purpose, the goal. Once you've achieved what you set out for, it invariably disappoints and you have to start the process all over again.'

'Killing people?'

'If necessary. Strategically. I don't like the idea of killing innocent people though - '

'But what was it you said about 9/11?'

'Let me finish, Ken. I said there has to be a strategy. You can't show the ultimate futility of capitalism without considering whether the destruction of a capitalist icon – like the Twin Towers – should be part of the strategy. The people were not the target, that's so, so clear.'

'In Bali it was a night club, Norman, in Madrid a train. Innocent people, every time. So many.'

'I can't answer for others' choice of targets. You'll have noticed that for my mission I've chosen the clinical approach - a high calibre rifle, not a messy bomb. But if my analysis is right, surgery has to be carried out to repair a deep seated malaise in the body politic. I'll trust the judgement of my fellow surgeons to use bullet, bomb – or aeroplane.'

'Is that how you see yourself? A surgeon?'

'It was Aqbar's analogy. He was a doctor in Lebanon before he came to Luton.'

'You said he's dead now?'

'I've never told anyone that story before, about Afghanistan, because it could be traced back to Aqbar. He'd have been hunted, harassed, punished and humiliated for his wisdom, even as an old man. But the forces of evil can't catch him now. He's gone to where he believed he'd be happy, at peace with Allah. He died... on my birthday, September eleventh. Two weeks ago.'

Flagg granted a moment's silence to his friend's memory.

After a few seconds Ken said 'He meant a lot to you.'

'Yes. He was a wise man.'

'And the coincidence of the date...'

'I'd already decided to do what I had to do. He knew that, so he died happy, despite the way it happened...'

'Despite what?'

There was a tear in the gunman's eye. 'I think he was murdered. I can't prove it, but he died in great pain. They said he had a heart condition and a simple stomach upset proved too much for him.'

'Well, that's possible.'

'It is. But I think the food poisoning was botulism. I think it came from a needle, the day before he died. He wouldn't be the first to die like that.'

'Who would do that?'

'In Luton? The British Government, of course. Aqbar had too many friends.'

'How old was he?'

'I don't know... 78? But he was a young man in his ailing heart.'

Ken decided not to pursue this line of conversation. Either it was bonkers, irrational and paranoid – or it was true. How could he tell which?

'Would you become a Muslim, Norman?'

'No, definitely not. I've no need for religion, never have. Religions are used to oppress and control, all of them, far too often for any to retain any credibility as agents of liberation. Are you religious?'

'No, I'm C of E. I'm sorry, that's a... family joke. I'm 'on their books', I suppose, but I don't go to church.'

There was no radio or television in the room. No newspapers lying on exposed surfaces. No telephone, landline or mobile, was obvious and no computer could be seen.

There was no connection between this room and the outside world.

This time the silence was longer than its predecessors.

Ken was reluctant to let his mind wander, which could only hurt. To make matters even worse it was patently clear that no cup of tea was about to materialise. Somewhere in the recesses of Ken Hemmings' memory something stood out like a sore thumb... a sore... it was indeed a damaged thumb, attached to a hand, attached to a loutish picket: Clapstone Colliery, 1984. Could it really be that he and Norman had met once before? Surely not. Lots of people have damaged thumbs - on their right hands - don't they?

Norman Flagg sat upright and stared more attentively as a police car, siren blaring, sped down West Street and turned right onto the sea front.

The temporary crisis of silence was over.

'So. It's twenty years since you had... contact... with the sort of people whom the press might call 'terrorists'.'

'Apart from my friend Aqbar, you mean? They would tar him with that brush.'

'Of course. But he wasn't... I mean, he was in Luton.'

'You're saying there are no terrorists in Luton?' Flagg smiled again.

'I think you know what I mean, Norman.'

'I didn't say it'd been twenty years. It's true that I did my research and earned my qualifications. After University I went to do some, let's call it 'postgraduate study'. In Bosnia, and in Africa.'

'My God. You were a mercenary?'

'Not exactly. As I said, I've never killed anyone before. Even today, I've nothing against the man himself, Blair, it's what he represents, what he is.'

'If you weren't a mercenary, what were you?'

'I helped support the forces of good, the people's forces. Hospital support, even PR.'

'Where were you in Africa?'

'Several places, very much behind the scenes. Civil wars can be very messy and white faces like mine stand out in a very unhelpful way.'

'So when was this?'

'Early eighties. You've seen my CV - it shows that I came into teaching late, some years after qualifying. My CV says that it was -'

'Voluntary Service.'

'Voluntary Service. You've seen it.'

'Of course.'

Norman sighed.

'Blair could be here at any minute. That's a pity... I've been enjoying our conversation.'

Narcissists always enjoy talking about themselves, thought Ken. But he could envisage no conclusion other than that which Flagg had planned. If only he could communicate with the Prime Minister, or even with his own son. He tried his very best to speak to them through the medium of telepathy, pleading from the heart, but he had no idea of whether the warning was getting through.

'What about recently, then? Are you in touch with anybody in 'the trade'?'

'I can't possibly give names, even to you or in a situation like this, but I have been doing my homework. For example, I spent a summer in North Belfast and a month in the Occupied Territory. This is what I've been doing for the last few summers, since 9/11. You might call it 'Work experience'.'

'Identifying directly with people with experience of oppression?'

'You're getting the gist, Mr Hemmings.'

'What specifically did you do there?'

'Where?'

'Let's start with Belfast.'

'I spent a few weeks as a community development volunteer. I was with a community centre in a Catholic area where most males were ex-internees, the press would call them murderers. That made it difficult for them to – wait a minute!'

Something in the street had caught his attention.

'No more questions.'

Nimble as an athlete, Flagg was instantaneously transformed into a shooting pose. His right hand was ready to fire, index curled against the trigger, abbreviated thumb pointing upwards for balance, the rest of the fist tucked under the stock and the right shoulder engaged to absorb the kickback and keep the focus. The left hand was elegantly allowing the barrel to rest upon it: the sight, on the tip of the silver barrel, was immaculately lined up with Flagg's nose and his piercing eye, which now took intractable aim. No longer was this a man with a weapon, thought Ken: it was a single, unified killing machine.

The distance between the retired policeman and the assassin was perhaps twelve feet. Four yards. More than one hundred impenetrable inches which a man chained to a large Windsor chair could never cross in time to prevent the tragedy that now loomed.

Even if he could move, what use could he be, what could he achieve? He might dislodge the gunman temporarily, but in a fight between a pensioner attached to a large chair lying and a fit man in his forties fired with adrenalin there could be only one winner, no matter how consistently and passionately this terrorist might normally side with the underdog.

It occurred to Ken that Flagg was intending to shoot from inside the window. Perhaps a thin pane of glass would be invisible to a high-powered weapon such that its brief impact would not deter the bullet by an inch. The weapon probably had a massive range, was far more powerful than what was necessary for Flagg to achieve his goal.

Flagg, intent, flinched. His finger visibly tightened on the trigger as somewhere inside the metal creature a spring succumbed to pressure.

'Oh, no...' Ken said quietly, his eyes closed, sensing warm urine running down his thigh as the crotch of his trousers became damp.

Before he could register another thought Ken witnessed in slow motion the event he'd been dreading ever since identifying the machine as a gun. The most outrageous assassination of modern times, more significant even than that in Sarajevo a century before, was happening,... And he, Inspector Hemmings of this Parish, could have stopped it.

There was a small explosion and microscopic splinters of glass seemed to fill the room. As they flew through the air like smoke the rest of the world was frozen and the needle of noise stuck in its groove.

There was a brief shard of silence before the stasis was released. Flagg had a rictus grin on his face which looked almost painful. He took a short, sharp, post-orgasmic breath.

Ken couldn't see what Flagg had done, but he knew what was supposed to have happened: he closed his eyes.

He could have stopped it, but he had not.

He could have stopped it, but he hadn't known how.

He had let it happen.

He was suddenly a much older man than he wanted to be.

Although it was only a moment it felt like an age.

Then a much bigger, second explosion blasted his senses and Ken naturally assumed that he had died.

Chapter 12: Aftermath/Spine

They call it white noise. Static.
Still.

Or perhaps it was the wind, blowing through the trees?

Still.
In the clouds.
White figures moving against a white background.

He was woozy, unfocussed, warm, but he was alive.
Lying down.
Soft.
'Shtungrenay.'

'Sorr…?'
'Dad? Are you awake?'
'Way… ek.'
'I was just saying, the doctor said you might be able to hear me. The stun grenade knocked you out.'
'Wha-as a stern?'
'It was a stun grenade that put you in here. I'm… sorry about that.'
'Pardon?'
'The stun grenade's affected your hearing, it's quite a blow, it's like… well, you can tell what it's like.'
'Yez…'
'They say there's no permanent damage, Dad.'
'A-right…'
'It's normal to sleep as much as this. After what you've been through.'
There was an edge to Clive's voice which was not reassuring.
'Dad…'
Ken was asleep again. It was approaching midnight. He'd already been unconscious for many hours.

The trilby, which had tumbled across the floor when Ken was tripped, had done its job. The transmitter hidden in its headband was little bigger than a needle; it had been remotely activated to relay a crackly signal for an hour and a half before its power had failed.

In a multi-storey car park in central Brighton, closed to the public for the duration of the Party Conference, a team of experts in a portakabin had detected the signal from the hat and they set about pin-pointing its source. The men from the intelligence unit had established, to within a few yards, which building that Ken was in, barely twenty minutes after he'd entered it.

It had taken a while to establish which windows corresponded to the exact room he was in, of all those overlooking the street, and to set up the necessary equipment on the car park roof without being seen. The target was eventually identified as on the second floor of the building, which was fifty metres east of the conference centre's emergency exit. That was forty metres, as the laser beam flies, from the officer who was now deployed to lie flat on a hotel roof, in blustery rain, behind a low parapet.

The officer carefully trained his vibration detector on a pane in the chosen window. This laser device would measure tiny vibrations of the window pane, identifying windows behind which speech might be taking place, though some types of glass and window frame lend themselves to rattling like an audio speaker better than others. It was more difficult with an older property, like this one, where different panes in the same window often exhibited different properties. Listening to the actual goings-on in the targeted room would rely largely on trial and error.

Although he couldn't see inside the room the officer could not assume that the reverse was true: he knew not how many people were inside although it was assumed to be just the perp and the old man. The officer also knew that either or both of them might panic if they saw a human figure on this very roof, directly across the street.

Dressed in black, the officer made sure his profile didn't break the skyline. Keeping prostrate, he edged his device ever closer to the parapet which was, helpfully, slightly higher above the ground than the target window.

Alongside the super laser microphone was a tiny TV camera, enabling him to fine tune the settings and direction of the device remotely, using a joystick and a screen no bigger than that of a mobile phone.

No technology is perfect. An hour after being despatched he was still patiently trying to get a clean signal.

Then he settled. What he heard reminded him of life as a teenager trying to hear to Radio Luxemburg, late at night, on medium wave, on an unreliable transistor radio, with fading batteries, under the blankets. This would be as good as it would get, it would have to do. After a while, what he thought he was seeing and hearing caused sufficient concern for him to radio to central control that there could be a gun mounted in the second floor room.

Operation Spine moved into top gear.

At two-thirty that Sunday the Conference had started without the Prime Minister present. This was not unusual - the busy man's keynote speech was not scheduled until the Tuesday afternoon. The Party Chair welcomed delegates and the local Mayor added her greetings, too. Tony Blair would be driven into Brighton shortly, from an undisclosed location, and was scheduled to head directly to the Conference Centre via the fire exit on West Street. However, the 'divert' protocol was now invoked by a Police Superintendent. This plan, prepared in case demonstrations around the Centre got out of hand, took the Prime Minister's entourage to the rear entrance of the Grand Hotel instead, west of the Conference area, at the opposite end to where the amusement arcade and the officer on the roof were situated. Although the PM would now be safe they now needed to deal with a frustrated assassin in possession of a hostage. The assassin might or might not intercept an alternative target - but he would want blood.

Two plain clothes officers quietly convened within the amusement arcade and calmly instructed the management to close the doors and keep everyone inside. They insisted that the machines, and their quasi-musical output, should be left active. In the street, other officers monitored the flow of pedestrians. A code word was used to ensure that only uniformed police officers would use the target door to the rear of the conference centre which was not, in any case, ever intended to be used by casual traffic. Non-essential use was now forbidden and all pedestrian access to the west side of West Road was routinely, unostentatiously, halted, hoping that the assassin would not notice. The oncoming rain would provide the police operation with helpful cover.

Within twenty minutes of the contents of the flat having been established - one gun, one assassin, one hostage, one hat with a radio transmitter in the headband - the PM had entered the Conference Centre via the alternative route. The two officers on routine duty at the West Road emergency entrance, wearing conventional helmets and raincoats, were quietly replaced by newcomers wearing bullet-proof riot helmets with heavy duty protection under day-glo yellow jackets; they were covertly armed. A trained observer would regard their slightly different attire as within the realm of 'normal' in this security-conscious age.

Now that the conference had started the crowds around the front entrance to the Brighton Centre were subsiding, so the situation could be better assessed.

An hour previously the Duty Superintendent had instructed Inspector Clive Hemmings to stand down from active duty as the situation had become clear. Clive was, however, allowed to remain in the nearby control room from where the neutralisation of the threat was being overseen. 48 hours previously Clive had followed his conscience, passing on his father's concerns to colleagues in Intelligence. The men from the shadows in London had already identified the subject. Norman Flagg's code name, for the last twenty years, had been 'Spine' - it had more of a ring to it than 'Thumb' - and they knew that he had intermittently re-emerged over recent years after long periods of obscurity. However, the security forces had not, hitherto, definitely identified him as a potential threat. Once it was clear from Clive Hemmings' reports that Spine had been AWOL for the whole summer, leaving his school colleagues in the lurch in an uncharacteristically irresponsible manner, eyebrows were raised and risk analyses carried out. A flight into Tel Aviv was identified, taken just a month previously, which was not in itself suspicious - but Spine had stayed just a single night in a Jerusalem hotel before disappearing until the return flight just a few days ago. Sources embedded within Hamas (and Hezbollah, for good measure) were asked what they knew of Spine but neither could report a positive sighting.

On Friday 23rd September, two days prior to today's stand-off, Clive Hemmings had been summoned to his Superintendent's office to be briefed by two men from Scotland Yard. They were concerned.

'We think of sleepers as like buzz bombs in the blitz, the ones that did all the damage to London,' the older man had said. He had silver hair and a silver tie, a crisply folded white handkerchief peeking out of the breast pocket of his pitch black suit. 'As long as you can hear their little motors buzzing they aren't a problem. The time to get worried is when they suddenly go silent. It means a bang's about to happen.'

Clive was told that Spine had been at school when he first came to the authorities' attention, at a time, 1977, when the Cold War was raging. A Home Office informant, a member of the same trade union branch as Flagg's father, had logged his concern that his socialist friend's son not only had an unhealthy interest in revolutionary movements around the world but was also studying Russian. As a result of that intelligence precisely nothing had happened. This was normal practice, not least as the person of interest was a minor. For a while, his file consisted of a single line of text about his Russian interest but then another was added, to the effect that he'd been wounded when witnessing a minor terrorist explosion in Santander in the summer of 1978. This had resulted, the record showed, in the permanent loss of a thumbnail and surrounding tissue. There was no suggestion that he was involved in that operation - almost certainly he had not been - but his proximity was deemed worthy of note. No one in MI5 believed in coincidence.

In those days it was routine for reports to be compiled on persons of interest at university, especially those who chose to do a degree in Russian. Even redbrick institutions had their share of paid informers. The note to say that Spine had 'gone missing' for a few days in Afghanistan, in early November 1979, was not added to the ledger until many years later - due to a filing error in the secret service's ever-busy Heathrow operation. Nor was there any recorded speculation as to what had happened in Kabul, though some years later his file became officially and retrospectively linked to that of the notorious, recently late, Mohammed Aqbar, a known Islamist in Luton with Afghan connections. Spine's record was 'interesting' rather than portentous. His campus political activities were duly noted in some detail, even including motions he proposed in union debates. When he joined the OTC unit Spine won even closer, if inconclusive, scrutiny - although his threat assessment remained low.

In the 1980s passports were less easy to track than they are today. Whilst Spine's love of travel to interesting places was registered, it was usually reported in arrears rather than in 'real time' and much of it was missed.

By the mid-1990s, with no evidence of any specific criminal activity at home or abroad, the file was downgraded; little was added for several years. His membership of the National Union of Teachers was on record but his later transfer to the National Association of Head Teachers never made it into the file. Nor was there ever any cross-reference to MI5's copious records relating to Arthur Birch or the Workers' Gauntlet.

When a police inspector in rural Sussex was found to have surreptitiously interrogated the Police National Computer about a certain Norman Anthony Flagg an alert appeared on a desktop in a troglodytic corridor, somewhere near Whitehall. The file labelled 'Spine' was re-examined. Unbeknown to Clive the labels 'interesting', 'inactive' and 'missing', were reassessed. Those who knew about these things now concluded that Spine's profile might indicate that he was a 'sleeper' or, as the older spooks called it, a 'buzz-bomb'.

The Inspector was interviewed by intelligence officers early in the morning of Friday, 23rd September, though no record of the exchange exists outside SW1. Clive was told to encourage Ken to keep trying to find his quarry, whilst he himself should exercise total discretion when talking to his father.

The most difficult moment for Clive had been the next day, Saturday, the day prior to the denouement. Burying the needle-like transmitter in his father's hatband was either committing Ken to a dangerous, uncertain and potentially brief future or providing the stubborn old man, Centre's link to a possible terrorist, with a potential lifeline. But which?

'We've profiled Spine, we think we know him well enough. Your father should be safe, as long as... He won't try any heroics, will he? I thought not. Spine's first instinct will be to achieve his political goal. I doubt he'll have seriously considered escape. We think he'll prefer the clean and clinical power of a high powered sniper gun to the mess of a bomb or a carbine. His mission will be calculated to be over once the gun has been fired. If there's going to be a second shot, it will be to top himself, rather than to shoot... your father. There'll be no going back for Spine.'

Back in the real time of Sunday afternoon, the topology of the building housing the second floor flat was quickly established. The tenancy of the flat was found to be in Flagg's proper name, so it was little wonder that Ken had tracked him down so easily once he'd gone down the estate agent route. As all of the flat's windows were to the front side, the rear staircase was invisible from the flat. The plan to terminate Spine's plot should not be difficult to deliver.

By now Ken had been inside the flat for some time. The Hit Team was summoned. When Clive heard that, knowing that they would be armed, his heart hit the floor. The planned use of stun grenades brought him little reassurance as, in confined quarters like the flat they could produce severe physical trauma, especially to mature flesh such as Ken Hemmings possessed. Significant hearing loss, possibly permanent, and the risk of a heart attack were also real possibilities. Lasting psychological damage was normally inevitable, too, though Clive reckoned his father was better placed to deal with that, thanks to the demands of his former career, than most men of his age.

He asked himself how he'd ever let his father get involved and why it had to be him. That was easy: it was because there was no one better. Ken had got himself into this without Clive's help. Ken was the right man for the job, in the right place, at the right time.

Make the car obvious, it had been decided. Officers cleared much of West Street but kept a group of faux pedestrians, colleagues, moving so that it didn't look like the place had been evacuated, whilst keeping well clear of that side entrance to the Conference Centre. A Rover with four motorcycle out-riders descended at funereal pace from the top of West Street, blue lights flashing from every corner. It stopped close to the target door and everyone paused.

The opening of the rear door behind the driver was the cue for the operation to enter its final phase; Spine would be concentrating on the pavement but would soon notice that no passenger was alighting - the bullet-proof car was empty apart from its well protected driver - at which point he would be apprehended.

Suddenly a shot resounded across the street. An acute observer would have heard a window shatter.

The scene was frozen.

Taking their cue from the gunshot a group of sweating officers had crumpled the flat's door with a heavy steel ram: before it even hit the floor six men in full body armour had entered the flat and a stun grenade had been deployed - wumph! - two seconds into the operation, landing inside the main room, half way between the two men inside. The disorientating flash and noise did their job. Several more panes splintered and debris scintillated out of the window and twinkled down towards the street, like dust, like smoke. That same observer might have noted that following the gunshot of three seconds earlier there had been no such cascade: any shards thus created must have fallen inwards.

Two further seconds after that, four men charged into the front room with snub-nosed machine guns at the ready. They wore black padded uniforms and helmets, their faces hidden behind reinforced visors, and they made straight for Flagg. The target was staggering around the room, bent double, veering about randomly around like a man with acute vertigo, clutching his ears, eyes squeezed closed, and screaming in pain. Two of the men pushed him to the floor, searched and restrained him in an instant, watched by the team leader. The fourth took control of the weapon and disarmed it. 'Clear!' he shouted. Then, to the senior officer on the team he said 'Skip! It's not been fired.' The final two in the rescue squad produced bolt cutters to release a barely conscious Ken Hemmings, prone on the floor, from the captivity of his handcuffs. The chair fell away as the snip was heard.

A moment later an officer kneeling beside Ken's body reported 'He's alive!' and another officer bellowed 'Medic! Medic now!' into his radio.

The officer in the driver's seat of the Prime Ministerial car felt his heart racing. He did not know exactly what had just happened in West Street, but something had. At least he had not been shot.

'Shit,' he said, from between clenched teeth, exhaled and almost fainted.

'All clear. Stand down,' said a voice in his earpiece.

* * *

Against the white sheets on the scaffold-like hospital bed, Ken Hemmings looked old and tired.

He spoke quietly.

'So, what will happen to Norman?'

'He'll go down. For a very long time.'

'Hmm.'

Clive felt awkward, coming to visit his own father, in his bed, whilst wearing his Inspector's uniform. He was desperate to know how much the old man blamed him for what had happened that afternoon. Did he hate his son?

It was not fair to ask, though he felt he had to apologise.

'Dad, I'm sorry about... today.'

'Your boys did a good job. Very efficient.'

'I mean - '

'I know what you mean, son. There was nothing else you could've done. You did your job. Really.'

'They – I mean 'we' – we put you at one hell of a risk. We shouldn't have - '

'Clive, please. I'm proud of you. I felt I was doing what I had to do and you did your job. We got a result. And I'm in one piece.'

'Yes...'

'A rather bruised and battered piece, but I'll be OK.'

'Oh, Dad...'

'I'll be out of here in a couple of days, I'm sure.'

'I do hope so. We'll look after you. No one was seriously hurt, so that's a good thing.'

'No one was hurt? Are you sure?'

'Spine, that's Centre's name for Norman, he sustained a few bruises and a perforated ear drum. Our lads – well, let me put it this way: his welfare was not their primary consideration when they barged into the room.'

'What about... the Prime Minister? I saw Norman shoot. He's trained with guns, you know. I'll bet he's a good shot. He must have fired the rifle, I heard the shot and the glass break...'

'Dad, he didn't fire, though we thought he had, at the time. He was about to, certainly, we'd lined up for the guys to enter the flat the moment the car arrived. But after all that preparation, he didn't do it.'

The pale Ken Hemmings blanched.

'But the window? I heard the window smash before the police entered, didn't I?'

'Well, maybe... Dad, this is completely between you and me. I don't want you telling Peter Elder - or anyone else, certainly not the press. I know you'll respect that. We had a sniper situated on the car park roof, across the road. It appears that he might have fired, believing that Spine was about to do so. He missed the target... though not by much.

The breaking window - the first breaking window - that you heard almost certainly disorientated Flagg.'

'Just seconds before the raid.'

'Literally: about two seconds. The entry team heard the window smash and took that as their cue.'

'Convenient.'

'As it happens, yes, Dad.'

'And the PM?'

'The Prime Minister wasn't there. He was taken into the Conference through a different entrance, the one the refuse lorries use to service the hotels. Business as usual in the Conference; it might as well be in a different world.'

'Some might say it always is...'

Ken's attempt at humour fell on deaf ears.

'So, Clive, you knew who Flagg was, all along...'

'To be fair, Dad, no, I didn't. At least... Not until this weekend. But the spooks had him sussed. You know when you asked me to do that PNC check, a few weeks ago? That rang some bells in some deep corridor somewhere, the system was programmed to alert the authorities if ever that record was accessed and... well, here we are.'

'You don't say...' Ken was almost beyond words. This was a lot of information to absorb in a brain that was still woozy with shock, trauma and relief at having no major injury to contend with. His son was standing there in front of him, in his smart uniform. Ken felt proud of him.

'So they called him Spine...'

'For twenty-five years, apparently. Most of which has been a resounding silence.'

Clive had to let his father ask and he had to respond. But he would save some of the choicer details – like the way he'd inserted the needle-like transmitter into Ken's trilby hat whilst his father prepared lunch on the previous day – until later, when the invalid was stronger.

'What time is it?'

'It's coming up to midnight, Sunday. You've slept for most of the evening, but you're basically fit, they tell me.'

Ken smiled.

'You're a tough old goose, Dad. Oh, by the way, you've already had a visitor.'

Ken, resting deep into a pile of pillows, raised an eyebrow.

'Peter Elder.'

'Ah.'

'He came by a few hours ago but you were asleep. He was pretty agitated.'

'I'm not surprised! He's lost a very good Head, but maybe he's already got another, just as good. Jane Moore will step up seamlessly, of that I've no doubt.'

'I'm sure you're right. The nurse said he talked his way in, they weren't supposed to let you have visitors yet. That's not just what the medics say, it was my boss's orders, too. So I went out and met Peter in the corridor. He was very anxious to see you. He asked me to give you this.'

Ken reached out to take the pale yellow, sealed envelope and started to tear it open but he was all fingers and thumbs. He was interrupted by a nurse entering.

'You're awake, Mr Hemmings.'

'I am indeed. Thank you.'

The nurse – Turner, according to her badge, Ken noticed – smiled and felt her patient's wrist.

'Inspector Hemmings… there's a message for you. There's an officer in the corridor, says he needs to speak to you.'

'Right, thanks. Look, Dad, it's getting late so… I'll get off, after I've seen to this. I'll come back and see you first thing in the morning.'

Father and son exchanged tentative smiles.

'Thanks, Clive. I look forward to it.'

Clive patted his father's shoulder, tucked his inspector's flat hat under his arm and left the room in a stilted, formal manner. His job was done for the night; his father was going to be all right. He'd also been told, by the authorities as well as his father, that any guilt he felt at putting Ken at risk, from the moment he had accessed the PNC onwards, was misplaced.

Ken suddenly felt very tired.

Nurse Turner helped him to sit forward whilst she adjusted his pillows into a position better suited for sleeping. She took the half-opened envelope from his hand and placed it on the bedside table.

The routines over, Ken and the nurse adjusted the leads which connected the man to his monitor and he started to settle down to try to return to sleep. Nurse Turner said her goodnights and dimmed the lights. Only a desk-type lamp over the bed, which Ken could extinguish or dim using a switch on the end of a cable, now illuminated the room.

What a day.

Not for the first time, Ken tried to piece together the events of the day. So far too much of it had eluded him.

He remembered the toast he'd had for breakfast and how he'd scraped the furthest recesses of the marmalade jar to obtain enough to cover it.

He'd checked the oil level in his car before driving to Brighton, a habit which, as a younger man, he'd learnt as routine, though it was all but unnecessary in modern vehicles such as he now owned.

He'd parked in the underground car park on the sea front, near the border between Brighton and Hove, the one he used whenever he came into town to watch the cricket. From there he'd walked half a mile to the Brighton Centre, despite the noisy seagulls, the drizzle and the blustery wind.

Goodness, the car was still in the car park! How much was that going to cost? Sod it.

In his head now was the distinctive noise of the amusement arcade, a sound which he'd never found attractive: clatter, clatter, tiktik, ding, ding, clang.

The anticipation he felt as he had climbed the stairs to Flagg's flat would stick in his mind for the rest of his life. On the other hand, much of what followed was already difficult for him to remember, the indignity of the handcuffs being a glaring exception.

Had he ever thought his life was in danger? No. Norman had never threatened him.

In his earlier years, walking in the Peak District, he had always obeyed the First Law of Rambling: always let somebody know where you're going and when you're likely to be back. Then, if you got lost, you'd be missed and someone would come and look for you; not that he'd ever tested this theory on Crowden, Bleaklow or Kinder. Nevertheless, on this occasion it would have been a sensible precaution. Not doing so had been stupid, neglectful, sloppy.

But who should he have told? Should he have told Clive? Someone close to Clive obviously already knew: how had that happened? The question could wait for another day. Perhaps he should have told Peter what he was up to? Peter had got him into all this, after all. Ken's recent deduction that an assassination was a possibility had been little more than a wild hunch which Peter would never have believed...

Ken deliberately ceased the train of thought.

Peter.

The letter.

Ken sat up, with difficulty. He was stiff from hours of inactivity and the wires attached to his body confused him. The letter was on the bedside table. He found his anxiety levels rising as he fumbled, tearing the primrose envelope.

Inside was a single small piece of matching writing paper. Peter's handwriting was bold, large, distinctive but clear. It was the script of a determined person, one who knew what he wanted and had the confidence to achieve it.

My Dear Ken.
You're a hero, you really are, thank you so much for what you did.
I should <u>not</u> have let him do it.
He won't get another chance.
Regards,
P.

Peter Elder was a good man: commonsensical, down to earth, committed. How strongly did he really feel about his cause? Perhaps he too was capable of passion, however clinical his approach to politics – and to life in general.

Flagg would certainly not get another chance, that was true enough. Ken's own evidence would send him down and life would certainly mean life. But Peter needed a good talking-to. This 'I should not have let him do it' business was totally uncalled-for, thought Ken. No one could blame Peter Elder for anything.

He folded the letter and put it back on the envelope, back on the bedside table. As he turned to seek a comfortable sleeping position he was surprised to see Clive standing there, in the dark. His son had re-entered the room and was standing upright, his cap held formally against his broad Inspector's chest, as though on parade.

'Clive?'

'Dad.'

'Clive! What is it?' Ken was now fully awake, perhaps for the first time.

'There's been a development.'

'A development?'

'Norman Flagg... is dead.'

Ken felt himself inhale in a short, sharp action. He was confused.

There was a silence. Ken now exhaled through pursed lips. Despite his condition and the late hour he was totally conscious.

'You said no one was seriously hurt... What happened...? I suppose he killed himself. He did talk about it. Well, I'm not surprised. But if he'd killed himself at the scene you'd have told me... So how'd he do it?'

'He didn't kill himself. He's been killed.'

Ken frowned, puzzled. Surely Flagg had been in the presence of police officers for several hours now. They would never...

Another parallel came into his mind. It was a story he'd considered more than once over recent weeks. An article in Workers' Gauntlet had brought it to his attention and, without mentioning that piece, he'd even discussed his own memory, of 22nd November, 1963, with Peter.

The President's open-topped car came round the corner, into the sunlit square, as part of a celebratory motorcade.

POTUS and his First Lady were young, vibrant, full of hope - symbols of all that was good and positive, of the triumph of democracy, the people's choice.

His was the face of the future, of justice, liberty and peace.

Every adult who was alive on that day remembers where they were when they heard that John F Kennedy been assassinated, one of those few events guaranteed to arouse the collective folk memories of Ken's entire generation.

From the grassy knoll – or perhaps from the book repository? – Lee Harvey Oswald had lifted his gun, taken aim and changed the world.

The President slumped in the rear of the open-topped car. Though the beautiful Jackie tried to tend immediately to her husband, it was to no avail. The back of his head had suffered a massive, fatal wound.

Hours later, in a Dallas precinct building, a tussle of officers, newspaper men and others surrounded Oswald as he was marched down the corridor.

And then Jack Ruby stepped forward to exact the revenge of the nation.

Or... was that not the motive?

Had it been Ruby's job to cover the traces?

There was a parallel, an ambiguous, ominous parallel.

Ken looked his son in the eye.

Even in the near darkness he could sense that the blood had drained from both of their faces.

'Oh, my God.'

'It's not quite clear how it actually happened. There was... a melée, as Flagg was being taken from the police station out to a van. There was a security lapse, a bad one. There were lots of reporters around. Unfortunately...'

'What was the weapon?'

'There was no weapon. The assailant used karate. He pounced, broke Flagg's neck in an instant. This was all on live television, just over an hour ago, apparently. The assailant then swallowed a liquid from a bottle, we don't know what it was yet, some concentrated, powerful acid, was the first guess, but it was certainly potent stuff. Flagg was dead by the time he hit the ground. The assailant is likely to have severe damage to multiple organs from the acid, massive internal bleeding. The doctors think he's unlikely to survive the night.'

Ken imagined the scene and put a face to the killer.

'Clive, you don't have to tell me any more.'

'I do, Dad. Just one more thing.'

'It was Peter Elder, wasn't it?'

Now it was Clive's turn to feel a shiver. His backbone was barely preventing him from collapsing, yet he wished he could wrap it around his dear parent at this moment of his greatest need. An emotional bomb had penetrated the very centre of his father's being and was exploding in his heart as surely as the stun grenade had detonated before him some hours earlier.

A chapter in Ken's life was over. Clive's continued silence spoke volumes.

'He won't get another chance', Peter's note had said. Indeed, he won't... now.

Ken held out a piece of primrose coloured paper.

Clive took it. It needed no further explanation.

Ken lay back and closed his eyes.

'His wife uses concentrated nitric acid for her etching. And he has a blue belt at karate.'

Now it was Clive's turn to be taken aback by the evening's revelations.

'So,' Ken went on, 'That's the end of that. I think I want to sleep now.'

From what Clive could see, the old man immediately slumped into unconsciousness.

Only the wavering trace of his oxygen saturation levels and the flickering of his pulse, illuminated on a silent screen, confirmed that his father was alive.

The Inspector stood, in dark uniform in darkened room, silent, rigid, tall, and watched. A small pool of weak light illuminated the man who had saved democracy, decency and civilisation.

And the Inspector felt proud.

Printed in Poland
by Amazon Fulfillment
Poland Sp. z o.o., Wrocław

62775837R10123